The Man
Who Was Not With It

Books by Herbert Gold

BIRTH OF A HERO

THE PROSPECT BEFORE US

THE MAN WHO WAS NOT WITH IT

The Man
Who
Was Not
With It

by

H E R B E R T G O L D

An Atlantic Monthly Press Book

Little, Brown and Company · Boston · Toronto

A selection from THE MAN WHO WAS NOT WITH IT was
published, in another form, in *New World Writing* #6.

ATLANTIC–LITTLE, BROWN BOOKS
ARE PUBLISHED BY
LITTLE, BROWN AND COMPANY
IN ASSOCIATION WITH
THE ATLANTIC MONTHLY PRESS

Published simultaneously in Canada
by Little, Brown & Company (Canada) Limited

PRINTED IN THE UNITED STATES OF AMERICA

For Sid

PART ONE

"I lay down in mud. I washed myself with crime. I played with madness."

To flee is to die. To discover is to make life eternal. When are we fleeing and when are we making?

And now the story begins.

1. Let me tell first how Gracchus became a father to me

THERE he is on the midway, Grack the Frenchie, talking for his countstore or his zoo while the loudspeaker clamored under his come-on with a *hee hee hee* and a *ho ho ho*. "Roly and Poly, the sole and o-nelly genuine Siamese twins from Siam in these great States — no adhesive sticking them together behind either, friends — and Little Bo Peep, the educated chimp, she's no geek, speaks five African languages — I'll translate for you, friends — move in there on the edges, you — lookee here at *me*, at *my*, at your friend Grack, friends," — and they looked.

This was the big show, if they only knew it.

"Lookee, lookee, lookee, friends!" He brought his hand with the horny nail of his index finger in a wide circle, swinging an invisible lassoo, looping their belly-eyed gaze and taking it at his eye. They were caught first at the spongy wart on his nose and then in his eyes, working it for themselves now like the flies caught wriggling in sticky-paper. That wart made a stiff flop when he tossed his head in beckon and hitch toward the pungent foot-darkened sawdust at the door

3

of Grack's Zoo, a gobble of cajolery up from his throat and the swollen Adam's apple.

Even that pretty monkey Joy, Pauline's pouting daughter, an agile child sneaking through the high stakes to womanliness, stopped in her roaming through this carnie where she dwelled and listened. Her dark face lifted to Grack while his lips rehearsed his words and her lashes veiled her carnie-brat's opinion. She knew his pitch, but he played in a pleasant new line for her now and then, and whirled with his immense mouth of grin to tease to her: "All green and life-defying, folks! All dreadful, friends!"

As Grack went to turn the crowd in, Joy scuffed off to where she would smile and nip the pleasant Southern air and take the tickets to Palmistry Pauline's mittcamp. "Psycho-palmologist Tells All, Marital, Sexual, or Mineral — but leave our Joykins alone," Grack chanted in farewell to Pauline's girl. "Oh diddle a hand, oh raddle a riddle, so step right up," — it made no difference what he said. The marks listened to him, his hand and his eye, not his words.

Ho, ho, ho. He adjusted the dial down. *Hee, hee, hee.* The machine now softly vented its hilarious spleen behind the platform. Pretty little Joy had smiled and gone. Again Grack opened to his sweet-and-sour hurry-up song. "Now you take them circus Siamese babies, you can't trust them, never could, folks —" He was a sallow stooped carnie with vapors fuming in his eyes and hard skinny hillbilly muscles, but he had a knack: he could chant them into anything. He could put them down hard on a paper dollie as quick as he could sell the gaudy clatter of Rosie's hips bumping, our grind-girl from the Boys' Farm in Hudson, Ohio. The index

4

finger and the wart and the eyes did the turn; he plugged them in. All he asked of them was to ease loose the marko's fist. The slum prizes dripped from their hands, taffy, teddy-bears, streamers of paper, and he didn't need the laughing machine to make the folks feel rewarded. "It keeps me company when I get lonesome," he said. "Sure, it gasses me, but you can die from the stupid marks you see out there." He said: "I don't booze, I don't mainline, I hardly even pull my robin, but I got me the right kind of mad on. That's my fix, boy."

"You don't get tired of it, Grack?"

"Sick of it. Sick of what, eh? Sick of them all and their pockets full of hanky-pank money — but you're a young fellow got his end before him."

"You get like that, Grack?"

"Got his end in front of him. I already come to my end, boy."

Even so, sometimes his thumb-and-finger snapped with a yen for the girls, and then there might be trouble, since the flypaper eyes were the smartest thing about him and they didn't reckon on anything but the sale. Me, I was a brat yet, not much older than Joy, a sawdust streetkid, and I asked too much of men in our world without women; that's ahead of the story. Grack, maybe he asked too much of the crowd in a world made, whatever he said, by individual men, just as one of them had made the rasping ho-hee platter which backed him up each workday evening, winters and traveling excluded.

How it happened with us is as easy as this: Grack, this fine talker, he stood in his box near San Diego and plucked a

5

tricksie in shorts as she wiggled by. He took the thin pants between his horny fingers, appreciating her ripeness by the plump distance she jumped straight up, and roared like a kid: "Snookums!" He patted. He pinched. He held on.

She had friends, it seemed. In that crowd, with Tricksie jostling them every chance she got — I've seen her on all my midways in these wide States — they were blowing for a fight. "Ouch," she peeped. "Oh me," — and she rolled her round little eyes to see what she could see.

"You goddamn bum," her marko friend yelled. "What you think you're doing, squeezing tomatoes?"

"Yeah, goddamn, you think so?" *his* friend asked.

Craw jerking, Grack said, "I'll explain it to you for the price of admission, children's rates. See me after the show."

They both jumped the Grack. He let go of Tricksie's prettiness and murmured, soft-like and reluctant, "Hey, rube."

Hey, rube! — with a ho and a hee for this carnie battlecry. Hey, you fearless rubes!

Dreamy in my high, I floated down from the next platform to kick the smaller mark where it would tell on him. I did it with my toes, as light as I could, though he did not appreciate this. It turned out that he was a real sociable fellow with a wide circle of friends and one of them came at Grack with a bottle. Grack whistled between his teeth. He had to rap the bottle baby on the knuckles. They were a party; we found ourselves with an old-fashioned hey-rube and obliged to move the show on that night. There was no patching it. I remember looking over to Tricksie with her pretty little hand tip-touching the black-and-blue spot, and I hoped that

6

she would finally let Grack fix the rest of her for her, but just then someone broke my nose and I went thrashing about, spouting blood over everyone and yelling my courage mixed with salty phlegm. How could I do any better? I worked toward the best pleasures on earth, ready for high virtues of friendship even if the sharpest nosebones worked *their* way into my cheeks.

"Oh, do it for me," Tricksie was saying.

Sam the Popcorn Man was throwing canvas over his machine and had it almost covered when a rube heaved a tent-stake and the popcorn blew like snow among us. "Hee! hee! hee! Ho! ho! ho!" Someone was windmilling an empty bucket. Someone had found a case of beer. Someone turned up the speaker at the zoo and it roared till our scalps shivered with it. "HO! HO! HO!" A small sliver like a fishbone had pierced my nostril in just the place where Grack's wart lay. I noticed it at the time. Tricksie was rubbing herself and murmuring happily, "Oh, my, won't you? Kill him for me, please." She was lonely because nobody touched her after Grack. Picking her hand through the broken glass of the popper, she stuffed her mouth and said, "All for me? Oh, you shouldn't hurt yourselves, boys. It's not right. Get the skinny fellow over there, he's the one. Kill him. I'm just a defenseless little girl. No, the one with the funny nose."

Joy dumped a jug of warm peanut oil on Tricksie's new hairdo. Tricksie stuck her tongue through it like surprised. Joy said to me: "Oh that must hurt, Bud. Bud! Let me wash it for you." She was crying.

Later Grack picked me for true and handed me a compli-

7

ment on the new nose. "You don't look like a kid no more, kid, never will. Thanks for coming. You was first. I really mean it."

"I was nearest, that's all," I admitted modestly.

"How was I to know the whole town was her friend? — in thin panties and fruitcake fat like that. We only just got in town. I didn't hardly see that mark with the bottle. I should of known, though, frisky like she was."

I blushed at this apology for the trouble and my broken nosebones. "You couldn't have guessed, Grack. You were busy with business."

"Business, kid, you mean monkey business. That there business finger got to look out for itself sometimes. Never did learn, did you?" — and he frowned at the dark hand with its pink ringed mounds of callus. He sighed, finished his study, and stuck his head toward me. "How's the face?"

"Still there."

"Looks fine, just fine." He sighed again and put his vaporous eyes upon me. He didn't con me with the finger, though. The wart lay sleek and still. "Just dandy," he said.

"Glad to get it for you, Grack." If I wouldn't earn this face and the skewered nose for him, then who could be worth it? I was lucky in this case that friendship and principle came together in a time of risk. Since love is the principle and Grack a man with a use for everything, my choice fell happy here. You don't always find it that way with grifters, family, and the others you meet in business.

The next mornings I took to crawling up on one of the rusty Ferris wheel benches, braked while the carnival slept, and tried to remember Phyllis and my faraway father in

8

Pittsburgh and the squares beyond. Motherless since birth, I dreamed only of my father, who was lost to me in the immobility of his mourning, his fleshly discontent, his business, and his shameful and secret watching over me. A five-dollar habit helped me forget and then remember. I was keeping cool and making the effort to give an answer like that of Grack's funhouse speaker. He had invited me to sleep in his truck, where we found room for two easy.

2. Had memories, old friends, and a bad habit

I WAS with it and for it. I was picking pockets in a wholesome diversification of ways, as the stockbrokers put it — countstores, girlie shows, even taking bets in the funhouse on how high a skirt would blow. (Saw many a frayed hem. Some girls are more careless with their underthings than you'd ever have occasion to know in another line of work.) I had risen fast despite my habit, from tent man and candy butcher to shill and apprentice inside man in a count-your-ball, rob-'em-all shop. I was no first-of-Mayer staying put with the rent at home until the spring made it nice on the lot. I traveled through foul September rains on the canvas. I gave myself to voyaging.

Only my tenderness sat flabby in the way, an overtenderness both to myself and to others. That was how, trying to keep cool and out of the way of such as Phyllis and my real pa, I picked up the habit. A businesslike five-dollar habit helped me mix the carnie hardness with the carnie softness which takes the place of the rules of courtesy in a traveling show. Grifting troubadours, bonnie princes of con with ten-gallon hats, we trailed our unchivalric careers through the dust of many counties. Grack could snip the fringe off a gypsy's ribbon and sell it back to her. My father, too, sold service — work service, loading his truck at any hour of the day or night in Pittsburgh, and never with schnapps even when Hizonner Volstead had made owning a truck and knowing the road profitable. Grack serviced for profit the marks with their greedy eyes and the dry lips of worried fraud.

Pauline, who liked Grack, said to Joy: "You just stay from under Grack, hear me? Get your first loving-up from somebody needs it of you, daughter-a-mine. You got cute shape, cute face just like your papa — I see nothing but trobble less you hold out for the genuine loving. And cover yourself afterwards so's you don't catch a chill — I see past, present, and future clear as glass."

Me, I booted the mark down the midway when I saw that squirrelly look which says: "Win it all back with the rent money because they can't, no they can't do this to me."

When the eyes fevered over this way, fright moving in on the larceny in their hearts, I dumped them outside and said, "No, no, there's a limit on losses here. Be a good loser now, sir. Go home. Here, take a nice babydoll to the wife and just thank the management."

It was policy, sure, to keep them on the move and smiling, but I was too quick with policy, and sometimes a mark would come back nasty: "Mind the wax in your own ears, sonny boy. Whose money and day off is it? Get back there behind the counter and set 'em up again." The kicks gone from it, I would have to sweep in the leavings of his cash, his watch, and his bad checks. I couldn't enjoy it anymore. Dad had done this to me, faraway in Pittsburgh, tiddling me with un-

11

pleasure for my pleasure and putting pellets of lead under my tongue and at the nimble tips of my fingers. Grack had no such troubles; neither did the others. If they had fathers, they knew what to do with them; they left them far behind and gave themselves over to proving who was who: *Gig and gouge, take your best hold.*

I tried to be different. I had an outlook.

You should have seen me rouge all over for the rightness of the world because Palmistry Pauline, the queen of our mittcamp, liked to tell the ladies nice things: he loves you truly, he's coming back to you soon, he'll be tall, dark, and with his hernia tucked in.

Later, washed by the dawn sky above me, in the truck with Grack or alone on a Ferris wheel mat, I knew that even sweet Pauline couldn't fix it for anyone. They all knew. She had her own troubles, a dollar-eating daughter to raise, the change of life, an old conviction for stag movies and illegal matroning. She demanded the minimum donation for reading the future, thus giving time and the ladies' hands a moral sense. You can see that we had a heart for each other's hearts, although Pauline couldn't do good anymore for anybody, not anybody. She went on trying. She could still be kind.

"Hernia Hoo?"

"Ropture, I said, modom. Tray-o-diemints. No more trobble."

"And for this you charge fifty cents?"

Still, paying the broads with tissue paper in their garters or telling *as if*, secure in morphine or other pacifiers, wobblies, ex-cons, gypsies, depression bums, freaks and cripples, guys with habits and light-footed guys and clever chappies with no place to rest their cleverness, gentlemen who were with it for every bad reason in a world of bad reasons, we found in the show that forgotten moral thickness for which so many of us were sick. "The Feast of Our Lady of Syracuse," Bigcut Stan wrote to *Billboard*, "the Biggest Feast in the East." Mindful of a sick past, we embraced this sick present, its festivals, sentiments, trials, and especially its divided religion which attempted to bring together a sublime freedom for elbow-room with a divided loyalty for friendship. "Those that know me, come on in," Stan the Bossman advertised in the springtime, "but no collect telegrams." There was society enough for the Sunday *Times*. For example, Pauline's little Joy tried to pass me a pop bottle during the hey-rube, poured peanut oil on Tricksie, later laved my nose and tried to mother it like a grown woman, still later whispered, "Here, have a sandwich, Bud. Don't you know you got to eat?"

"Nose hurts and no appetite. Thanks."

"You *got* to. Minced ham on white, peanut butter and jelly on cracked wheat, all those nourishing vitamins."

I watched Grack winking and grinning at this nervous-kneed girl who wiggled like a woman to offer me sandwiches in a bag and jelly on her wrists. Although I had only a couple of chinhairs and summers on her, Grack's grin made me stiffen away and pull my mouth down, saying, "Little girl, y' bother me. Got my own vitamins."

"Okay, Bud," — dipping.

"But I mean to thank you anyway, little girl," — but she had already gone, fast on small feet, a shy monkey, quick and busy and pretty little mug coming to an angry pout.

Grack was still shaking his head and scratching. "Now you hurt the filly's feelings," he said. "Little boy, you're plenty rough. You don't want to hurt a feeling like that less you *really* like her. You only nip like that, puppy, when you're —" He stopped and grinned.

This is what I mean by society just like yours even among all us complacent oddballs. "Shouldn't worry you because it tickles me to watch — that kid was making up to you so sweet," Grack said. Our cooktent had a pleasant business warmth, too. For other examples from the society page of Stan's Famous Truck Show:

The wedding of Roly and Poly, our Siamese twins, to the Hayworth Brothers, who were billed in the West as "Those Gallant Aristocrats of the Trapeze," until Chet Hayworth accused his brother, Poopface, of having eyes for Roly and the act split up. Or the hey-rube when a farmer took off after Red Rosalie, the belly-dancer, and Rosalie blushed, pouted, bargained, and finally consented. We heard the mark's howl from the Ferris wheel to the last countstore when he discovered that Rose is a man like the rest of us, or nearly. "Dincha know?" Rosalie lisped when we got him subdued. Or the long sleepy drinkdowns during the slow Florida winters at Jacksonville, when, if off-season and off-luck meet, the very richest carnie you meet is like to sell his pins and buckles and rings and end up a wino at the salvationists by Feb or March. Or the boosting from the A & P, when we put bets to see who could get away with the most bottles of vanilla extract in two hours; no fair buying, fellows. I used to kiss Pauline's ring for luck; Joy wasn't looking — she went to high school wintertimes. Or Casanopopolous, who had a pair of the widest nostrils for a mark in a crooked show, who sniffed them out and vacuumed them in, who drove a trailer and ironed his money at the end of each day. Yes, he put out his board and heated the iron on a stove and smoothed out the rough places. That man hated creases. Once or twice in the season, and every season, he was looted. Broken into. All gone. "Why don't you lay it away in the bank?" I used to ask him. (This happened every year.)

"Don't trust banks," he said.

He knew too much about con to fall for that one, but he never managed to save a buck. We all felt sad sometimes to have sneakthieves among us, but what can you do with a mark besides giving him a chance to enjoy his flatwork or win a free Indian blanket?

One day Grack strolled over and stood spraddle-legged at my booth, grinned to show his friendly black tooth — I was warming up to the empty air, "Try a free one, they're all free, folks" — and laid a finger to the fat-bellied wart and his mushy eyeflesh. He snapped it away to kid my ears empty and my head ready. Making me watch, he closed his mouth for a moment; he was the rare carnie who could live without brag. He carried the talent of silence with him. He reached for my arm, rolled up the sleeve, and poked at the sore places on the veins. Gently he scratched the scabs. "Why don't you kick it?" he said finally.

"Don't know how."

"It's an expensive habit."

I was thinking: Expensive to myself without the habit, too, Grack. I touched my nose healed flat but still sore.

"What say?"

"Didn't answer yet, Grack."

"Come on along, kid."

"You know it ain't easy, Grack." The trade had already wandered away. It was a windy afternoon, the shadows still short off the mountains, and they were just looking things over with their palms not itchy and hardly a dime jingling. I said: "But another thing, now you're asking, what do you do what you do for, Grack?"

"Wha-what?"

"Grifting, you know it. All right, so let's cut up a jackpot. How long you been grifting?"

This made him frown and rock softly on his heels. "Listen, kid, I studied for priest, but I didn't like it. It didn't agree. So? I did it for my mother."

I leaned to him over the board and shook three marbles in my fist. "You think you can always make it like this? You ready to go on for always?"

"Get myself a skillo, get myself a patch in every town, what more do I need?" He looked over the apprehensive afternoon crowd with its know-it-all faces and its pockets joylessly buttoned. They weren't even buying balloons, cobweb candy, or Spicy Artist's Views. He took the pencil from behind his ear, under the Texas hat, and tapped my knuckles with the marbles in them. "You make good money on a skillo wheel," he said carefully, as if I had touched a difficult place in his way of thinking. "I love, really love to see how the mark runs and then he's headed off by a wideawake patch."

"What I mean, Grack," — and I took the pencil. It changed hands. "What I mean is what's in it for you? You

16

got yourself no habits. You just like the feel of the crowds maybe."

"That's it, friend, I love to let the crowd feel me. With a ha ha ha and a hee hee hee. I love to let them do it. You hit it there now. I wish I could dress snappy like a priest, but they'd never trust me. No, you'd start slow and get away slow. . . ." He tipped back the hat and shaded his eyes with his hand and watched the pickup bums setting down the Ferris wheel. "They're going to tear that thing apart like that, not now, I only mean someday. No, you can't dress queer, you got to look like the marks only wear a big-brimmed hat to show who you are, in this case Gracchus. I ain't no sweet seminarian no more. I'm with it and for it." He grinned and brought the finger around to his eye. "I ain't forgetting, kid. You talk it up like a longtime grifter, real dealing how you talk it up. Listen here to me now, you. Kick it before it kicks you, kid. Before it beats you white. You can do it, you're the kicking kind — that's my bet on your nose."

I wondered if he meant it, and tested him. "You can't do it all by your lonesome, Grack. I mean me, I can't."

"I don't know it?" He scuffed the waffle chips at our feet and pinched me with his Tricksie fingers. "I know it needs help, kid. I'll help. I can sit you out. I used to join out the odds, had myself a stable of clappers for the gash-hounds too dumb to do their own howling, that's how bad I needed it from those shyster country docs. I did it myself once, now I know it needs help and I'll help you."

"You a pimp? I never would have thought you needed anything that bad, Grack."

He adjusted the hat with a ticketstub for a feather and

did not answer for a moment. Maybe he was busy blushing under the many-weathered reddish-brown grimace. "Here, give me back my pencil," he said at last. He watched the Ferris wheel going up in the wino's hands.

"Can I do it, Grack?"

"I'll mash it out of you, kid."

"Can I do it?"

"We'll say goombye to the habit together, kid. I know how." He pinched me and grinned and dragged his fingers along the little scabs from the hypo; they burned like ants on the blue flesh of my inner arm. I winced and my heart turned close inside me, because goombye to the mainline would give me the chance to goombye Grack, pocket-picking, and the spoiled life which was my fond own. He knew me.

"I like being with it and for it," I said. I wanted to be with it someday like Grack, all there, hard, dark, and sure of himself under the sun with the marks turned up at him like daisies in a field. The fat wart on his nose was their moon, his eye their mortified sun.

Grack grinned and winked. "Tell you what, kid," he said. "*Nobody* likes it."

3. Kicked it near Grack's knife in a cabin

ON the morning after Grack had decided for me I went swimming at the backed-up bend of a stream. It was a hot early morning, dog days coming; the carnie slept under dusty canvas just beginning to take on its suneaten scorched smell. The cooktent woke first after me — rattle of grates and coffee being measured. Maybe this would be one of my last mornings in the carnie, I thought, flapping and blowing water and pushing from the treehung mudbank to a gravelly shore a few feet away. My habit kept me cool, but the morning water was nice outside our lot. I could float half-submerged under the dapple and sparkle of sun through leaves on water.

Like a monkey little Joy came swinging down from one of the trees.

"Get away, I'm nekked," I yelled to her. "What do you mean spying on me?"

"Not my fault, I was just sitting in the tree," she said calmly. "I like watching you, anyway — ain't my fault. How's your nose in the wet? All grown over already?"

"Get away, brat!" I yelled, splashing her as she kicked off her moccasins and started to wade from the gravel side.

"I already saw you, anyway," she said. "You didn't know I was watching, Bud, did you?" I windmilled water at her. She laughed with small white teeth. "Now listen, Bud, you're getting me wet. This dress has the starch in it. Pauline got it for my birthday at that Sears in Ogden."

It was true; she was a nice little birthday girl in her flowered $3.99 cotton instead of the usual kid shorts or blue jeans. I went on shoveling water until the dress was slicked down to her legs. "Oh! oh!" she said. "Now *stop*."

"Then *get*."

"Why? I like you."

This made me stop. I ducked to my chin in the eddying water and said, as if repeating her *why*, "Why?"

"You let me fix up your nose. I like taking care of people. You're nice to me."

"That just ain't possible, little girl."

"I *like* you, Bud."

"Get away from me now, you bother me. What are you, sixteen years old carnie brat and you got hot pants already?"

She ran crying to Pauline. When Pauline asked her why, she claimed stomach ache and Pauline answered she was too young for bicarb in the heart and would have to grow up. But she got mad at all us carnie heroes despite her jokes and there were some bad fortunes told that night.

A couple of days later Grack came visiting and said: "It's time, Buddy boy." He started it like a vicious mama and the baby's bottles. "No-no," he said, scowling off that long galled face. He broke my hypo in his hands and paid no mind to the skin cuts and the splinters. He let me see how he paid no mind, how he did it. He broke, pinched, crushed, and scattered. He even got rid of the powdered sugar which I had used (but less and less) to cut the dose. "All gone," he repeated. "No-no, goombye."

"Fine, fine," I grinned for him.

"You like it fine now?" he asked. "Wait." He watched me sideways and dusted his narrow hands together. "Wait."

Then quick, while I was still cool and stepping dainty off my last mainline, he took me on the trip. He had rented a cabin there on the slope near Winter Park, Colorado. It was summer; I felt all in one piece under an eggshell sky. I didn't care until I saw him pack our gear. He put in a knife, a long black hunting knife with a long white blade sharpened for funny hunting, for monkey business. He looked up to see my face on him, and the black wart shimmied. "What's the matter, Grack?" I asked. "Something wrong? What's funny?"

"You," he said, shrugging as if offering me a free throw: Try it, just try it once, Mister. If you win, fine; if not, well, the house pays, I mean the management.

"Me?"

"You're the matter. Wait till that stuff wears off. You'll want to eat the mountain down. You won't be pretty, friend."

"Sharpen it, Grack." I even shared the laugh now in his need to protect himself from me.

"Don't you worry, kid. Just remember."

By the time we got to the cabin on the hill — far enough from brotherly love and its occasional nosiness so that I could bang my head in peace — I was jumping. I jumped. By the

21

time we unlocked the door I was begging. I begged. By the time he unpacked the knife I was in the thirsty way. My mouth filled with crumbling.

"Maybe you brought something for me, Grack?"

"All you can do now is kick it," he said calmly. "I'll wait. Got nothing better."

"Maybe you brought something in case I couldn't do it? In case it got too rough? In case it was maybe hard on the heart?"

"Nothing at all, boy. But I aim to wait here with you."

He had put the sheathed knife in his jacket pocket, trusting his eye to protect him, that Frenchie eye which had submitted to the voyage of his fingers and the adoration of the farmer-boy waggles. My legs were coming rubbery and I geeked out the first time: "Grack, I can't make it."

"Sit down, friend."

"Grack, it wasn't a good idea."

"I like it."

"Please, Grack, listen to me!"

"Sit down. Pretty soon you'll start shivering, it'll give you something to do. Lucky the carnie got rained out." He stretched himself on a cot with his legs propped on one of the logs of the cabin wall. Now he held the knife handy on his chest. I kept looking at the wall and feeling my head ripe and tight and wanting to do this foreign thing in and break it the way you pop a pimple. Grack would stop me. He said I was the kind could kick a habit. I got through the first vomiting okay, Grack's hand hard on my forehead, but my body let go everywhere else.

He waited for me with his eyes half-shut, wide-awake.

First shivers and gooseflesh, no blankets enough. Then fever and howling to ease the weight on my ears. I tore my clothes off because Grack wouldn't help me unbutton; I remember how my belt cut me in half. Skinny ribs were mine, bare chest was maybe mine, heart cracking was someone else's; and no strength to push lungs against those somebody ribs and no chance to unglue those someone eyelids and whose white dust on my lips? Fever's! Mr. Fever's dust!

"Help you to the faucet," somebody said.

Under the roar of white water pasting my hair back, I gasped alive and said thanks. In that dripping instant, with the forced ebb of the fever under cold water, I was human and spitting bubbles, and thankful to Grack.

Two steps away, hair glued, the fever came up again and the water dried with a sizzle and crackling in my ears and it was no longer my body; and three steps away. Another. Another. A hand on the ribcage held me and guided me. Who was here with Mr. Fever and Grack? Not Bud, not Bud! The roar in my head had the gift of tongues, then suddenly came clear: "Let's not and say we did," — the puerile suburban voice of my childhood. Then the gooseflesh again, and a whole day when I knew that the touch of cloth would kill me. And I begged him to kill me. Howling: "Oh my god help me someone." Crying: "Help me someone."

"You're doing fine, kid," he said.

My brains turned to soap and came out my ears. My legs turned crazy. *Let's not and say we did.* His eyes were open and on me. I put my head down and stumbled to butt the wall. There was the sweet moment of an epileptic's bliss when I came out of it enough to feel, not only hear, my head against a log. Grack picked me up and I squirmed wet in his arms and he threw me onto the cot. I felt myself sobbing but could not hear it. I twisted to the floor. I pulled myself up, Grack everywhere my eyes rolled, and went for the wall again. Grack everywhere! Then quick I turned — lucid now! sly! — and leapt toward the knife. His boot stopped me hard. He led me outside through a gray drizzle and held my forehead and then wiped the mud from my knees and wrapped me in blankets. It was night; there was no light in the sky but an airplane beacon toward which I had knelt. "Look at the scenery, kid, you did it all over the Continental Divide."

It's lovely cool country up there near Winter Park. The folks come to ski in winter, they say. Run special trains — hot coffee and college girls and lots of harmonizing around the fire.

Then I remember how he pulled the raspy Army blanket about my shoulders. He turned the cot over on me and sat on it to keep me down. All I thought to say was, "Oh my god help me Grack," — and felt the running in my ears.

"Yep," he grinned, bringing his finger to his eye to help me hate him enough to stay alive. This wouldn't kill me whole, but the pieces of me were dying. He looked and swore to me that my ears were empty. He kept on promising me.

"Let's do and say we did," he murmured, grinning.

Then it was better. I think I slept. When I awoke he was eating, his jaw full of sandwich and making a click of eating work. As soon as he saw me looking, he swallowed, showed his teeth, said, "You got the jaundice, that's your color, big

behind Grack and the show — had brought the pieces back together again. The nose was still squashed flat.

"Now when they try to give you the stuff, just for joykicks maybe," he said softly, "you can ha-ha in their faces."

Hee, hee, hee — I tried to smile by thinking this phrase. All the graduates of his seminary together couldn't have done what Grack helped me to do.

"But you'll dream about the sugar yet. You'll wake up hot for it. No joypopping, hear? Stay off, kid."

I thought the word *cheese* to help make a smile for him.

"You don't need me no more," Grack said.

No, fact, I didn't want the carnie anymore. Even a nice living picking pockets isn't such a nice living.

"You need to be square," he said. "I want you to get out of this world. Get."

"I'm going, Grack."

The carnie is a feudal domain, with rules of easy power and Grack the courteous lord at the top. I named my desire Gratitude, and said goombye. My ambition, uncured of hope, dreamt of the wide world away, in my father's house and near Phyllis and where the marks whom we scorned did better than the best skillo man in the business. I felt strong enough for this republic of markdom which Grack and the others derided; you might put it that I lacked their energy of despair. As you like it about me.

"Scram. You got somewheres, kid. You need out. I got noplace but to the seminary twenty years ago. Get the hell out."

"It's a long way on the bus," I said, as if he should pack

27

me a lunch for it, the complaint read correctly by him as: *Why do this thing for me?*

"That's all right. You'll do it for the Grack maybe someday. I like giving one more push instead of the kick. That's all."

"You got some long black ideas in your head, Grack."

"Think so? You too, kid, but maybe it's all tongue. We're buddies now."

This time I could smile for him without any tricks about it. "Then why do you want me to get?" — what could he give me that was surer than that junior word, *buddies?*

"Scray-out, kid. Beat it. Get from the life. I said already it's for Grack, too, and I can see by the fuzz in your ears you heard me. Listen, I can tell it to myself how I did it once before it was too late. Keep me warm winters. Keep me sleeping sometimes nights, a trick like that. Listen, I want to send one back just for me, for the Grack."

"One what?"

"One you. Just one. You're the one I'm sending back to mama for me, kid."

Now the smile came for true, for no fun, with teeth. "Grack, you might be making a mistake." I really wanted to warn him. "I never had no mama."

The dark face winced and turned shrunken with frown like a monkey's or a newborn's head. "Never had a mama? Kid, they been telling me a lot in my day, but that's one for the geeks. I don't want you even kidding me on that one."

"Fact. I'm kidding on the square, Grack."

"Shut up. Shut up. You're going home now and big Grac-

28

chus is sending you back, kid, and shut up now," — the fury taking his dark face and twisting it and breaking the voice, so that I said only:

"It's a long way on the Greyhound."

I bought a cardboard suitcase to carry an Indian blanket East to my father. Grack didn't say goodbye although he took me to the bus stop. He had shaved. He whistled and rubbed his dry hands, but did not touch his eye. He gave me a paper bag with the knife inside: "For going away quick, kid." It helped me that he wanted me to go, and his whistling said: I'm sending you for me, kid. His Adam's apple and the wart were all wiggling; then he swayed from behind in the nervy carnie dance of breaking down the show. Goombye, I thought back to him. The knife was sharp enough to be wrapped in underwear so that it wouldn't poke through the suitcase, across half a continent in the presence of many other travelers, on a long ride back to Pittsburgh.

4. Then visited from the jungle to jungles

W<small>HERE</small> you been?" That's what my father said to me. "Hello, boy, where you been all this time?" But, fluttering his thick oily lashes, he got out of his chair to take my hand in both of his. There were gray pouches under the eyes. His eyes had the scared longing of a man still a male but living without a woman. Noisy with feeling, his breath came over me as he touched my hands, my arms, my shoulders. When he pulled me toward him I leaned away and he stopped. He sighed and croaked, "What you been up to?"

"On the road," I said. That tied up three years of it for him.

"What you got to show for it, son?"

"Nothing much."

"Not even money?"

"Just only penny-one."

He tucked in his undershirt over the heavy gray flesh as if greeting a creditor — petulance, unease, but none of the anger I needed from him. "You never even wrote me but one little tiny old postcard. That's all right, now you'll settle down. That's something is worth priceless, son. You have gained you some experience. What the devil did happen to your nose? —

used to have one like mine, a nice nose. But you didn't bring back any cash?"

"Couple dollars, Pa, with my penny-one I was telling you about."

"Like I was saying to my driver just the other day, son, that ain't all in life, I mean cash. . . ." — and the tears came blue and fat down the slivers of beard on his cheeks. "It's good to see you again, boy. It is." His face was blotched purple and the tears came dripping and his eyes were squeezed up, red rim against red rim, but the voice went on calmly telling me his good news of Pittsburgh. "Money or no money in your pocket, it's always good to have a son for a father in his age. I been missing you all this time, boy. Your skin is marked there on your face, on your arms over there. What happened?"

Did to myself and now I say I didn't, Dad! But I just heard him out.

"You were born with a nice clean body, not a mole on it anyplace. Your mother was like that, too. If you're hungry, let's be having something to eat. I'm going to fix me some sausage and potatoes now, boy. Will you have a bite with me? Come on to the table and sit down while I fix it," — the thick body, heavier but still muscled, flap-flapping the slippers and the heels showing pink across the floor.

"Still putting it away, eh Pa?"

"Doc Fink says no more deep fry, and he *knows* that's how I like it. Salt, butter, bacon grease, too —"

"So what do you do now, Pa?"

"Deep fry it, boy. You really come back broke?"

All I meant to think was, with a jerk of regret: I spilled

31

my money into the sewer through those nicks on my arm. But the jerk turned out to be a movement of gratitude for my friend Grack, and a hi-dad for my father, too: Thanks for beginning where we left off and with food. If you can eat fats, then so can I.

The old man had grown older, the stubble white on his cheeks and a way of talking which spoke for the hopelessness of words and the hurry-up which the sight of death gives us. He had the slow movements of a strong man who has worked hard, and is tired, and no sleep but one can mend him. Even now he refused himself the compensation of anger! The nervous lift of my head to his was regret for this, was the apology which could never reach him, was, above all, greeting.

Still in his apartment at the corner of a street of side-by-side houses, his fire-escape door open to the flies in summer and the twice-a-week maid, grease in his pots and fat on his thighs, he ran his trucking business for pleasure and went on dwelling in his other habits of a lonely something-to-do. He moved without touching the narrow walls and the accumulation of furniture in these rooms which he knew with his feet and roaming desires. He had no one. He had nothing. He was not sufficient unto himself (no man is), nor was I good enough to make the ghost of my mother stand back. He had nothing to do but to pass back and forth in time from my mother (so pretty she was, and you'd never believe how light on her feet) and then to the rest of life (so heavy, so long). And I was all that was left of his wife and I had come back to him. He leaned the bull chest and the head with its unshaven cheeks toward me. He was trying to smile. "See this old slicer, son? Remember when I got it for a premium? Your mother always wanted a set of nice cutlery, but I got it too late. Couldn't afford. Look how I honed it down so she's no more'n a wire on a handle. Makes you wonder about steel, don't it?"

"I remember, Pa."

"It'll sure be a day when this blade goes crack, but it's coming, I know it. I'm glad, so happy, you come back before all the old things wore out, boy. Coffee?"

"I'll take it with thanks."

"Sit down, sit down, you don't have to play formal manners with your own dad. Sure, I know you're not used to home ways."

At first I watched through his talk for him to try to convince me with the index finger to his eye. But this was the new world of America at Pittsburgh I had come back to, a suppleness in its demands and a sternness in its ways. The house would not move. Dad would wait to see what he could do. Grack's older world had all its morality faced to the one commandment — *Be with it and for it!* — and the way or the why unjudged by the other solitary judges. Unlike the carnie, the Outside practiced a ritual which could never be learned because it altered with each day. I had to get wise all over again, my pocket-picking wisdom insufficient. He fed me. He learned to talk without questions except for the future. There were proposals, courting hints, and much patience in a heavy man with gray fat and muscles going bad in his age.

Would I like to sell pants? He knew a fellow, a clothier.

How about clerking in a high-class shop? I would just have to sweet-talk a little, pour it on the way I knew how.

What about the post office? a factory? soliciting by tele-phone? a working job or a selling? "You pick it, son," — and his mouth was that of a swain, soft and half-parted as the lips waited for me.

Back to college, if you really want that, — and I watched choking while his finger, plump and knuckle-thick, came to his eye. There was a lash to rub out; that was all. My father, bald and shaving what hair he had, lay in the cushions like a cheap rubber doll with thick, oily, pasted-on lashes. He walked, he talked, he did his duty, folks. White slivers of beard lay flat against the falsely hale cheeks.

"No, I don't want it. I think I'll hang around awhile and see, Pa," I told him. "College, I mean I don't want."

"Just don't you go back on the road, son," — and the doll-baby lashes fell shut. "You're all I have in the world. I'm not counting my possessions. I almost got the detectives on your tail, but I couldn't afford it. Sure, business was pretty good, *pr-retty* good, the trucks were hauling sometimes twenty-four hours a day. . . . Stay here with me now."

"I came back to see you, Pa."

"Don't go away. Find yourself something. You won't have to stay here so long, just till your old father —"

In a hurry, reproaching and interrupting: "I'll get some-thing in mind to do, Pa. I haven't got it yet, but I'll get it." By this time he should have known that I needed something from him.

"It's a pretty good business I got here for a young man. Two White Motor trucks, dependable drivers, a name for careful hauling and paying my bills on the first. Got me a better spot in the depot since you left. You wouldn't want to work for me, would you, son?" — again, as he said this, the soft shy smile of the fearful swain. I was grateful for the *you wouldn't would you?* I loved him for it. But, as is the habit of men like me, it drove me to strike at him harder.

"No, I wouldn't," I said.

And his lashes fell thick over the opaque eyes, and the smile sank away within his cheeks.

I needed his anger just because he strangled it for me. I had to twist, to butt, to dig it out. Looking through to his eyes was like standing in the sun, trying to peer through a screen after the girl who has just slipped inside. I remember doing that in Montgomery, Alabama, one time when I followed a girl to the julep-and-Buick part of town because she looked like Phyllis. Otherwise I forgot about Phyl.

"I saved your postcard in my wallet," he was saying. "Want to see it?"

One thing more about my father now: He showed his happiness by talking easy and going as light as he could on me. He couldn't help the sticky eyes and the disordered smile. I had made so many judgments on myself that I would not have been able to take even the predictable ones from him, those judgments of nag which never did for his fury against me. The fearfulness in my sight and the thick lashes were the most I could handle. I had given up on his telling me his anger out. Burdened with enough sense to know gratitude for the way he waited me through, I never said anything when I caught him trying to figure me over his newspaper with the teevee, his creaking slippers, and his flabby, money-used face. The soiled furniture of his world swelled about him in damp pillows and upholstery and loose whining springs. He settled among these things of an evening, groaning with pleasure in what I (mistakenly) thought of as power over the future through the abdication of risk. "Just horse around, figure it out for yourself," the baby-faced blink said to me, the combed lashes sticking together over his eyes.

Well, this girl in Montgomery — like girls in Rifle City, Colorado, and San Diego, California — had made me think of Phyllis as I did now while my father was patient with my peering about the city jobless, stiff-necked, and cool-headed. *Think* of her, I say: those others turned me back despite my habit to the side-looking cast in Phyl's eyes, her black hair short-cropped with a calculated wildness, her eyes, too, calculating in their defect but playing at one time only for me. Home now after three carnie years, I made no effort to find her. Nevertheless, while Pa worked and I pulled with two fingers at the padded roll of dollars I had brought home with me — padded with singles, *this* small — the backward-bending part of me looked to the small bones quick in Phyl's cheeks, the small mouth bitten full and pouting, and the intelligent grace of the swimmer in her movements across a room. Deep-breasted, deep-clefted, knowing it and using it, she leaned, laughed, or bent her black curls with the cast of her eye wily in thought. I did not call her or try to find what had become of her. She might still have been too lively for me.

Meanwhile, first I told Pa I didn't have penny-one. Lie. Then I told him I had a fat boodle of gain in my pocket. Lie. He nodded and looked, his head thrust forward on his thick neck, always believing me. I think my mother was also

too much for him, and died in pity of him at my birth —
but that's the sort of guess you make when you live overlong
in a house with a man who deals even with pleasure as a sort
of reverence. Lies, lies, and true enough.

Anyway, no man can escape the woman he considers too
much rused for him: tear her down or run away toward her
if he can't meet her head-and-hind on. I was coming back to
Phyl as the Kansas City legionnaire, stupefied by banquet
and toast to the Old Battery, sleeps, sweats in it, dreams of
some pert French *fifille* that he thinks he remembers. She
is light to hold, and dance to our dream. She is the prize
of an easy war. Remember, Frank, how we took Saint-
Tropez?

I was speaking there from fancy. The leap and high-
buttoned soar of Phyl made me think of the poor dreams of
Vet convention stag parties, where being together makes
each wife's man snore after the same faraway girl.

I called her at last. No, she was not married. Yes, she was
claimed. She was to go East to be married in October to a
man in the litigation business, she said. He was a lawyer
working for a fine organization. He didn't interest me; it
didn't change anything about Phyl for me, either, whether
it was a mote or a lawyer in her scheming eye. Even by telephone I could feel her presence, the smallness of her, swollen
with sex, and the thirsty face which came clear astonishingly
sharpened with surprise over the telephone. I heard her
breath — Fifi transported from the dream! It was the surprise
of long anticipation. I had the good dizziness of the barker
watching the marks file in at his promise of a high-ly ed-u-ca-
tional French can-can from Paris, France, the half-boy, half-

37

girl which sometimes does it like me and sometimes like you — yes, *you* — plus the genuine man-eating octopus from Japanese seas in added attraction.

Yes, she would see me. I picked the night.

The victory of a barker, however, is an end only in the carnie world at the canvas places where distinguished marks congregate: nothing at all to look roosterish about yet. I named an evening not too near and waited in the dark, my father's black shades drawn and my Prince Edward butts sucked gray in the dishes, while he went to work; he came home; he watched and waited for me to be a son to him. "You thinking about something, boy? Getting ready? That broke nose trouble you some in the change of weather? Planning things out for yourself?"

"Probably does, Pa. I'll do the supper dishes tonight."

Often I walked. I roamed the city at all hours, remembering when I came this high to a fire hydrant, seeing how the lot where we played stick hockey was now a four-story apartment, finding the corner where I had first dropped Phyl's books and tried to kiss her. I had succeeded, but she had spied out my astonishment at how little good it did us. Then a kiss doesn't move the sky and make a boy seven feet tall and smart! And a kiss does not unite the two of us in spirit forever! Her laughter was incredible.

At the cliffs of Pittsburgh, black with coal and red with ore, ruled by the mills to which came slope-jawed workers and the snappy commuting engineers, I lazed near the steel-makers while they sometimes cast an indifferent glance at me and away. If I caught an eye, I turned with Grack's scowl and Grack's grin through the changing weather, bringing my finger in a wide arc to the tender corner where the tear duct flows in the wind. They turned away. I didn't mean business.

Still I could have made a fortune in the carnival business. I have tongues, as Jake the Japes once told me; I could run a mission house, be a Captain of Sally. That wouldn't be being a son to him, Dad's long-lashed following of me insisted. "It's good for you to think things out. See that girl Phyllis Whatzername, too. I like it," he said.

To go away once more, talking the money from their pockets, this would be to fork my tongue forever and to put out his eyes — or so I thought that late summer in Pittsburgh. I believed it was now or never for getting with it. An absolutist, I did not yet know that life keeps on giving us another chance, just as with kisses, as with love's fumbling to be love — and just as with love's failure to be more than love. I ate every day. The liverish yellow disappeared from my eyeballs. The scars on my arms faded and vanished. All this should have been a lesson to me.

"What do you call her? What did you say her name was? Son! You're not listening to me."

Grack too wanted me to be good to myself even if he could not himself answer to this good. Like a saint devoted forever to his vice in hell, he wanted me to be a visitor and to carry a moment of his revery up with me to the purgatory which is what is best on earth. (Jeez! I had forgotten to kiss Pauline goodbye.)

Pa and Phyl were waiting for me. Grack, dwelling in cunning and sloth, busy in despair, waited in the rains of North Dakota. I looked around and dozed in the fat pillows of my father's chair and waited.

39

5. Evaded my mail and the liability to love

IT was nice. The day for Phyl came golden clear, a September interval with the dirt of the city upwinded from the smokestacks and the sun sailing free. In Indian summer weather the vegetables of the suburb turned crisp and obedient to the sun, all of them, hollyhocks, commuters, schoolchildren. Vacuum cleaners awoke with a wail and the quick-deciding kids were already sick of Crafts and Social Studies. Hoots of gang and band shrilled among the birdsong of electric wiring behind the apartment building; someone cried, "Give it here!" and the nostalgic critter wanting out within me thought, *Lookee lookee lookee*.

The one thing I did for Dad, having wrapped his old flannel bathrobe about my skinny flanks, was to make his breakfast mornings before he went off to the dispatcher's office. We sat blinking at each other over coffee. "You all riled up about seeing that girl tonight, son?" he asked me.

"No more'n she's worried about me, Pa."

"That's fine, fine, it's called taking things in your stride. Like I did when my driver twisted a trailer off into the ditch

40

coming out of Youngstown and I'd forgot to renew the insurance. What did you say her name was? They're only women."

"That's all they need be, Pa," — and his gray face wrinkled with the complicity of laughter between father and son while toast crumpled between the plump cheeks.

Later I went down to the mailbox. We all have dreams of lotteries, longlost Oklahoma uncles, delicious fawn-eyed models from the perfume ads who have found our address, and we reach behind our names even if all we find is the electric bill. The top letter was addressed to me. I turned it over for the fun of receiving mail, the abstract breath which a word can carry from person to person, the pleasure teased through a pen until it comes out grammar. This envelope had been smudged by hands unskilled in writing. The return address was a jail in Kearns, Utah. The letter was from Grack.

And he had set me loose only to drop the net on me?

I stood in the hard September sunlight of the suburb, the scratch of a rake next door and the tasty stench of burning leaves in my nostrils, and knew that all this was slipping away — money and plan and Pa and Phyllis, and the suppleness of decision of which I have already spoken — as my fingers slipped over this envelope which Grack had sent to bring me back. Then he couldn't! — I knew this without opening. If he couldn't do without me, how could I be expected to do without him? I looked to the leaf fire down the block for a flame to reach out for this paper in my hands. The dead leaves crackled, and the green edges hissed and sang. If his will had sent me home, how could I remain in my father's house in the suburb when his will called me back? Or had he given me something he could not so easily Indiangive? —

some alteration in my moral chemistry which this humor of his could not dissolve.

Freeing me, he thought now to play leash with old affections and gratitudes. I hustled my breath in the autumn like a shill pushing to buy. But I would not buy.

And, watching my hand move with the letter, I discovered that in these doings I had decided myself. Boggling my father and Phyl, ambiguously loosened but unfree, the stiff-limbed gestures of the suburb were my only trust. I practiced the skill of meanness. The gesture was one of putting away, thrusting off, closing. Grack had seen in his moment of pity for me that I needed my childhood more than I needed him. And now that I was making the effort, I choked with anger at my own injustice to myself which had sent me from morphine (of which I still dreamt) to Grack (who signaled our carnie past like the thrilling daytime memory of a dream, and beckoned). This letter had come to take me down once more. He was in jail; he needed help; he asked me to risk myself as he had done, with only a knife between us, during those days and nights in the cabin. When I left he might have picked up a habit himself, as if the number of habits is fixed, and the rule strict that he take my place in the one I had given up. The transmigration of joypoppers! — He had no rights now. I asked my respite and time to work. To answer the call on friendship for him meant to foreclose my own mortgage. I tried, like the suburb, to hate those not of our way as much as those in our way. Sacred fear universal, terrific, and purificatory! My choice was declared now, to return evil for good and callousness for kindness, in justice or not, or be never a man or nearly one.

Besides, the eye was faraway and the finger blunted by unsuccess.

Without opening it, I slid Grack's letter back into the mailbox and strolled down the street toward the dry cleaner to pick up my pants, rinsed in gasoline and creased for Phyl. I didn't hurry. A pair of trousers draped over my arm, I felt light and tricky in the ankles, healthily underfed, ready for any flight. I poked about the neighborhood, still carrying pants. The trees had thickened, the bark cracks turned darker, in the only three years since I had been a college kid visiting here. I bought a newspaper. I enjoyed the sweet images of childhood pressing back on a lazy day — roller skating in the streets, garages nicked by scout knives in this season, legs suddenly long with Phyl under the streetlamp evenings — while I enjoyed (yes! relished!) my feebleness of resolution in putting Grack's letter back in the box.

And I found the same kids in the street, wearing the variant faces produced by the hormones of chlorophyll, wheat germ, and dextrinized chocolate secreted since I was a boy devoted to Wheaties and Big League Gum, playing the same touch football under branches aflutter with dying leaves. There were the small quick curly-headed ones, the slow long-legged ones, pensive and pimply in adolescence, the hungry hot-headed athletes, all of them frowning with what the suburb does to children while their mamas talk on the telephone and wiggle to help the gas pass itself, as they wiggle for nothing else. I put my pants on a Home Edition of the *Press* and yelled, "Let me see it!" I was a big fellow to them. The ball came in a high arched spiral, unwobbling, and I caught it hard against my chest. I could still do that! I could throw a

43

long pass, too, proud of myself in touch football. (Girls watched! — children sprung tall whose knees and other corners were beginning to take kindly to flesh. A pale blond girl, in blue jeans and her father's shirt, sucked at a leafstem and waited, learning from us the interest of her coming age.)

"Again," I called.

They threw it again.

"Now try this one —"

It was a flagrant weakness to postpone the moment when I must again confront Grack at the mailbox by my father's front door. What else could I do now but undecide myself? How long could I wait for the decay of paper and ink, the corruption and dissolution of an appeal from my friend? I danced attendance. I played football in the street while I imagined the letter blowing away in the wind, stolen, burnt by fire and forever unopened. In the meantime girls were looking; it was autumn in the suburb, a golden dust and spinning birch leaves in the sky, while someplace the carnie was moving south, moving southwest along roads with ditches on both sides. In the meantime a studious pale blond girl, sucking a leaf, held herself and learned how men could perform. I had found an old game, a consolation for violence violently subdued, during my walk through the autumn sure of its frost and of its renewal. Having left the letter in the box, I pressed the hard lacing of a football against my outstretched palm. I loved myself for the twist which my body recalled with a long high pass far out to the smallest of the players. Let Grack make it himself now! I had grown up in touch football and still knew it well. (A pretty little girl watched and said nothing.)

44

"Again!" I cried.

They did it once more.

"I'll show you the sidewalk play," — and without waiting for their reply I explained how the ball carrier takes the center in the street, darts across the curb and the lawn to the walk, beyond the row of trees, and then wings a straight low pass to his right end far down the sidewalk. "See? Now let's practice it. Get out to the double-u," — furious with pride, the strong sweat staining my shirt and stinging along my jowls.

No one moved but the girl chewing at her leaf. A man with a briefcase had stopped and was watching, grinning, tucking, zipping, and buckling because he had just done business for "the Singer people" or "the Hoover folks" with one of the housewives. The child plucked a fresh leaf.

"See it here, I'll show you the way it's done. You get the other team out of balance. I'll explain it again."

They stood straddle-legged with their mouths like movie heroes in abstract know-how and their hands loose on corduroy hips. Endlessly the leaves were spinning down in each vagary of breeze on the trees turning away from summer above us. Screen doors slammed to; a slipshod infant fell, bawled, was hushed; somewhere a television roared, was tempered.

"Go on out, I'll shoot you a long one," — and the prickle of sweat at my jaw turned chill all at once.

Even pride had to admit their sense of me now. One of them spoke in a murmur compounded of high executive condescension and the remnants of his boyish impatience: "Go home, Mister, we're in the middle of a quarter. Give us Jimmy's ball back. He's letting *us* use it." Another came grin-

45

ning toward me, holding the Home Edition of the *Press* as a cradle at arm's length before him: "Here's your pants, Mister. They'll get dirty on the ground like that. We already heard about the sidewalk play."

"Nosy!" — this one down the street.

Surely it was as they thought: the intruder had no rights. They played touch only for touch and that was all, while I made of their sport a spurious triumph upon the world of my absent, vacated, forfeited childhood. "Who is" (the question was a titter) "who *is* that Joe?" Still their skill was at more than football; they knew how to use my risk of self at the game for their purposes of vindictiveness, as they used the game itself to console them for foregoings, for waiting to grow up, for traveling hard against each other.

"Nosy! Oh nosy!" A shrill cry careened down the street after me with my pants and the paper, and it came from the witty smallest one, to whom I had first thrown a fine long pass. "Lookit his nose, lookit! Ja-ever see it?" The delicate blond girl turned her regard sweetly upon him.

Home much later, my elbow had already begun to stiffen from the football and from my unnatural carrying of my cleaning. I had even been down to the river with it, where the freighters and the pleasure craft moved and seemed not to be moving in a commerce that never ceases, even at the bend of the stream downtown. I had hung my pants on a starved dogwood branch until I heard the heightened end-of-day whir of traffic on the road above, and then I went home. It was time to shower for Phyl.

The mail had been removed from the box. There was

nothing on the table for me but an advertisement for a tie pool: exchange two old ones for a grab-bag Kravate. ("Be sharp, stay sharp, think sharp, men, at a minimal cost for terrific accessories.") Dad was pretending to doze in a chair. "Any mail for me?" I said.

"What? Just what's on the table." The letter had gone away, exactly as I had prayed it would. I knew the heady triumph of the gypsy whose enemy dies after he has stuck pins in his image, burned his fingernail sheddings, crossed his shadow with a strangled cat's tail. And his chagrin: think of the gypsy returning to the woods for the head of the cat and fondling it to say, *I remember when that man was a friend.* "You're late, son. Been doing something?" He wore the drawn, righteous, self-tormented face of a diplomat or of a sick old Tom.

"Been out all day. Played a little touch football, limber me up again."

"That's fine, get yourself some air," my father said. "Trouble with work is you get muscles but no air. Those kids know how. Best thing in the world for you."

Rioting within, I ran to my shower. Done for me once more! I didn't care what he had made of Grack's letter: I had dreamed right and proven that even a day of indecision could end in irrevocable decisions. The letter was gone; I needed never ask of it — it had never been delivered, it had never been written, it had never existed. Like the nose before my flat new one, it was vanished from my life and no good to me. I could forget it. (I shaved in the shower without cutting myself.) Had I ever guessed that my delay before the letter was a way of giving another my decision to make? The gypsy's cat was only an instrument. I sang and soaped myself, even to the grainy hairs, oily and bulbous at their roots, a chief, a desired player at least in this realm.

6. Tried the sidewalk
play once more

I DIDN'T have to talk. It had been years, but sure, she was still ready to be my Phyl. *Ready:* but not yet or ever mine. The side-looking cast of her eyes supplied what explanation she needed, and she murmured, very fast, the polite words for a neighbor after a voyage. When she had spent them all, she smiled, showing the budded teeth through her small swollen mouth, and slyly added: "You're thinner around the hips, Bud. You used to have some fat, some curves there. Quite a rear you used to have — quite a rear."

"It was only baby fat," I said. She looked fine to me. Even the subtle new lines about her eyes (those black calculators) gave well to the vital quickness of her movements, her bones, and the organs within. She tossed her head, and her body rippled, and she was still a girl despite the deepness at her breasts and the lace at her eyes. We avoided talk of her marriage. He was in New York. That was a mistake, I think — I mean our not speaking of it. Disbelief in explanations was one of our habits, although we were no better than others; we needed them. We never tried explanations. They had seemed inappropriate since our grammar school days together, when we had played Hospital through the long summer afternoons and had cured each other of indigestion, broken arms, and wanting anyone else. Once we had eaten ice cream and smeared it and then tongued it away. Inexplicably children together, we had even slept side-by-side touching in the grass through the heat of July and the swarming grasshoppers.

Now, an unskilled sleeper, I had been roused from my carnival dream (Grack did this!) and walked imperfectly awake, stiff-elbowed, thick-tongued, and dim-sighted despite my looking. I was walking without Grack, his approval tight in my fist. "I wanted to ask you, Bud . . ." She wondered how my father was making out; I told her great. He was making money, I said, and preserved by his life and not growing old too fast. The letter was not part of this speech, nor the love and dread of me in the sight of my mother's photograph on the dining room shelf.

"I'm hungry, Bud," she said.

"Do you want something to eat?"

Her laughter rang out as we strolled a business street of the suburb. "If I want something to eat for being hungry," she cried, tears wetting her study of me. "Well, I'll make a bargain —"

I had forgotten my father's automobile parked at her home. Out of old habit, we had begun strolling as if rewarding ourselves for high school homework finished.

"There's Doc Dinny's," she said. "Listen, let's be as if I mean it when I say I'm hungry." With a schoolgirl playfulness she announced that she could eat only half of a bacon, lettuce, and tomato sandwich. Would I be responsible for the other half? Yes. By the time I had finished two mouthfuls, she had devoured her share and I offered her mine. She hesitated, her eyes glinting sideways at me under the crooked lids, the cast in her left eye emitting Grack's wary glitter while she waited in simple hunger and in the pleasure of it. She studied the ragged edge where I had eaten; then just where the mark of my teeth was most perfect, she took a bite. She smiled at me, her lips salty with bacon.

"Let's get out of here, Phyl."

"The jukers bother you? It's pretty loud," she agreed. "That was good. You always bought me a good bee-el-tee, Bud."

Did we need this talk after so many years?

We strolled and kept cool ("Let's not and say we did") to the alley which we both remembered for that first time, grown-up, that I had jammed her against the wall to kiss her. When I had finally loosened my arms and knees to let her go, she had clung to me and followed me away and then, with a laugh wild as any hey-rube call, pulled me back until I felt the crumbling brick against my own head and shoulders.

We turned into the alley together as if it were home.

When we came out again, bent and blinking against the streetlamp, she had agreed, though only for tonight — this was her condition, her paltry economy, a holiday welcome to me home — and we walked back to the automobile, chattering as old friends do after one has emerged from a long illness or a long quarrel. I reminded her of how, in high school, when all the girls practiced keeping the boys waiting, she had run to the window to watch me turn onto Buena Vista Street, and then gone to the piano to serenade me up the walk with "Themes for Two Hands from the Great Symphonies."

"You like me the way you always did, Bud?"

"I never forget anything, Phyl."

"You just remember me, that's all?"

"It's always new to me, Phyl."

"You talking about me now?"

"You now, Phyl."

The kiss, salty with bacon and her swollen lips, her flesh which loved my motherless cruelty trembling, had signified more than our jokes and our teasing. She agreed to the cabin, but only to the same one, the old one we knew, as if our past of cabins, a traditional right, pointed the way for her to be decent although engaged. Precedent it was. A lawyer it was.

Only our memories had rights — this her dearest mistake; how could she hope, in our return to what was gone, for a matching of histories as we had used to match homework? She shuddered in the morality of a suburban romantic, far from the strife of business and love, a well-rested heroine fresh from her waiting, although she knew to move close and her hands played greedily. Greedy all over me and impatient for the profit of it. "You're beautiful, beautiful, beautiful," I think I was saying in that alley we really still knew. Spite, spite. But I believe we really remembered it there and together.

Then we drove through the city and the whiteness of frost on the highway and the empty lots (but it was only moonlight) toward the roadhouse — LIQUOR! TRUCKERS STOP HERE — silently gossiping in memories and, for the moment, content with our strangeness to each other.

52

"You look a little like a girl I know, Pauline's girl, Joy is her name—"

"I just remind you of someone? You've traveled a lot?"

"Not so much. A little. She's just a kid daughter of a friend of mine. Anyway, how could you remind me of anyone when I've known you ever since—"

She interrupted. "Yes, ever since," she said. "It's really been a long time you've known me, Bud. Other girls should remind you of me."

I looked a question at her, but the eye was turned inward and it seems that she was thinking of all that time without thinking of me, no matter what she said to make what we were doing nice. She moved next to me. Had we always been so strange, shaken out of time? No, in those days we had made demands for trust, thickened flesh and mingling breath signifying great ambitions toward mingling of heart, abstractions and ideals to the flow of finicky adolescent blood. "Themes for Two Hands"—and from the great symphony. She slipped her hands into my shirt and let me slip my hands, too, and brushed her mouth down my cheek, and a moment later she slipped away to tilt her head in order to show me her lips pouting because bruised, because amused. "You never did wear an undershirt," she said. "I always remembered that about you." She had learned early to bring politics to the play of love. She laughed in that time after parking, before stepping out onto gravel, and told me that the new sudden laughter was not for the undershirts I didn't wear nor for the fine combed-yarn tee-shirts that she had once given me (the last one worn out and used to wipe a windshield in southern

California my first winter in the carnie), but for the lessons she had taken because her parents could spare the two dollars a week and I liked music. For this: the piano. "Never play it anymore," she said. "I played it for you."

"Let's get out of here."

Knowing his cousins from Jacksonville to San Diego, I was easy and my voice loud with the keeper of the motel behind the roadhouse. A bloated, purple-faced wino with a stained white knit shirt open on a chest bald and plump as a woman's, he drawled, "Checkout at noon," — rocking on his heels and grinning from me to her and back. Phyl kept cool, studied her face in a purseflap mirror, didn't touch her lipstick. "There's a rag there to put under the shower if'n it drips. Noise aggravates some folks, t'rists I mean — sensitive that way with that driving and all." He pronounced "tourist" as if it were the newspaper word "tryst," his unwieldy mouth wearing the jealous leer proper to the keeper of this place, whose sign declared itself *An Approved-Type Motel. A Home For Your Car.* Phyl snapped the purse shut and waited.

He retreated, still grinning, his fat back wobbling. Phyl moved near to give me the flex of her legs and the soft cradling of her breasts in latex when she stepped forward to pull the cord on the mosquito-lamp. Faintly came the music from the roadhouse across the lot:

> "And lead me to the valley
> Where the still waters flow
> Oh I got a gal . . ."

For a quarter in a slot we could have had the use of a radio. My arm burned where her softness had passed, and my thigh took it, too, like the shock of an unsheathed wire. There was

54

no mailbox at the door of the cabin. Even Grack could not find me here.

Stung and hot, I stood at the door, drawing breath, thinking: *Free*. And not even curious about what Pa had done with the letter. I leaned gratefully into the damp night air, turning at the smell of hops which seemed to flow back past the few scraggly pine between the roadhouse and us. The sign — LIQUOR! TRUCKERS STOP HERE — was flashing behind a wooden building. It signaled itself to me only by the bobbing red halo above the roof, a smoke which drifted nowhere, but I already heard the steady click of the mechanism from my long looking out of flopster hotel rooms and down midways at closing time. STOP HERE! the smoke said stubbornly, then paled, then repeated. I knew at that doorway while Phyl was busy behind me the awfulness of being absent within my body under the stars of this continent, neither at sea nor at land but rising like the imprisoned neon smoke, red to a click and black to a click, falling and rising, in love with land and sea, in love with sky and cloud, while imprisoned to a click between them all. I thought: *Stop here!* I thought: *Click!* and then thought it again. The sense of hopeless love was in this, that I did not even know for whom this love burned or whether it burned or drowned, although my skin had been scorched by her warm flesh and my places were swimming for her places. And I was cold in that doorway. And I was hot there, shivering when she put her hands on me.

"Hiya, Bud," she was saying, "good to see you again," — the cast-ridden eye calculating my disarray. "You haven't told me anything yet."

"It's a long story."

"Close the door."

"It's a long story, the carnie's hard to tell," — while I turned impatiently to her, thinking of Grack and the scars on my arm and the hazards of a rusty Ferris wheel and Pauline and old Popolous and his lost ironing. And how I teased my way into the pockets of a thousand marks or two, and squeezed their larcenous hearts in my fist until they squirted green money. "Save it, honey, save it, some other time, Phyl."

Curl-lipped, petulant, she exhaled through her smile. "That's not what I mean, Bud. Oh dear me, of course I want to know all about it —" She pouted maliciously, but not with malice. "I mean, I mean about *me* . . ." I took her to kiss, as she wanted to be taken. This was the story she needed me to tell, and the rest was hurry-up, was patience, was the dance of blood which the world and nature require. Even Countstore Bud responsible to it! Even this electric-headed black Phyllis! "Oh dear me oh dear you . . ." — with her schemes and her cast-eyed ways.

"You're a funny critter."

"I fancy you," she whispered. She twisted and fooled like a coy child because this was a costume party for her. (I was a machine for judging: I know that costume parties are important to children.) Engaged to a lawyer, she celebrated her blood with me although, pious in a way she did not guess of herself, the ritual signified more than advance and retreat, supplication and avowal, a drinking from the cup and an eating of the bread. Turning, turning, she kissed and pulled under the throb and pulse of a neon flare: "Oh! Hurts! Now tell me about me!" I shook my head. I was unwilling to re-

TO THE LITERARY EDITOR

This Atlantic Monthly Press book
will be published on

February 16 $3.75

Do not review before publication date.

Tear sheets or clippings of your review are
requested.

Please do not quote more than 500 words
without special permission.

In giving credit to the publisher in your
reviews, please use the words
"Boston: Atlantic-Little, Brown"

ATLANTIC-LITTLE, BROWN BOOKS
ARE PUBLISHED BY
LITTLE, BROWN AND COMPANY
IN ASSOCIATION WITH
THE ATLANTIC MONTHLY PRESS

Little, Brown & Company, 34 Beacon St., Boston 6

turn to what I named the world in order to play a part in a dance, even her pious dance, even the one that was our bounty since we had discovered ourselves in each other behind a willow in a suburban field.

I have often been mistaken about human beings. I must be wrong about her, too. As you can see, I *need* to be wrong about her.

A shower was not reason enough to leave me then. We kissed once more, but not enough.

"In just a minute," she said.

"Stay again, please."

Despite her soft yielding within the arm thrown across my chest and her hard hot holding as she opened and closed her eyes next to mine, the eye each time was overwatchful. "I'll be back in a minute, ten at the most."

"Don't go, Phyl."

"But it's been so sticky tonight."

"Stay with me, Phyl."

"But I want to be clean."

"Don't go now, Phyl."

She let the odd clothing fall from her body before stepping over the tricks and straps and little lace into the bathroom. This was to keep me busy while I waited. Congested with health, she moved briskly away from my own scrawny, hairy, unripe, and renewed readiness. She grinned at her one hand's gesture of shame, but then used it to reach for a handkerchief and said nothing. When she blew her nose, with conviction, her hips seemed to expand. She returned my handkerchief and went to the shower.

I waited to this hiss of water beyond the door and, in my

unleashed revery, to its brisk steaming off the tanned partial face of her body. Flesh is a face. After silence and longing it must think of love before soap. She should not have left me there. She should have decided me quiet first. Exhausted, red neon in my head, I went again to look at the mailbox. There was no letter; there was no box. I knew the cabin; I moved quickly in it. I coughed, astonished and agape, to find no letter. Where had I lived in a cabin like this one? Not with Phyl, no. I spat into the swept-up heap of rubbish in the fireplace.

Grack had thrown a cot over me and sat on it to still my writhing, and then he had trusted me with his knife because I could kick a habit. I heard her singing while the prickles of water invaded her domain, the proud flesh rising on her round arms and down the long, tennis-playing, suburban legs. She should not have left me then, even for a shower.

I thought of Grack watching me while I butted my head against a cabin wall. His smile had helped me; the knife was only warning. My eyes swarmed, my sight eclipsed, I had a headache, I was sleepwalking. She was sloshing about and soaping herself and working the soap in her soft places. She should never have left me.

And then I heard the sound of my habit: a low wail of someone tormented in sleep and unable to wake. *There*, there again. I listened with my head twisted for the enemy. The shower hid it from her. Once more: and this time no mistake. It had come from my own chest. Now I needed Grack to protect me from that dreaming which is too real to be known without the coolness of morphine's double sleep.

It could still be warned away. There was silence as she moved onto the shower mat. "You there, Bud?"

How could I answer *yes?*

"You there now?" — and she must have been dripping and rubbing with a towel in her hands and her back arched. Soon she would open the door, cool with water, hot with it, and come for me with her woman's huge-faced body, the eyes palpable, yearning and blind, the mouth mannered in its secrets. She should have stayed with me in the room all the time.

I heard the bite of gravel under my heels and the thin harangue of hillbilly laughter from the roadhouse. LIQUOR! STOP HERE! I fled back to put five dollars on the table for her taxi home, and then out, into the automobile, and roaring down the driveway and back to Grack's letter. Only much later did I imagine what she had thought, naked within a towel while a moth headed furiously into the light, when she saw the money weighted under a hotel ashtray on the bed-table near where we had stood and been together.

7. *Decisions as we like them: My regretful imagination sees true*

I SEE the letter this way. Pa comes home panting in the heat, already unbuttoning his shirt on the sidewalk before he enters and rubbing the sticky gray belly-hairs. The air is not that hot, but the afternoon has been long for a man with a son lazing at home on his money. He mumbles it this way: "A no good, no account boy I raised. I raised him, poor kid he had no mama, I did it to him — that goddamn bum," — a man soft because his son is his only chance at lasting beyond his days, hard because his son is to blame, being present and an instrument of all the bad tidings of his life. And worse than either the hardness or the softness was the dread of seeing these things naked, love or hate, in a moment which would fix them forever. The love he could not speak was as hateful to me as the slow seepage of detestation for which I feared him, worried him, and from which I drew all hope for him and for me. "A tramp, a drifter is all he is. Why don't he come to work for me? He knows I'll give it all to him someday. Waiting for me to pass on. How do I know he ain't just home hiding out like I seen it in the movies? Poor kid, he's still a baby — what can an old no-good like me do for him?"

He is shading his eyes and looking to the window for me. I don't stand and wave to him; I'm not home. He sees, he *thinks* he sees my shadow.

Up the front steps, the stain spread and crusted under his arm, the tip of the evening paper tickling his bared chest, he is still murmuring to himself, a heavy old man, sick with no one to talk to since his wife was taken away. The mailbox, that outpost of magic, replenished each day: Shirts Factory to You! Are you insured against Acts of God? Pick your own Pattern! Our subscription manager is thinking of *you*, Mr. Alert Citizen, in the events that lie ahead. Satisfied Users say (and we quote from unsolicited comments in our files). Ignore this notice if you have already complied.

But Grack's letter, the return address a jail in Kearns, Utah, has already caught him and he lets the others trail down across the rug as he goes to sit hunched over it at the kitchen table, the bare bulb behind him hot on his bare head. We were not rich except in desires toward each other: the bulb is uncovered; the linoleum bumps itself under the stove; the light switches go *click*, not softly squashing themselves into place as in some houses I have seen.

He studies the envelope and turns it over in his hands with no design at first but the passive one of awe. That my boy should get a letter from a jail. . . . That these should be his friends. That he never speaks of these people, of anybody anymore, that kid. A father should know his son's friends, shouldn't he? A boy that wants to be a son to him, normal thing to be.

There is no decision to open the letter. His hands simply pull it apart. (There is no impulse to steam it, to read it

61

through the light, to woo his son by ruse or trick.) The sheet from a child's school tablet comes flat in the horny blackened fingers. He is breathing heavily through pursed lips which help with the reading, but his eyes are slotted against the glare of light off ruled paper. His mouth breathes with it. Grack is asking money to get out of jail. His lips are moving:

> — a run of luck and stuck with the fuzz. But I know a
> fellow needs another store, we could do it together,
> friend. I'll buy in for the both of us, that's how I'll
> piece you off square. Come on in. We can really ride
> it high together and get on fresh in the springtime —

I imagine the letter that way. He needs the money bad, so bad that he offers me a friendship which means pulling me back — it turns out that to send me away had judged and cost him too much. My father understands what the letter asks. This is enough for him.

In my father, as in me during that time, there is little capacity for decision. We learned from ourselves, if we learned at all, by observing what we had already done. He sees himself — as I see him now — opening, reading, putting his hands on his hairy forearms while he knows what it means for me to receive such a letter. It means I would go. It means loss; it means his final bereavement. He looks up to find the letter stained with fat as he clings to the rough paper with his fingers. The penciling is oiled and smudged.

Now look! he is tearing the paper in his hands. He is rending it into scraps. He pedals the garbage can and lets the pieces fall among the sodden summer refuse of a week's eating. *Here* is the brutal willfulness which I need: this turning of my back on a friend, because not to turn meant my fall

62

into the pit from which I could only climb once. Grack had lifted me out. But I have not opened the letter, and my father makes for me the heartless decision that a father can arrogate to himself. I have left out one event from this argument in the kitchen, a decision which I could not imagine because I hoped my father altogether risen to the cruelty needed for the love of fathers and sons. He too, like the rest of the world, moved about me as an idea among other ideas.

I did see that he picks the scraps from the garbage can after a moment, finds them dripping already and rusty with decay, and tries to burn them. They will not burn. He crushes them back into the unemptied can.

I have said that these kitchen doings were decisions as I like them. I aspired, as I imagined these events, to a moral brutality of judgment. It is a duty to allow a man the privacy of his thoughts, his friends, his mail. Displeased by my terrorized agility before Phyl, my fright and my flight, I was calmed by the parallel act of disloyalty to Grack which my tenacious and overtender father could perform for me. By such confrontations — I prayed for my father — he might master his loss and his contrary passions. Living in the hope of this and of my own acquiescence, by such evasions might I separate myself from Grack.

I parked the automobile and heard the comforting squash of my rubber heels against cement as I strolled through the midnight yard. My fright had been stilled in power over the automobile, and I could imagine now without revulsion the thrust of Phyl's heels in the gravel near the roadhouse as she waited for a taxi. I went to the heap of mail and dealt through it.

Hushed and creaking, the apartment lay swaddled by darkness. I knew its furniture. Step here, step there, don't crack your shin. The hoarse breathing of my father was soft in this womanless place. Everywhere lights were out, and the reflection of the clear September sky outside on the belongings of our life made me remember what almost was, when I might have had a mother and my father a wife. I tiptoed to his door. It was ajar. He stirred, busily feigning sleep. No words between father and son, no sign. But I stood in gratitude for his confirmation of my wish, and went to bed at peace with Grack and Phyl.

I slept the sleep of a dutiful son in the late summer's heat. As I imagined my father then, so I assented to him.

8. Came with it one more time

My wrath was a foot gaff. I diddled it and tossed; it could not stop the wheel on anything but a number which lost for the house. My sleep was a skillo owned and operated by a carnie with stiff joints when the wheel most needed to be stopped. Night after night I crawled into bed toward the practical sleep of the just, fell sound dead at once, and awoke an hour later with the morphine gooseflesh hard on my limbs and my sleep no good to me. But I was cold for another answer this time. No morph, no! I had really kicked that one, and would do my own traveling from now on. Self-dread, self-loathing, these shudders took me; the memory of Grack was a honed belt tightening about my middle. Once I even whispered, as earlier in the cabin with Grack: "Oh my god help me someone." Whispering myself awake: "Oh help me someone." The wailing in my chest had put another habit hard upon me: the habit of conscience. I called it regret; I called it the willies. (Phyllis, someone said, had left town to marry her lawyer in New York. Or maybe it was Washington.)

Grack appealing, I had refused. My father had turned my back. Soft for me, he knew that I could not resist the word from another world. He had saved me by heeling me; there was sickness in my stomach; I thought of killing him. I loved him — that he could do this hard thing was a glory to me. Even Grack had failed to be devoted and cruel enough. My sense for Phyllis, for Grack, for my new-found father revolved in my head and chest. I was busy with people; this was a step. The people were all inner folk — the rest, the outward touching, was yet to come, if it would come. I even thought of Pauline and that shy treadmiller, Joy. And I could think of them now because of my father. One evening he had been magnificently mean for me, and then could go on grumbling at suppertime about sand in the two-ton's transmission and the guts of Standard Oil. We heard bells from the Ukrainian church on the next block and he had said: "Funny thing, son, how you sometimes notice and sometimes don't —"

"When you know a thing well," I had answered.

It was working. In the hard-awake aftersleep I arose silently to rummage in the clothes, my feet cold on the floor. I sat in the kitchen on the chair like a child after punishment, wise to hari-kari, stealthy and grinning, holding the knife Grack had given me. In a way he had taught me, I practiced a kitchen stunt: sharpening the long knife against a glass tumbler. And considered: Did my father have the right to do what I had asked of him?

Even a priest would have made me read the letter, I decided, unless, in full avowal, I pleaded aloud to be spared this knowledge-the-pride, knowledge-the-sin. Never enough words for us. At least one Canuck priest would have taught me to know and to sin with pride. I had run from it; I had seen Grack's finger against his eye. Some slaves, they say, came back at the sight of the master's eye. And then penance.

66

No morph now, not this time, not that blind fleeing with the naked white back exposed.

The white steel zipped like a pantleg against pantleg in the silvery night as I sharpened it on glassware. I had worked it to slicing the hair from my arms. Sometimes I went back to bed and sometimes I slept. Many nights together I practiced to find that with which I had begun: my heavy-fleshed father had conquered Grack for me. In destroying the letter unopened, he had done for me what I needed to do: spit in my love and anger, all to be collected with the garbage and digested in a truck. Again I returned to bed with the glass left on the table and the knife under my mattress. Often I thought: no! And then: yes, yes, this is the way. I could forget Grack now.

Phyllis, or someone like her?

A job of work, or something like it?

For the moment I found a place as dispatcher in a Greyhound station: "*A*mbridge, *Bea*ver Falls, *You*ngstown, and Warren. Cleveland. Sandusky. Toledo. *De*-troit. All a-bohrrd." I sat on a high stool in an air conditioned booth with a microphone in my hand and the cord between my knees.

Dad had done happily for me, and I carried a lunchpail and whistled my way to the bus. The fast money and the dirty money of our carnie otherworld belonged to those mouse-biting geeks out there; as for me, I took an interest in union politics. This was better than pocket-picking in a countstore, pedaling the skillo, or any of the other short-con moments of which Grack had told.

Then one day I came home earlier than my father from our separate corners. Jaunty in my cap, a lunchpail in my hand and a pay envelope heavy in my pocket, I manipulated a familiar thought. Grack would have approved of this way, the sanitary no-reply which pretends that the absent burden is dead in another life. I was no longer with it and for it. Grack must have understood, I decided, and served out his thirty days in friendship to me. He at least would have felt as tact my father's brutality, and ascribed it to me, thinking: I never knew the kid could do like that. . . . Pride swung my pail for me.

At the mailbox I found another letter. Grack wrote to thank me:

> I figure you're just too busy in business joining out the odds or some monkey business to say hello, but that's all right, we had ourselfs some times together, you sent the money. Real sweet of you, kid.

A cool reciprocity in this acknowledgment:

> I know a fellow needs another store behind his midway, like I say, we could make it in twos, friend. I'll buy in for both of us, that's how I'll piece you off. Like I told you. We can ride it clear when you come on out.

And he said further:

> You should have said something.

By reproach I was knotted to him now like the infant to the mama. He sent me with murder in my heart to ask my father: "By what right do you answer my mail?" — not open it, read it, guard me from it, but *answer* it. He must have sent a money order in my name to the jail in Utah.

In my ignorance, he had saved me. In his ignorance, we were all but Grack judged. Having aspired to my heavy-

68

fleshed father's simple way (I named it brutality), I found betrayed in him the same equivocation which kept me flowing between the carnival and Pittsburgh, fleeing from my worthless sheets to Phyl, and then away. I revised it clearly once more: He would give me the letter; he won't. He will simply destroy; he won't. He will ignore it; he sends money in my name; he returns me to him with a son's curse on an old man's head. A few dollars! It was for this mimicking of me that I had to destroy him.

Again Grack showed me the way. This was the decision as I liked it, thick with blood, heavy in consequence, and irretrievable as the five-dollar bill for Phyllis on the table by our bed.

9. Put out our eyes henceforward

THE truth about my life — I fear all but facts — was this lie which I tell you. We who live waiting for decisions to be made by others have already lost our parents, mother, father, or someone to love. Self-made, crediting only our dismay, we will end unless we learn in bondage to the fat black wart on Grack's nose or the abstract glitter of his too-much-looking eyes. The carnie is thought to be a rough-and-tumble fellow or a tendoned dancer. We are neither. We are fatherless; we are motherless. Our fond hands touch the padded boodle for love and leap like minnows to the mark's defeated bawl.

Unless, unless. A will to live in is the great thing a father can bequeath his son.

The house, on that night of which I speak, was humming dark again with the breath of my father and me, and as I crawled from bed, fully dressed in the black corduroy pants which were my carnie garb, I stumbled my shin against a bedpost to give pain to my rage. "Oh!" — this head cocked, jerked, lay flat in its own hiss. The *oh* was for fury that Dad could have done for me, could have raised me up and destroyed me and slept on; a purple blotch on the bone of my shin gave me a sign of life amid my starvation. I thought of John Wilkes Booth leaping to the stage after shooting Abe, crying out in Latin and plunging away on a broken leg. A sham: while splinters of bone violated his flesh! My father could have freed me, had he been hard enough. All my body ached with Grack's reproach that I had given only money, neither offering myself to his need nor reminding him by turning away in silence that he had once been master enough to let me climb on his back from the pit in which the carnie dwells. I had struck Grack cruelly at his pride. Dad! I forgave stealing the letter!

In a purchase of conscience, my father had sent money to buy silence from Grack and to ransom the freedom for which I fought; at that postoffice was I destroyed. He miscalculated! Choice was a dilemma for him, and my father could not be strict and serene enough to make an offering of meanness which it happened that I needed. More than that, his deceit struck at me with the sort of miscalculation which has always calculated us apart from each other, from the world of meaningful doing, and from ourselves. What was it to him that I thought him a father? — that poor fat sack tumbled into bed, that gray sick old man with no son for his trucking business.

"I did it for my boy" — the broken bedsprings would pitch him in his dream — "and tried never to hurt nobody. . . ."

It was so dark in the house that I released the shade to give substance to windows and mirrors, silver and the other metals and their alloys in faucet and lamp. At the shelf which ran halfway down the wall of the dining room — a shelf once used for the family plates — I leaned blindly to its one burden, my mother's picture. Yes, I made out the flash of light, a tinkle of sense in the dark. There remained of her no memory but the smudge-eyed girl caught in the photograph and her moles painted out later.

I had pulled Grack's knife from someplace where I kept it.

"What? What? That you?" my father called in his sleep, turning, his thighflesh thumping in the mattress, unwaking.

The zip-zip of corduroy leg against leg moved me toward his room. All thought of him had turned to regret and love now that I had no choice left about him; there was but one more turning for me, although the end of the moving was still to be made between us. I could think of him with tenderness as I crept to his door with a cruel knife hot in my hands, held low to jab belly-upwards.

"Wha? What, boy?"

I stopped, choked once more with gratitude, as if it were his tact to make his sleep talk, thus giving me thoughts of risk and mummery to stuff the weak knees of my regret and reversal. (*And the dead shall rise; they will speak, the mute, the dumb.*) Booth must have choked so, even while latining his deed! I stood stiff behind a door and waited for him to fall again. The dark swarmed within me in this house where I grew up, swarming as does the body in that instant before pleasure, as the mother's body must swarm when the child's head comes beating through. This swarming came, and I leaned my head against plaster. Webby and crumbling, the dirt hidden under a beam invaded my hair. This unclean apartment had housed bereaved men for too many years since the photograph on the shelf had been touched or tinted. The dirt slipped in hair and across my wet face, soft now, dusky to the taste when I caught it on my tongue.

Again the heavy cloth on my skin and the taste of rotten lint showed me the way to the blessedness of decision, the forgiveness of others which it allows, the freedom to be responsible to the deepest desire of self-forgiving. "Wha? What?" — but that was my own voice.

But it was time. *Hurry* was my thought.

Hurry was too fast for a son looking at a father's door in the middle of the night, come to enact dreams of truth-telling, dreams of evasion, and the great dream of murder which every sulky son knows. The door, varnished dark but swirling with its grain and its rings of growth, stood with the years out of color between us. Behind this wide door he had conceived me; beyond the stained wood he slept alone. My shin ached. The pantleg was sticky where it was bruised; it oozed. It attended poor Dad and his poverty of sense for me. Again the reminder: He had thought to get off easy and cheap against both Grack and his son. Did I drop the knife then? Did I pick it up? "O-oh." I heard his groan in sleep and his heavy turn behind the door. I dropped the knife; I picked it up; I carried this knife in supposition, but I really carried it. (Did I retrieve it at the door later?) I want to think that at least once we did not get off cheap and easy against each other. However the knife was managed — swallowed, hidden, sleeved, juggled high, escamoted in the carnival of my intentions — I opened the door softly to carry assault with me. It swung without a sound. I had oiled all the hinges in the house.

Cunning and self-deluded by desire, I wore assault like a knife close to me. I came dizzied with hope to peek and peer at my sleeping father, to tiptoe near him and be tender by

73

his bed and to let my eyes widen in the dark and feed on the thick rolls of flesh and look him awake. I came with my own image to search out the resemblance in his features battened on years of eating, years of work, the years of his age, and fattened awry by his years of denial and deceit. I was only in the doorway. I came to look murder at my father.

Now! Hurry while the dream endures!

In the room quick now, I sang up the shades and the three o'clock starlight came flooding through. "Ain't you sleeping yet, boy?" He rolled in his bedclothes, the hairy old legs uncovered and the stench of an old bull's strength rising off lonely sleep and his weary overmuscled body. Waking, he wheezed hoarsely, and I had the sudden terrible thought: He's sick! Could die before I reach him!

"Dad, you never said you felt bad —"

"Son, I wanted to explain to you, I knew from your face how it was —"

"You been seeing doctors?"

"Now you come prowling in my room, I know what you're thinking. Where you going?"

I whirled from the door, accused, and cried out: "Noplace!" Could it be that he did not see the knife in my hands and the point shielded deep in the flesh of one cupped palm? It was noplace; it was away; it was dropped with my watching at the door.

"You going away? What you looking at me for?"

"Nowhere!"

"Son! Son! Don't leave me," — the croak of a sick and lonely old man. "I'm sick, son, take care of me. The doctors say I got to stop everything, and I can't do that. I worked

74

all my life. Stay. Don't go now. I could die by myself. All I got now is you and the job."

I wasn't going yet.

He sat deep in the wornout springs, leaning against a pillow, unmoving except for the heavy wheeze of his breath in the pale alley-light of stars and a streetlamp through the window. This watchful stillness let me know that he admitted the letter and knew my thought about it. He tried to smile; his mouth opened at me. This was one last tact: no word of the money he had sent Grack in my name.

"I'm sick, son."

It was as if he had been waiting for me. He had no right to threaten illness and death now, to die owing me my anger, to die like me, incapable of sufficient cruelty and unable to be tender. Even in this decision I failed; I stood only to look murder at him. I measured his cunning at the postoffice, signing my name to a money order, and his shush-shush tread in my presence since, thinking himself clean with me and with Grack and with himself in this dirty house. I only looked my thought at him. His hairy legs were moving; he would climb out of bed; he would try to wrap me in the sick purple flesh of his arms.

He did not touch me. He said: "You're a fool and no good, you were the death of her —" And he clapped his own hand over his lips. I believe to this day that these words, wrenched against his hand, would have saved his life anyway, even if I had not already failed my intention and begun the far lodging in evasion. His admission of anger, the somber truth of his love for me, let our hatred be spoken between us.

"*My* fault?" I yelled.

75

"How could I know what to do? I lived here all alone so long. Get out! You did it!" — and he covered his face. "Don't leave me, boy."

"You never should have been that way, Pa."

"You're no son to me. You're no good to yourself."

"Pa —" I wanted to explain how we nursed failure between us: How the brutal silence for which I had wished him strong — he might have shouldered the blame in his age! — could have saved us both and made Grack grin, cluck with approval, whistle a tune, and forgive us his waiting in the memory of his powerful hope for me when we had last been together. I stood at the bed to say how too much kindness, a money order over my faked name, meant deceit and defeat.

"Shut up, you! Don't look at your father like that!"

To be patient with him, and to be tender in my decision, this was to do more than look murder at him. And more than fending off his anger which came too late to help me, but not too late to spoil this night's work. "Pa!"

"You got no right. You had your say."

"Pa, listen to me —"

"I listened already! I'm deaf from it! Listen, boy, I sent your friend the money and I said from you, but I couldn't tell you, I couldn't let you go back to him —"

"Don't!"

"I knew you would leave me —"

"No!"

"I knew you'd go back to him —"

"Don't say it, Dad!"

"But stay with me now," — the words so constant in him that this was his cry as the pendulous cheeks swelled in

76

his astonished face and the heavy legs catapulted his body upon me. I thought that I plunged the knife wet and deep into his chest, once and then I could not count, into his eyes I thought, many times for all our illness that no telling can ever heal. Please believe me. My intentions were perfect, were final. The knife, fumbled and fallen at the door, had ripped my shirt as it flew; it had not even taken my own blood. In the reek of bodies and of his wakened flesh, I was beating him back into bed with tiny fist-flurries, spiteful, cool and malignant because this man's son was like him even to failing with knife, clawing with fingers at his bull chest with its fine, tight-curled hairs and then at the horny silver-bearded skin of his head. I think the old man was crying; the springs groaned beneath him; he made sick stifled noises. Our truth together had always lain unused and fetid between us. He let himself be struck. There was commotion on his bed.

Then, at last, he opened his mouth, and up from his chest came the thick roar of the mastery which is every man's right, murdered in us by the life we made, his lungs crashing to the tide of his love and his devastation; and the fall of our years together, damned like unto like, carried the flood of his breath and his saliva to my face: *"Son! I could kill you with one hand,"* — but he would not strike me even now, even for the years dead in him since my birth, and the cry was broken by his tongue clamped between his teeth.

All my larcenies, having despoiled him of an enormous admission, were still no good to me! His over-tenderness no good to us! I put my head an instant against the wet cheek, and then I ran loose.

77

10. Am never to be stilled?

BACK to Grack, who wanted no one.

I ran, ran, ran with the bloodless thing under my shirt. I ran until I tasted it on my tongue, the blood. It was the last wisdom of the body which kept me moving, turning and running, looking behind and hearing, not feeling, the branches across my face; and running.

I ran with the knife toward Phyllis once more in that moment before dawn. I stood under her window and whistled as I had many years before and waited for her light. A baby bawled; a lamp came on behind pink nursery curtains; I ran again. I was at the switchyards, still running, and then I was clambering in the coupling of a moving freight.

Phyllis had gone away, and so had I, as had my father — not for having lied, not for having cheated, not even for having wished murder — but for failing to lead our lives to be hard with a hardness, willful with a will, and serene for others and self. I was running to a world where no one desires or looks, all the blind ones plucking with our fingers at our eyes. I had not yet been found. Grack taught me how to tease you with a glare which I now possessed equally with him, then to count you into winning scores or foot the skillo soft, with a ho ho ho and a hee hee hee, with it and for it and nothing else until we are to be quit of this life.

I was young. A certain yellowness, a phyllisness, a sonnyboy trust that I had the right to be helpless — these were cured. Undone murder and all, I had learned something about doing my will.

My liver had grown back.

Now I had a road to go.

PART TWO

"It should be every man's ambition to be well enough acquainted with himself to be his own doctor."

Take your best hold.

Go peacefully and score on Saturday.

Those that know me, come on in, but no collect telegrams.

11. Now time to eat grass

Like a sick dog, I went out to the country to eat grass. And I carried my few bucks of money the way a dog carries his sex — where he'll spend it in the springtime for a little pleasure or sympathy. The fleeing hindquarters sensation of running away from my dream of death to my father and my reality of no more desire for Phyllis and my wee-wee-covering backlegs scratch into the Pittsburgh of my childhood had made me a dog again. My tail was between my legs and I was running. I was headed down to Georgia where I would pick up the Wide World and Tuscaloosa Too Shows again, Grack again, Pauline again, with it and for it again. There would be no pleasure for me until I stopped.

The very next night, however, my brains came to interfere with the pure aimless pattering of flight. I heard Grack's voice and saw his eyes and the wart, all three bearing down in sleep from the shadow of the Ferris wheel where he had told me: "They see the fleas clearer on the skinny dog, Bud. Better be a fat dog."

Dogginess, skinny and fat, may be all right for some, even for Grack himself, but I had other ideas for myself. Wanting to kill my father and not doing it was a great big idea. Want-

83

ing Phyl and turning away from her was an idea about my life. Trying to play touch football again and seeing how the kids took me was a good hunch toward an idea. Getting back to the carnie was getting back to the only home I now knew, there to eat my grass and take care of my liver.

First thing, before I could get new ideas, I had to eat. Spraddle-footed and shivering, I scrambled down from the freight. You haven't hit bottom if you still know you're hungry. I ate parochial school lunches that a sad-eyed nun gave me; she might have been Irish or Italian and a girl under her robes, but I would never know and remember only her smudged, sad, married-to-Jesus eyes. I ate handouts from sarcastic kids and angry women: why can't a healthy boy like this work or go into the Army? I ate what I boosted in small cans from the A & P: caviar, cheese, mincemeat, and similar unhealthful delicacies. Oh, my liver. In the early morning, for example, having slept under the mats of a bowling alley with my head on a pin, I stretched and hummed "John Peel" while I swiped milk from the porches of small-town houses. I was beginning to feel better. "John Peel" is a nice song for a man who has avoided killing his father.

After the first angry night, before John Peel came to keep me company, when I was still a dog and nothing but canine, I stayed away from freights because they mark you with railroad dirt and make it hard to meet nice, respectable people. "Do ye ken John Peel at the break of day?" I hummed to myself this question. I drank my nice milk and put on my nice college-boy face and hung out my thumbs for rides, breathing the mountain air and moving toward the seaboard and Route One.

84

People didn't much care for me at first. They must have caught the milkfed puppy smell, sour as a kennel, of a man who wanted death to his father but couldn't do it. The inner yipping of a man who had assaulted the Pittsburgh of his babyhood may have given them obscure desires to kick me. Turning tail from Phyl caused nobody to love me in the whole wide world of men and women.

So I ate grass in several states of the Union.

In Washington I did get a ride from a man running away from his wife, drinking from a bottle of fine stuff and dirtying the upholstery of his car, but we didn't see eye-to-eye on things. First of all, he too believed that oyster sandwiches would calm his stomach. "Gotta put a lid on it," this fugitive explained. Grack had that idea, but it was one from Grack's Almanac — he didn't drink. "I'm sixty-two years old and never had a day's peace out of my life. Money I made, got me a Buick franchise — no luck at all. Daughter married at eighteen to get away from her mother." Then open would go the glove compartment and up the bottle and down too fast again and the lid came flying off. Second, when he felt sad he wanted to love me up, which is not my way. I quit him after a hundred and fifty miles of nursing and saying *too bad* and leaning against the far door, not any surer than before that I was to be a member of the great old human race.

"Like this and like that," Pauline used to tell me, reading without looking at my palm or the cards, shimmying her loose bare arms of which she was so proud for their milky flesh, "like this, like that, and ziggety-zaggety. What do I mean? Don't ask, I'm not charging you, Bud."

"Then what good does it do me?"

"Find out yourself! Trobble, trobble! It's all free. Make your own fortune!"

But it had cost me to go back to Pittsburgh, although I had rec'd value. The old neighborhood, increased thick of tree and gray of stone, apartment where the stick-hockey field had been, was not something I dwelled in for free. My eyeballs had hardened and saw the old place differently. The new kids, fleet skinny punks, were neither my friends nor Bud Williams. I had gone backwards to walk sideways, ziggety-zaggety, and maybe Pauline would say:

"I told you so, and I never charged you. Make your own fortune! Look how my Joy is now a big girl!"

I quit the man with a bad wife and a franchise in D.C. and sat on my suitcase until I was tired of sitting. I walked to the next bend in the road.

You may ask why I took such pleasure in being a dog and singing, "Do ye ken John Peel with his coat so gay?" and wondering if I were really a human being or something else that had no decisions to make. I didn't seem right to myself. Ungrateful for having a head and heart. Unfit and wounded in the world, and yet ready for more. It just seemed to me that leaving Pittsburgh meant leaving strong feeling for a while, and it was a thing necessary for me to survive. A young man has to stop killing his father sometime. I got away. I got to scheming again. I was doing better. Funny thing, too, how the carnie fell away now that I was no longer doing what Grack thought I needed to do. I talked American talk again. The carnie was for the carnies, at least until I would get with it again, and then it would be for everyone.

"Come on in," Bossman Stan would say, yawning to show

86

his gold inlays, "but no F.O.B.'s, C.O.D.'s, junkies, lushes, agitators, and collect telegrams. I'm the only signifier I need around here. You still want in, Bud?"

"I heard your song already, Bossman," I would answer. "And you heard me count the balls already, too."

Well, Bossman could wait while I dogged it awhile in the country. In South Carolina I walked down Route One from a dirt road where a farmer had turned me off. He didn't even take me to the gas station at the crossroads where I might have picked up a trucker. "Gimma a quatah," he asked.

"Ain't got no money," I answered him right back.

"Ain't got no luck then either," he said. "Right chere," — and he dropped me down together with a jet of tobacky juice.

"Yessir, no luck without money, that right?" I started to ask him, being friendly with my thoughts of dogs and John Peel, but his truck was bumping down the road in a funnel of dust, and it was just as well. I didn't want to be rewarded for philosophy by being grabbed by the sheriff to work on his peaches. They do that in the South when you haven't got twenty dollars in your pocket. Vagrancy. The charge is called "Unlawful Refusal to Work."

I pulled the handle off my split cardboard suitcase under that hot wet sun, a mile to go to the crossroads. I was in the clerk class among bums: suitcase, friends. But it made walking hard, even with "Do ye ken John Peel in the mo-o-rning?" The thought of being safe in the great hobo bourgeoisie didn't make me any less hot and sticky where I moved. The grass drilled into the sand and nodded its head — it was corn or tobacco or cotton grass, what difference what? — but this thought of vegetables does no good either when you're hungry and hot and tired and the sweat is trickle, trickle, trickling into your eyes and your feet are swelling in your shoes and you feel your clothes wet all over when you bend to untie your laces and the dog has a thorn in its ear and the hell with John Peel. But I mean hot.

It would never be a surprise to find Grack anyplace. I didn't find Grack. But I did find, and I was surprised to find, something growing in the field. It helped distract me from my thoughts of being a sick dog with a heat that no amount of tonguing the breeze could cool. There was a weed in the field. This weed with languishing Latin eyes and a caved-in middle, squeezed by a belt, massacred, grass in its hair and its shoes off for comfort, was almost a man. When an ant bit it, it scratched just like a man can. It had sad puppy eyes and bones sticking out all over, each knob for a kick, a disappointment, a regret. It was a pimply boy of maybe twenty-two, and it would be a pimply boy until it died.

"Why hello," I said.

"Yuss."

"Yes what? What you doing here?"

"Waiting for a hitch."

"Me too, but do you expect a truck to come poking off the ditch for you in the grass? What's the matter with you? Stand up and beg like a man."

He groaned and flopped in the field. "I'm too tired, too hungry. I'm weak. I'm sick."

Oh-oh, I thought, serves me right for asking questions and not just moving straight on my way. Looks like a refugee from the boys' farm or a vocational school. Looks like a meek who will never inherit the earth. I fingered in my pocket for my one dollar and six cents as if I didn't know how much it was — three quarters, three dimes, penny-one. But it made me feel still less like a dog and more like John Peel to know that I would buy him a cup of coffee. I didn't admit it yet.

"You just dreaming asleep like that?" I asked.

"Once I was a man in the Army near here. Quartermaster Corpse, eats drinks sleeps. Boy, I never had it so good, that's what I been thinking."

I had served a term at Fort Bragg, up near what we called Fagleburg, not so far from there, but I didn't tell him. "Whatever got into you, kid?" Grack used to call me kid, and here I was, calling a kid kid! John Peel and music did this! — and maybe winning out a little with my father and Phyllis and the touch players in Pittsburgh after all. "Howjaever come to crawl back to this here red sand, kid?" I asked him.

He gave a thin, pale, weak, and clever smile from the weeds in which he still flopped. He pinched an ant between his two fingers and wiped its fastidious oozing. "You must've been in too if you call it red sand," he said. "That was our word for it in the Service."

I began to laugh. He was so beat that he rolled in the weeds without protest, letting me take in laughter his starved girlish belly, pinched by the belt, his overlarge girlish eyes, his hungry mouth, rosy-red with fever among the bluish dimples about it. I prodded him with a stick. "Howja come so low after the Army and the Quartermasters and all? You probably could live on the jump boots and blankets you sold, especially with that Hahvahd accent of yours."

"Laziness," he said mournfully. He was too weak to stand up, and my prancing about him gave me an advantage he

89

finally admitted. "Laziness, unlucky in love and other businesses, bad salesmanship, nervous. That answer your questions, nosy?" He seemed to feel better and braver. Confession is good for the soul, conversation nourishing to the body. "It's not Hahvahd, either, I'm a Wop Irisher from Boston. What a family tree!"

"Okay, no difference at bottom, brother. Can you get up and make it to the crossroads? I'll buy you a coffee, you need it, but I'll be damned if I'll carry you. Up now!"

"My name is Andy," he said.

"Up first!"

He arose and lifted a bundle wrapped in a dirty shirt and carried it by draping the sleeves about his neck. This boy looked for liabilities, that was the only answer. The hobo who doesn't have a cardboard suitcase loses his chance for all kinds of luck with hitchhiking. For example, it's well known and widely appreciated that a female motorist will never crawl into the back seat with a lad who has his bindle wrapped in a dirty shirt, and therefore she will never give him a sandwich after the fun. And that's only the part about love — there are jobs, money, friendship, a future with sunshine and happiness and movies on Saturday and plenty of other commodities to be lost. Go without socks if you have to, but get yourself a suitcase: that's my advice to young men who want to get ahead and a piece.

"My name is Andy," he repeated hopefully. He was long and yellow and big-eyed and sick as he unwound and swayed to his feet and finally loped by my side down the Carolina road. He was going to cost me a sandwich, too; I had seen it coming; but it's funny how sacrifice for others is good for a man. Phyl and Grack and my father were hidden by the dust his big sad flat feet churned up. I was no dog. I had eaten enough grass. I was John Peel, the man, himself.

"Andy," he said, ready to cry because I didn't answer him.

"Oh yes, my name is John Peel," I said.

"Boston Andy, mine is," he said gratefully. "I was borned and raised in —"

"Pittsburgh, me. I'm not really John Peel. Bud Williams. You still talk like Hahvahd, Andy, even when you say 'borned and raised.' "

"You never been in Boston, it just proves, Mr. Peel. I mean Bud. They got neighborhoods there. I'm weak from hunger and not eating."

I squinted across at him and shifted my suitcase. "Yeah, that's what you're weak from," I said, wondering how much food it would take to kill the weakness my pal Andy brought with him into the world.

The place at the crossroads turned out to be one of those Colonial-type drive-ins, white pillars and cozy curtains, they put up for the tourists prejudiced against social diseases and to whom the important thing when you get a cup of coffee is the ultraviolet irradiated toilet seat afterward. A fancy-lettered sign said HARVEY JOHNS, and to the fast reader, inexperienced with American ways, the way most Americans are, it was Howard Johnson, especially with the lace in the fake dormers and the orange captain's turret and the pastel tiles and the girls with powder on their noses so that they looked positively clean. Also paper napkins in dispensers and plump creamers on each table and at the counter where Andy and I sat. Only Harvey didn't have to pay Howard for the franchise — why not save a buck? This is the land of opportunity even for a Carolina hillbilly on Route One.

"Yes," the girl behind the counter said, eyeing us to figure whether we really were bums or only sports in disguise, "sir?"

"Let's eat," I said. Pride kept me from telling Andy how much I had. A brave man would have been able to bear that burden, but I was afraid Andy would break down. I protected him from the facts of my life. "A sandwich and coffee," I told him sternly, "a cheap sandwich is all you're worth, Andy."

"A hotdog?"

He broke my heart with dopiness. "Not that cheap! I didn't say that, Andy boy. You can have cheese — American, pimento spread, cream, you can have a hamburger, you can even have a cheeseburger. What the hell, let's enjoy, kid." I didn't say it, but he must have guessed that this was likely to be our last meal for a while. In a way it was a good thing, Andy being the kind of stiff who, once his belly is full, starts to crank out the story of his life, that is, how he was born for one reason only: to be misunderstood from coast to coast. The more you give him to eat and drink, the sadder the misunderstandings. "Eat up, kid," I said, "don't forget to nourish yourself."

He ordered a hotdog and coffee anyway. ("They are very nice today," the countergirl advised us.) I had a hamburger and coffee, and slyly I watched for the relish and ketchup. Andy ate half his sandwich before they came, stuffing the bread and pink pork down without letting his mouth get the good of them. I put my hand on his elbow and whispered, "Listen, kid, learn the truth about life. The ketchup and relish are free with all their vitamins, minerals, and encouragement for the intestinal tract."

"What kind of a track is that, the intentional track?" he asked through sour spice and the smell of breadcrumbs chewed with pork.

"Please, Andy boy, you don't have to kid. Be nice and pour it on."

"Thank you," he said with that prim girlishness which only got worse as he got courage, "but I'll just take some mustard on my wienie, thank you."

"But mustard is no good for you! No calories at all! You need strength when you're starving, Andy, otherwise you can't do it right."

He pouted. "Just pass the mustard, please, Mr. Peel," he said. "I always loved a little mustard with my wienie."

I munched my own relish and ketchup and looked at him disgustedly, thinking that only a Danish doctor could make an Andy into whatever he already was. "Look, let me explain about eating, friend —" But obviously he felt that I was trying to push my deep philosophy on him just because I was paying, so I shut up and ate in silence. It's depressing all the same when people can't get the good out of what you do for them. It made it hard for me to get the good of my burger sunk in a red swamp of ketchup and pushing up a jungle of relish: best things in the world for a quarter, too. Even if they make it of pure trichinosis worms in Carolina drive-ins.

Finishing his eating with a sigh and a dainty pit-patting of napkin at mouth, Andy waited before his coffee. He gazed glumly into the full cup, adenoidal, dog-eyed, girl-dog-eyed, while I peeked into the mirror behind the counter to see if the food was doing me any good. It was. The mirror looked clean. I felt better. The mirror and the waitress both gave me my reflection back. Neither knew about my troubles and both seemed to like me. In the meantime, Andy developed a nice steamy look on his face, innocent of pain and trouble now that he had a hotdog in him, although there was no more flesh on his bones and they stuck out against a world which had been rough on him. He sucked his teeth; that was all; but the sweet smile was gratified.

He sipped his coffee.

"Oh! don't!" I said.

"What's the matter, Mr. Peel? I don't do anything right to suit you, do I? I'm just a Boston Wop Irisher."

"Never mind the genealogy, kid, put cream in it."

"*What?*"

"Put cream in it!"

I nodded jerkily to the creamer, which came full and free on the counter. First I poured as much as my cup would hold, then sipped a bit, then poured again to show him how. "Nourishing, the best thing for you," I explained. "Vitamins, calories, minerals, strength. The coffee is just caffeine, it'll pick you up and let you down, but the cream comes straight from the mama cow. Drink up." I handed him the creamer.

"I like my coffee black," he said. He blushed.

"Put sugar in it, too. You need sugar for the bloodstream."

"I prefer my coffee the way it is, sir," he said. He didn't move. I knew he was a dope, and I was tempted to pour the cream for him. Let me put it down right here that I respect other people, even the dopes, even Andy. Human beings have their rights, idiots included. Every soul is free and equal on this earth, except that some of them will never come down from the sky, like Andy's.

So I didn't pour it for him, but I said: "Didn't you hear my explanation to you, kid? I had a year at U. of P. with hygiene required."

His cheeks burned. He was ashamed, but he was for pulling his pride on me now that he had eaten. He refused to drink the cream.

I guess that was the only manly thing I ever saw him do, so I shouldn't be too hard on him now. The cash register clanged and Andy looked over to our waitress, touching me to look also. She was nice. Heavy hips, heavy breasts, hot in their rubber cradles, heavy sleepy face and her hands in the cash. It surprised me that he could be interested in her. He wasn't. "Look at all that money," he said. "You like to try something?"

I wasn't a holdup artist, never could be. He wasn't either; this was just his way of apologizing to me and showing me he was right. He was all wrong. He wasn't looking at the girl and he wasn't looking at the paper money. His greedy eyes dropped into the puddle of quarters and dimes; that was as high as his imagination could strike. "Okay, never mind, finish your black unsugared coffee," I said.

But all the same he stuck at that place, and I respected him for it. When he said black coffee, he meant it, and no good sense could dilute this integrity. He liked it that way. We walked out, me bloated with ketchup and cream, Andy jittery with garlic and caffeine, back to the road with our bindles and me wondering how never to see him again. It was nice to find the born jug of the continent and to decide even about him: he knows what he wants.

When we got outside I finished shedding him. It was an affair that required adrenalin and the squandering of part of my hamburger. "You're a dope, you're going to expire," I said.

"Yes," he said, drooping by my side at the road. "So will you someday, Mr. Peel."

"You think you're going to buddy up with me? You gone crazy?"

"I'm sorry, Mr. Peel, I'll leave you. Thanks for the hand-out."

I yelled at him, "You think I'm going to buy you hotdogs without ketchup or relish and coffee without sugar and cream all the way down to Georgia? You think I came onto this planet to carry you around like my suitcase? You think you can follow me everywhere?"

"No sir," he said, "I'm going. I hope you find what you're looking for, sir."

"You think I'm going to spend all my money on a bum with a Hahvahd accent?"

"I already explained about that. I'm truly sorry."

"Get out! Get!" I screamed.

He started back down the road to the patch of grass where I had found him. I put down my suitcase and chased after him, crazy mad, and said, "Here!"

He didn't protest. I put the rest of my dollar-six into his palm, turned pale up at me like his gaze. He never allowed himself to suspect that it was all I had and now I didn't allow myself even penny-one. I wanted him to hate me, because a little gratitude would dilute his blood even more. Not that it made any difference. He looked at my fraying cardboard suitcase as if it bulged with treasure, or at least pencils and laces to sell. "Thanks again for the handout, Mr. Peel," he said, "but say, did you notice how that waitress looked at the cream pitcher when we got up?"

Then he lowered himself to sit after the palest star-flicker of a smile. Yes, it was a pleasure to see that even Andy was human; therefore I could hardly be a dog forever.

I turned without goodbye and headed toward my privileged place at the crossroads, singing and tasting ketchup and cream, sure that I had already hit bottom. I would never see Andy again. I stood hexing the cars on Route One, humming them by and not impatient because suppertime was still some hours away:

> "Do ye ken John Peel with his coat so gay?
> Do ye ken John Peel at the break of day?
> Do ye ken John Peel when he's far far away
> With his 'ounds and 'is 'orn in the mo-or-ning."

Naturally the ride came along. It was a colored man, plump and sweating in a white linen suit, who laughed at my talk and finally asked me: "Did yall know I have a juck joint of mown? A fish fry?"

"No, I never knew in my whole life before."

"Yall lookin for a job?"

"I want to get back on my feet, sir."

"Ahd jest *love* to have a fine old wide boy washin dishes for me."

He must have liked me right off to talk that way and lean

97

on that *love* with such a friendly tongue. I accepted, saying, "I'm not a white man, I'm a former dog."

"Can yall wash in hot, rinse in hot, nevah touch the cold? Fish makes a turrible scum and greasiness."

"Yes."

"Yall is hired, wide boy."

I stayed with him two weeks. Mr. Sammon was good to me, feeding me and giving me a dollar a day besides. He lent me the vaseline bottle when my hands were burned. He gave me an aspirin, too, when I had a headache thinking about my pop. The dog that I was stayed with me, but I put it out on a leash. I waited on tables and picked up tips, besides. The colored are generous. I plucked my new little boodle and finished my grass-eating and got ready to rejoin the show in Georgia. I knew their schedule. I waited to get with Grack and Pauline and the rest. I slept in the back of Mr. Sammon's place and ate up good. Not scared anymore, I knew Pittsburgh was done, done, done. Andy had showed me that no one could ever hit absolute bottom until dead, no matter what, and I would always have some sense and take the cream if it was for the taking. Waitress frowning or not.

I said goodbye. I thanked Mrs. Sammon, too. He drove me to a truck stop.

"Ah knew Ah couldn't hold you, wide boy. Yall is smart. Yall go far."

I went for Athens, Georgia, and Bossman Stan's, which this season was called the Wide World and Tuscaloosa Too Shows, because it had not been going peacefully and had tried to score on every night but setup night. There was trouble on the show.

98

12. Can't step down the same midway twice, the philosopher said

FROM outside the fairgrounds there's a stomach ache of music of the calliope and carousel; it churns and stretches, trying to relieve itself. I took a breath of the salty air. There is also pocket music in the marks' pants, quarters jigging dimes, jigajig. I listened for Grack's come-on and the hee hee hee.

Now you might guess I then sauntered with my restaurant cheeks and other fat right through the fume of sawdust and the haw and yaw of the midway and said to the first man I saw, "Listen to me now, old Ferdie, and let me tell you how I am glad to see you." And he would say, "Bud! You back with it?" And I would grin and touch my new hat and say, "With it and for it, friend." And he would say, "Wait'll they hear you're back. Wait'll Grack sees you. Let's cut up a jackpot, Bud. Listen, that little Joy, Pauline's little Joy, she ain't stopped bleeding for you, kid, and" — winking and rubbing a finger on the stubble of beard — "and kid, that little Joy there, she went and grew up since you left us. Got a cigarette?" And I would say, "Smoke nothing but big two-for-thirty-five cigars now, Ferdie. Here, have one. Got a boxful in my duff." And he would say, "Figuring on taking over the countstore again?" And I would say, "Course I'm figuring. Owner will always make room for an old countstore hand." And he would say, "Then come on in! Lug it in! Get with it, Bud!" And he would put his hands to his mouth and give a tremendous screech:

"Hey you first-of-Mayers, Bud Williams is back!"

Well, you might guess that way, but how wrong you'd be. We were in Georgia, many counties from where I had left. Ferdie at the gate, on the lookout for hey-rubes and smart kids and the county cops for their birthday payoffs, was no longer doing duty. He had evaporated. Ferdie had just dropped away. The carnival smelled the same, and the rain-streaked sign swung there — WIDE WORLD AND TUS-CALOOSA TOO SHOWS — but another fellow stood lookout at the gate, a cracker this time, skinny and suspicious, hateful of marks, not seeing me at all. They know a carnie when they see one. He didn't see me. I was just another mark to him.

I strolled past, hoping to catch his eye. I stopped with my cigars sticking out of my Texas shirt, the cigars I had ready for Ferdie and Grack and the rest of them, and he didn't even stop spitting. He had unhappy wiseguy hands that kept finding his pants, fleeing, finding and sticking again.

"I'm with it," I said softly.

He looked and spit and his hands grabbed himself.

"With it and for it," I said.

He showed his gums and covered his mouth and turned away. "Been reading books lately, feller?" he wanted to know. "Go in and have yourself a time anyway. Best thing for a feller. We got games of chance and skill, pleasures, girls, everything you could want or desire."

It was only months since I had left. A carnie can tell by the tilt of the hat and the walk if you are of the carnie, with it and for it, and he had not told about me. I was of the crowd and went in.

Parked on a low flat just outside town, the fair had its two wings of trucks drawn about it as for Custer's last stand. The sawdust was sprinkled so stingily that bald patches kept poking through, smelling bad, and snake-holes, rat-holes, gopher-holes or whatever were enough to make you turn your ankle just from looking at them. The earth showed for poverty under the carnival chips. It was late afternoon, nothing much doing but everything running. I mixed with the kids. Pink cotton candy muffled a few sticky mouths. Finally I saw Sam the Popcorn Man and asked him, "Where's Grack?"

"Grack who?"

"Sam! It's Bud, don't you remember me?"

"Grack ain't with it no more," he said, and went on pouring the raw corn into his popper. I stood and waited and he said nothing but: "Danged chicken corn. No good for nothing. Wetness inside and out. Gives me the heaves. Sure, how could I forget you? Last name of Williams, you always claimed."

I moved down the midway, remembering how they were all friends during our hey-rube and I bloodied my nose for Wide World and Tuscaloosa Too Shows. It wasn't natural to be put out and away so fast.

"Hey, Chet!" I yelled. Warily he turned around slowly at my repeating his name. "Chet Hayworth, it's Bud!"

101

"Ain't I got eyes?"

"How you been, boy? They biting?"

He looked drier and older. He had never had any love for me, jealous of my talent as a talker. "We're sticking it," he said.

The sweat was running down my back and my hands were slippery on my suitcase. No one said to put it down. No one said how about a mess of something and coffee. Was this because I hadn't stuck it out? Because I had left the life? Didn't they see I wanted to be with it and for it again? "Where's Grack?" I asked.

"Grack who?"

"Grack *who*? What's the matter with you, Chet?"

He shrugged and walked away. "Don't give me no lip, marko. Been back to college?"

I moved on down to the owner's trailer. Stan would have some sweet talk for a good countstore man. He'd yawn and show his swollen tongue and tell me where Grack was and why he hadn't rejoined the show. It beat me and made me hotter how I didn't seem to know anyone. Even Joy wasn't around. Nobody wanted to know me under the clash of afternoon sun, the mote-laden rays striking guiderope and stand while I wandered about with my forehead burning at the creases. Stan's trailer was closed up tight and he wasn't for the asking. Maybe he had gone to the fixer, maybe he had just heard I was coming. I headed around, puzzled, hearing a strange talker in Grack's place before the zoo, while the growl and roar of the record clamored below him: "We got Siamese twins, friends, they're from Siam and joined at the vital organs. We got a ape talks real good, friends. We got a Wild

Man from Brainwashing, China, he eats live rats. We got all things educational and instructive, step right up. . . ."

Grack would never do it. They had a geek in the show, biting off chicken heads and rats, some poor boozer. I felt a flush of anger under the Georgia heat that they let a dead-head like that voice take Grack's place. Maybe the jail trouble he wrote about was more serious than the usual carnie peddling, boosting, or unlawful refusal to work. I worried and poked down the midway, no better than a rube. A tuft of shirt trailed from my suitcase where the hinge had buckled after many wettings. The kids with coins in their pockets grinned and elbowed each other at my coming. If the Show wasn't for me, I would soon be carrying my bindle in a shirt like any poor Andy.

Sometimes a show dies under you and you don't know until it begins to smell bad or is simply rained down into a gully. Carnies tell of such shows, a four-trucker that blew up for no reason at all out in Corvallis, Oregon; a certain Benedict who now pushed French postcards but was once boss-man on the biggest power-generator Sunday school show in the Southland. Losing a Grack could diminish us sorely.

The velveteen Georgia dusk was coming on, dreamy, rosy, frayed at the edges where the heat of earth had worn it away. I could have been invisible. I was alone. No one knew me, and I was starting back down the midway when I suddenly thought, *Pauline*, and there she was. Her tent, all colors, purpled and silvered, spattered with stars, astrological enough for kitchen maids and cautious matrons: PAULINE SEES THE TRUTH! Yes, she reads your palm and tells you. She deals the cards and makes you know. She plays the horoscope for you. . . . Set off and away, her tent was a distant thing by several feet and an angle of planting, magically clean, magically nightfallen amid the bustle and palaver of carnival doings. She had more mystic figures than a Masonic convention, more half-moons than a manufacturer of outhouses, more glory and queerness to her tent than the Milky Way. There was nobody around. I stopped to buy a ticket outside.

In the little booth I saw that furry, bristly, swarthy animal called Joy. She was scowling and smiling and she had grown. She was a girl, she was a female already, and I knew I had been away for many months. She turned red at the sight of me. At last someone meant welcome home. I opened my eyes to look better and saw that she was no taller than before, or only a little. But she was a lady. There were bird-buds of breasts blossoming, cheeping, and her mouth was parted over her teeth. I had been away only a couple of months, but they were those couple months in a girl's life when her funny sprouts become woman things and her ideas get womanly and her legs begin to scratch. She was hot and hungry. She said in a soft husky voice, that of a child who is shy before its old friend after a week's absence: "Hello, Bud, you come for a reading?"

"You doing palms, Joy?"

"No, Mama still does it."

"How've you been?"

"The very same, Bud."

"That's a lie. You've went and grew up on me while I was gone."

"Did it on purpose, Bud."

104

There was a silence. She was blushing and squirming and glad to see me.

"Tear me a ticket from the roll, I want to see Pauline."

"Bud, oh dear, you don't need a ticket."

"Give me anyway." I was talking big for no good reason. I paid my quarter and she shrugged and gave me the ticket. She was displeased by my swagger (I knew it), as if she could read my hard times in it. I turned and left her without saying so long.

Pauline was in her gypsy headdress and smoking her cigar, which she stubbed out rapidly, breaking off the ash and then blowing to clean it for the next lighting. She started to push herself from the deep pillows. "Buddy boy!"

"Wait a sec, Moddom Pauline," I said, "I bought a ticket and want my answers straight."

"Buddy, what the hell you been doing with yourself?"

"Business first, moddom." And I extended my hand over her glass-jeweled, sequined, sweaty-from-palms table. "I paid my way in."

She sat down and looked at me with a fat grin on her face. I could see a speck of cigar leaf, stuck between her teeth and waggling as she breathed through her mouth. She took my hand in her paws, ready for the joke, but it was no joke to me. If they thought I was a marko from the other world, I'd never get in, I'd never hear the news. But if I could tease Pauline into telling me, engaging her in a play at reading my palm, then she might break the rule of the carnie and treat me as one with it. She began: "I see a lifeline that trails from Capricorn to Pittsburgh, sir. I see many loves intersecting thees lifeline. The future is cloudy, the past is disarranged.

For feefty cents payment I will cast the cards, which never fail, which always tell, which conform my diagnosis. You maybe bite?"

"Where's Grack?"

"I see a talker in a great show very very onhappy when he lose his friend. I see him not himself no more. I see pins and needles —"

"Grack got himself a habit?"

"I see snow white as sugar —"

"Cocaine? Heroin?"

"I see snow white as pain. . . ."

"What's he doing now? Where is he?"

"I see blackness, darkness, the swift deep —"

The words and words of the game were not funny to me now. "Pay attention," I said, pressing my hand to hers, "pay attention to my palm and tell me what happened to Grack."

"In the night there is a noise. *Whsst.* Someone cries. Someone lights. The talker is gone with a box under his arm and his arm spotted with holes."

"Listen, Pauline, did Grack steal from someone on the show? No, I don't believe it." This is the unpardonable sin in the carnie universe. To betray the rest of the world is business and pleasure; to betray a comrade is black as nightbane. It could poison everyone. It could kill a show — just the thought of it. Now I understood why they were not glad to see me and why the show was limping. They connected me and my habit with Grack and his habit, and my leaving with his leaving, and my memory with the sin and malediction under which the show labored when the Great Grack did this. "Listen, Pauline," I said, forgetting my game, near to

106

tears, "when a man has a habit he don't know what he's do-ing. He can't be with anything but his habit. He's dead, he's gone when he's got that thing on his back —"

Fat and impassive, but her upper lip beaded by the effort of gypsy mummery, she went on without listening. "I see a Greek man shouting and weeping —"

"Casanopopolous! The ironer! That guy always hangs his money out to dry, just waiting to be took. It's his own god-damn fault, Pauline, but I *know* Grack didn't do it the other times. It was rubes did it."

She rubbed my hand to comfort me. I put my head down on my arms. "So, so, Buddy boy," she said. "The Grack turned bad after many years of good. So. It's rough and tough, but we're getting along. We picked up a new talker — not as good as the Grack, sure, but we're getting used to him. The Grack shouldn't have done it. Now, now. Grack should have held on to himself better. Now, now, Buddy boy. Grack should have just gone on, but maybe he felt he wasn't going noplace. I never saw his palm or pulled the cards on him, but that's my estimate. Stop taking it so hard now, baby Buddy boy. . . ."

I did. I peeked through a slit in the curtain and saw the careering sun turn orange and brave before nightfall. Joy turned at the waist on her stool to see what we were talking about so long in the dusk of Pauline's domain.

"It must be a funny show without Grack," I said finally. "Is."

"I don't get him as thief at all."

"Neither did any of us."

"It's the habit that did it."

107

"It is surely the habit," she said.

There might be business waiting for Pauline, and yet we sat and looked at each other across the table. She was soft on me. People claimed she still had a no good man someplace, a man to grieve for. She had always been a friend to me. "Whatever happened to your crystal ball?" I asked, fingering the worn spot on the table where it had rested.

"Broke," she said. "Rolled off on my toe once when we were just setting up."

"Lots of changes. Poor Grack. I been away longer'n I thought."

She shrugged her weighty shoulders and leaned toward me, spreading perfume and cigar and showing me the dark cleft of her breasts. "I've got a new speciality, Buddy boy. Head raping."

"Phrenology?"

"Tells the truth through contact with the spirits that live on dandruff. Moneyback guarantee if you don't like your fortune — that's the gimmick. Want me to try?" — and she reached for my scalp.

I dodged away, laughing, which was what she wanted. "Better to give me something to sweat out my troubles," I said.

"Trobbles! If you think I'll give you hard drink, you're wrong about your fortune, Buddy boy. How about some nice tea? You have trobbles at home, boy? You not like Pittsburgh when you get there?"

"Listen, Pauline, there's no moneyback guarantee about anybody's fortune."

"You disappointed in family at home in Pittsburgh, boy? You didn't get with it there?"

I nodded my head stubbornly. Grack's trouble was enough for me to think about now without messing with my father's and mine. "I'm with and for a cup of tea," I said.

She shook her hips and went to light the alcohol burner. She set out three cups, three spoons, and a box of cookies. The water boiled fast. She caught my eye on the third cup and said, "We're closing up for a few minutes, why not?" And she poked her head through the curtain: "Joy! Come on in here, brat." Before Joy could close the cage, Pauline waddled back to kiss me on the forehead.

13. Joy came in

Joy lifted the curtain and waited, smiling as if she didn't know which way to go but hoped to be invited. She knew, and she was going fast toward womanliness. The hair of this fierce, swart, berry-dark girl was cut short and grew like electricity low down her neck and curled about her ears. She may have come from a gypsy father. She wore a man's shirt, the sleeves rolled up, and a skirt cut from cheap rough blue cloth, the stuff the Southern mills make for the crackers still further South. Her legs were rounding. Her feet, tiny and without socks, padded in tennis shoes. I could stand up and peek at the little-girl breasts: but they weren't a little girl's anymore, as they had been a few months before when she had tried to tease and run from me. She wasn't running now; she was standing and using her teeth to grin, biting her lips. She had a lovely taunting mug of a face, drawn forward to the mouth. Oh yes, her father was a gypsy. Her lips were filled with blood; she was all filled with blood, sweet and hot, and the blood whirled dizzily through the new curves of her.

What was it she had said to me once? Soda paste good for my broken nose? Playing-at-Pauline words.

"Sit down to your tea, honeys." I had stood up. "Sit down, Joy darling. I'm putting cream in your tea, Joy."

"Put down that can of condensed milk, Mama."

"You need the strength for the years ahead of you."

Joy grinned, but leaned like a cat spitting: "No, Mama, I like it without."

Pauline turned to me, proud in defeat. "She wants to get her own way these days. I was like that, too. It only brought me trobble and trobble and trobble telling the good fortune of others when I had nothing but bad luck for myself."

"And I'll put my own sugar in, too," Joy said.

"But one thing about her and me," Pauline said, "I took care of her like my own child all by myself. A man helped me to her, true, but she was only mine, for I did give him the boot and heave-ho a couple months later. Trobble? Trobble! Later he came back to look at Joy and wanted to make her his daughter, but I would never let him take advantage of us."

"Mama, is there any of that marmalade left?" Joy was hungry, snatching at the cookies and looking for more.

"No more marmalade, honey. I'll have to send into town. Then one yellow carnie oddball after the other tried to be man to me and poppa to Joy. I said no. Sometimes they used to come and peek down into the box where the baby was sleeping and I'd catch them feeling her cheeks, I'd catch them thinking, figuring a kootchie dance or a sideshow come-on or some other wormy fig carnieness in their noodles. No *sir*. Joy gave me nothing but trouble — pardon, *trobble* — but it wasn't her fault. She was always sweet, loved and appreciated her mother from the very start, and I catch how rare that is from my clients. A delight to me."

"Mama," Joy said, "just let me have the jar and I bet I can scrape out enough for one little heel of bread."

111

"Shut up, honey, we eat at eight o'clock."

"Hungry, Mama!"

"Then have a cookie. Eat. No one else wants them, they're soggy and stale."

"Not my fault if they're stale. You went and hid them so I wouldn't finish the box."

Pauline turned heavily to me, asking approval, as she said, "Just wanted you to eat your veggy-tables, honey. Listen to her, Bud. Listen to me. Joy is the finest little filly ever got with it, plus the hungriest. But that ain't my fault, it's her age. And ain't been deflowered yet, either, have you, honey? No sir ee. I give you my guarantee, Bud."

I pursed my lips judiciously into my cup and finished the tea, warmed now by friendly gossip and a hot infusion. I huffed out the tea steam and cracked the sugar between my teeth. Joy was looking at my nose to see how it had healed. Pauline must have understood that my anger and teasing when Joy tried to take care of the nose were a warning to a mother. Teasing and anger in children are a sign of good things to come. She was saying:

"I left my first husband, her father, for how he looked at other girls. Then I left any one of my other men if they took a look at Joy the wrong way. *That* way. It wasn't mean jealousy, it was my mental picture of this daughter of mine. Having mental pictures, by the way, is how I always ran a reliable mittcamp, read your hand good. Yes, Bud, she's as pure as her heart, she's as pure as my conscience, she's a fine young thing and that's the truth. Bud, you maybe won't believe me what I'm here to tell you, but this here daughter

Joy of mine is a goddamn virgin if she been telling the truth, and she wouldn't lie to Momma Pauline, would you, honey? I see all, know all."

Joy was choking with laughter, her black eyes squeezed up tight but not daring to open her mouth. It was full of cookie.

"Here, have some cream," Pauline said. "She calls it condensed milk, the stubborn critter."

I showed her my empty cup.

"Drink up anyway. Give you strength. You want maybe another cup of tea? I got sugar to spare, kids, plenty of sweetening. Joy! Manners! Eat the cookie before you swallow it."

At last she fell back to look upon Joy and me in silence, smiling all over, adjusting the fortuneteller's skirt of mystic blue, tilting the turban which had fallen over her cockeyes in the effort of drinking tea, scratching her swollen ankles, and caressing the varicose veins which came of too much sitting and holding of her own troubles while she predicted the never-never happiness of others. She returned from her commentaries with a dreamy look, like that of a very high flier, and she said, "I bet you're not hungry, you two, after all this eating? I bet. I bet you want to know each other better after so much absence? I bet. I bet you need a walk in Georgia, since there's nothing more improving, before you can have any appetite at all for dinner? I bet."

"I can pick up my supper in a diner someplace," I said.

"I bet," said Pauline angrily. "You eat in Pauline's mitt-camp and noplace else, boy. Now go for your little stroll and don't worry about me. This is no afternoon" — and she sniffed the tent-hot air — "this is no evening for business. Even the mosquitoes smell like no business, but we'll pay ourselves to have you back."

"Thanks, Pauline," I said.

"Give me a kiss." I did touch my lips to that vast prairie of a cheek, pock-marked and scuttled, badly hurt by face powder and conflict all alone with men; and then, when she turned the cavern up to me, I kissed her creviced expanse of mouth. "Thanks, Pauline," I said, meaning the talk and the dinner and the finding of a friend.

She rocked with laughter, slapping her loose thighs, which must have been how she knocked over and lost the crystal ball, crying out, "When I was a girl, Buddy, a man never thanked me for a kiss. Not Pauline, boy! He just took it and howled for pain."

Joy and I lifted the flap and walked out. She waited for me — not like Phyllis! — and we slid through sideways together. We bumped and said, "Oh, sorry." She was shy and lovely and fierce as an animal with her tawny skin and its light down pink in the last slanting columns of daylight. She could make me forget Grack and Pittsburgh, and then perhaps even remember me enough to unforget them again. It was the good part of a suburb to take a walk in the evening, although this was the suburb of a midway in deep Georgia, with a Negro wilderness outside and a white wilderness surrounding it and my next decision up to me.

And up to Joy.

14. Calliope and coffee, with sounds of counting

AT evening, together with the dark flash of calliope music and the whir of the Ferris wheel, turning to lure the lovers with strings of colored bulbs against the sky, comes the carnie's second morning. It is the time of dinner and a further awakening to the pitch and burn of the carnival night. Camp stoves smoke; steam of frying and tomato sauce rises from trailers and tents; men in riding breeches and women in chenille bathrobes yawn, stretch, sigh, and complain. Someone kisses someone: *Wake up!* Accustomed to each other, there is privacy despite the elbowing and tripping against friend and enemy on the narrow path to the latrine. Stroll slowly through this tight knot of working men and women, drawn together to do battle against the Indians, and find its familiar housekeeping: a pretty blonde shaving her legs with the trailer door open, a freak deepening his tattoo with wash ink, Lucy being hit over the head by Frank with a rolled copy of *Billboard* because this made three nights in a row for spaghetti. A couple of tenthands are taking their flannel shirts off a line; they tell the news: *Still damp at the collar!*

Wake up, wake up! Another button gone, Harry! Beyond the second morning of the carnie, purple and dusty, lay the Georgia countryside at evening, hostile, murmurous, and mark-laden.

I remembered Joy's long tomboy step because once I had watched her carry a box of pink babydolls for prizes, running down a path in Indiana with her narrow feet bare and her arches so high she left a print like feathers tipped with toes in the Hoosier loam. Her step now shortened by the weight of woman she carried, she was still slender and easy under the shirt with its rolled sleeves, and she worked her knees without great care against the denim skirt. Her mouth was small, sweet, and heavy to look at. It pouted when I looked. "Wait up!" I said, making talk. "Maybe this lot is a pretty good place for the setup."

"There's water okay," she said, knotting a handkerchief about her throat, "but the town doesn't know the color of money."

"They want to have fun?"   .

"Every day is Good Friday," she said. "They have to get liquored up before they laugh at anything more than a Yankee falling off a ladder or a broad getting tickled. Where you going?"

"There's a stand of pine over there. It must mean water."

There really was a thick knot of pine, and I had a sudden fiery desire to put the Georgia countryside and the carnival buzz behind us for a time before I began work in it. Nothing was settled yet; I had not even seen Bossman Stan; but I had felt the way Joy knotted the handkerchief about her throat and the pine looked cool and I wanted to ask her a few

116

things. "Pauline looked like she didn't mind my bothering her," I said.

"Mama always liked you."

"Nice Pauline." I walked faster, embarrassed because she had to say it and it was true and I knew it was true and yet I had managed to make her say it. "You think Stan will let me have a go at the countstore again?" His habit of looking at me was for lushes and first-of-Mayers, not the finest way for an owner to look at a talker.

"Maybe not," she said. "You ran out once."

"That's not reason. Every man who ever got with it tried to chuck it once. Why not?"

"Maybe not," she repeated.

"What's reason then?"

"He talked against you."

"So? I was gone, wasn't I? Now I'm back."

She paused before saying: "Grack turned bad after you left. . . ."

"That's not reason, Joy."

"No," she said, "no, you're right. That's not reason. But Stan — you know Stan."

"What? Why? He's a smart boss, how else would he get his own show? Why would he want to do more'n complain? I'm a good talker."

She shrugged. "He's been jabbering at me." And then there was the coy, flirting, childish hitch of her shoulders, her hands in imaginary pockets. "You ever hear how we got with it with Bossman Stan?"

And she told me from the beginning the story of Pauline's looking for a steady place for raising her kid. We walked in

117

Georgia and I saw it happening six years back when I was a pimply high school kid only thinking about college:

— Want clean American mittcamp? Pauline had asked Owner Stan. — Use Pauline, me here. I sell and foretell. I go peacefully. I only score on Saturday.

Joy had wrinkled her nose at Stan, trying to flirt at age twelve. — She has to score on Saturday to buy me a dress. I grow out so fast. I do, Mr. Bossman.

Stan had not smiled, but he yawned, crunched down hard on his cigar, and said yes. — Okay, you're on. Listen. Rules of the show: no junkies, lushes, signifiers, or agitators. No bad habits. No gypsies but one. . . . He had cocked an eye at little Joy. — Don't solicit for your kid, she's too young, but you can let her help you turn the tip.

And finally the lids and flaps of his thin face had lifted in a smile for Joy: — And how does your mommy score on Saturday, carnie brat? Treasure maps? Mexican prisoner? Syph cure? Or does she just pick a boozer's pocket while she feels for his fortune?

For all Pauline's years on the show now, Stan had been after Joy with his teasing. — And when do we score on Saturday, girlie?

And Joy always answered with the carnie command to ease up or get slapped down: — Go peacefully, Bossman, you're not ready to score. . . .

When she finished her tale I kept my peace. You don't often hear ancient history on a lot. I walked with her and considered this beginning against my own, all that wife of Pauline without a husband, all that husband of my pa without a wife. And the kids always making out someway. We

118

moved together across the burnt-over Georgia field to the clump of woods. Joy was sighing and gradually coming back to the present season. "I don't know why Bossman would want to talk against you to me. He shouldn't have picked me, Bud. Wait up!" Now it was my turn to be speeding from her on my own nervous feet, as if she were suddenly Phyllis, but she stopped me with a sober straight-on question: "Bud, listen, are you sure you want with it now? You really need a countstore now, Bud, for picking the pockets of the marks? You want to work like Mama?"

"What's the matter with Pauline? Your mother's a lady, Joy."

"Honestly you want to get with it and for it, Bud? That what you learned in Pittsburgh?" I was moving fast, not caring if she followed, wanting her to follow without her questions. She touched my elbow. "Wait up, Bud."

Yes!

"Did you say something to me, Bud?"

"Yes, Joy, that's what I want right now."

She shook her lovely mug and the shorn black curls shook. "Well, that's all right then, Bud. I'm with it, too." She walked with stretching steps, dodging imaginary rocks in the dirt, winning bets with herself. She had retreated and would not say any further for now. The last dark stain of sun was finished in the sky.

We walked in the deepening silence until I decided to chance another question. "Did you see much of Grack? What made him make trouble all at once, Joy?"

"It wasn't all at once."

"What made him start so much trouble? He was a friend

119

to everybody. He was the straightest guy on the lot — hard to be a friend to, okay, but straight."

She shrugged her shoulders and took a deep breath of pine as we turned into the patch of woods. We both stopped, blinked, and waited to see in the dark.

"Answer my question, Joy."

"You're just going to answer it yourself."

"How do you know? You a mitt reader like your mother."

She took my hand, stared at it, puzzled over it, laughed, dropped it. She laughed again because she knew this made me jump when her fingers explored my palm.

"You think I had something to do with it? Grack liked me, sure, but he wanted me to get out and that's no reason for picking up Casanapopolous's boodle. You think he wanted me to stay around with him? Listen, Joy, you don't know how he worked to get me free of the show."

"I remember something about it," she insisted softly.

"All right, then how was it my fault? How then?"

She stopped in the shadow of the rapid night, falling swiftly under these pine branches, and her feet slipped on the mat of brown pine needles, and she said, "It wasn't your fault. If he had known you'd be back he'd have been just as bad about it. He wanted you to stay away. It would have been worse if he knew you were coming back."

These words were no longer those of the child of a few months ago. Joy was telling me. She was learning something in Pauline's mittcamp, but she was learning more from the rub of years against her mouth and the slanting black gypsy eyes. "You think he'd have minded if he knew why I came back?" — and my voice was hoarse.

She let me move against her, then moved away. "Why was that?" she asked. "Why'd you come back, Bud?"

"For you."

She stood swaying next to me, stilled by this, astonished, dizzy (I knew) because I was dizzied by her, and then suddenly burst into an agonized clatter of laughter: "Liar! liar! liar!" she pealed out like bells at the hour. "Liar, when did you ever think of me?"

She ran down the path deeper into the woods while I ran after her, trying to explain, "Yes, it's true I'm a liar, but I'm thinking about you now, Joy. You like to hear me lie like that, don't you? Don't you like lies?"

"You never thought of me, never!" — and her laughter grew more and more breathless and light as she fled slithering and bounding on the pine needles. I had seen her run before; she no longer ran like a lanky boy. Her arms were held high and her elbows away and, nimble though she was, fleet though she was, she ran with a woman's high ripe weight at her throat in the darkening woods. Suddenly she stopped. We were at the edge of the pool. It was covered with moss and the greenness was silver in the precocious night. There might still have been a trace of day in the sky, there always is, but here under the pine it was midnight and only a wisping of dampness that rose from secret warmth and coolness. Out of breath, exasperated by her laughter, I caught up and stood beside her, not touching her once, as she looked into the pond. She was bending and looking and pondering sweetly on things that matter to girls. "What do you see?" she asked me.

The carnie had wised her early, but not prevented her from

being an American girl who would think, Are you happy? What do you want? Where are you going? Why?

"What do you see, Bud? You're not talking to me. In the water. That green stuff moving around like that, it —"

Stupid and caught, not looking into the silver-green mass, thick with heat and growth, I could think only to answer with a question: "Did you see much of Grack?"

"When? What?"

"Did he talk to you after I left?"

"Who?"

"Grack! Listen to me, Joy."

"Why weren't you listening to *me?*" She straightened up to defy me, stretching to raise first her fierce small white teeth and then her tiny nose with its long narrow nostrils flaring back, and then, on tiptoe, the eyes black and level with mine. "What would he have so special to tell me, Bud? I'm nothing but a carnie brat, a kid to him, a former baby of somebody else's —"

"Well, he might have said about me."

"Ah!"

In a movement of rapid impatience she stepped back to the edge of the pool and began pulling off her tennis shoes. Then she stripped the shirt and girl-clothes beneath the shirt, shaking herself free. She was angry and laughing and wild; she showed something pretty to taunt me. She unpinned and stepped out of her skirt and kicked it onto a bush with one touch of her toe and pulled off the rest and stood there a moment, just laughing, just mocking me and my nakedness of curiosity. She knew that I could see her and that I was drunk with seeing her.

"How did you happen to grow up so fast?"

"Just happened, I guess, Bud." And there was the beginning of a confidence until, still caught, unfree yet, I said:

"Grack used to —"

"You want to go swimming or you want to talk about Grack?" She waited. I started to undress, slowly, and she had pity and jumped, her head splitting the algae at the surface, burrowing a hole in the green fur, her fierce small animal's face blowing water and gasping. I undressed, scattered my clothes, jumped in. The water was chill. Backed up from some underground stream which emerged here and then hid itself again, it circulated heavily and powerfully beneath the overgrown green surface. The stream below pulled at our legs, and I had the sense that we could let ourselves be guided by it into chill, green, underworld regions. Dog-paddling, cautiously making a trail in the algae, I watched Joy turn, puff, laugh, her teeth bared and her head black and dripping with the wild curls over her forehead and about her ears. She opened her mouth, tongue daring, and then she disappeared beneath the water and I turned to look but felt instead the slim animal swiftness of her speeding between my legs. Dared, I kicked; back she turned, and I tried to clasp her between my knees, a shiver of voluptuousness taking me as her hands thrust me away. She came up sputtering and laughing. "Wait!" I said. "My turn!"

She dog-paddled and I dove beneath the surface, opening my eyes but seeing first the violent green sparkle of water striking the eye, then only a kaleidoscope dazzle of eyeball music. I knew where and how she was. I found her and, turning sideways, put my head between her legs, my teeth at her thigh, thrusting them apart; but then she tightened swiftly and her long legs were wrapped about my shoulders, persevering and squeezing as if to have done with me by drowning. The violence startled me; I was taken by panic even in play and rolled over, blowing bubbles and reaching with my hands. She held still and more tightly. I dove deeper, carrying her, dragging her under, and then wrestled loose and we clung to each other, embracing with bursting lungs, dim and caught without breath and flying like minnows in dizziness and fright. I felt the long wet coolness of her body even in my despair of breath. At the surface where the night air struck us, she broke away and swam the three or four strokes to the edge of the pond.

She scrambled out, shivering. She ran back and forth to dry and warm herself. I understood her sudden violent shyness, timid myself, and sad as a wet dog I climbed up at the other steep and slippery side of the pool. I shook, rubbed, and slapped myself for warmth, my back to her. Then I turned and she was pulling on clothes. She gave me just the glimpse of her girl's fur and heavy flesh in the starlight beneath those arms of Southern pine. I did not move to her. I put thoughts of Grack and Bossman between us, and they vanished then like smoke, but I did not turn to her anyway. I did not try to touch her more.

We walked back now, stumbling on the narrow path, tired with chill and restraint, our wet hair plastered to our skulls and our breathing hard and hoarse, tired. We talked. I told her again that she had grown up. She told me that I had grown up.

"Me?"

"You've become a man."

"It's only been a few months. How could I change?"

"Then you're not a man, because you weren't. But you are."

"What do you think, Joy? You want me to change from the way I was because I had me a few troubles?"

"Yes."

"You think that makes boys men and girls women — just trouble? It takes joy, too."

She shook her head at the joke about her name. I did not intend it, but it seemed right for laughing. She was pleased. "You tell me I've changed," she said. "So did you, then, and I can tell you. You better see Bossman tonight. He'll wonder why you didn't come to settle with him straight off."

Pauline was rinsing her mouth with salt and soda and spitting it out like plaster at the flap of her mittcamp when we returned. She said she had finished dinner already; she was preserving her teeth and her babygirl breath. Maybe Pauline, that expert fortuneteller, sees all knows all, had guessed that we would miss the evening meal and that was why she had put forward the tea and cookies with such motherly stubbornness. She glanced with heavy eyebrows at our hands because they were not touching. I was already looking ahead to my negotiations with Owner Stan. On my way I realized a funny thing — the coffee and the cigarette which I had taken from Pauline were fine things in life. I thought of my coffee with Andy, the marko hitchhiker, and realized that I too liked it without cream or sugar except when scared of starving. The tang of smoke and the dark

125

bitterness of coffee took their sense from being taken with ease.

And they needed Joy. It was the swimming; it was pleasure; it was the way she judged, considered, worried, and decided. Joy made the sawdust fume of the carnival evening beautiful to me. I had not even noticed that this was being done, but only that now the slow bulb-strung turning of the Ferris wheel against the sky pleased me. I thought this just before I recalled: Joy's legs gripped me! "Come back and tell me what Stan says," she asked shyly, and I promised and intended to honor this first responsibility to her.

"I will."

"Be hard on him, Bud."

"I will."

And now I would see Stan and sit down to his table if he were eating. I would get what I wanted from him, which was not to play touch, and he would have to give it to me no matter what he felt about my friend Grack. Stan could never talk away the desire which comes of decision and a will to be good for Joy.

15. *Count you to win and I win*

THE countstore was my business, but I haven't been overeager to talk business here. Now, on the way toward Bossman Stan's winks and yawns, I should tell how a countstore gets after a mark. Okay.

It's a nice yellow summer evening; you have the itch of gain; you come up to the stand with your woman pinching your arm. You want to try your luck. You roll the marbles, and each one falls into a numbered hole. The numbers are summed by me, very fast, "Two and six is eight and three is eleven and ten is twenty-one and five is twenty-five and —" If you reach a winning sum, you will be invited to carry away one of the genuine Indian blankets, the Winchester rifle, the electric grandfather's clock, or maybe fifty dollars in U. S. of A. cash for your two bits of risk. It depends. And with some numbers you may get two prizes — the ones with stars on them. Easy? Just roll the marbles into the holes.

The winning numbers may be 1, 4, 9, 25, 105, 179, and so on. You are all suspicious. All right, step right up, try it just for kicks. Now I count up your total, as above, finishing by: "Twenty-one and five is twenty-five and you win, sir! Congratulations! A nice new Indian blanket, straight from the reservation! Ooops, I'm sorry, so sorry, oh dear, but you didn't bet that time. It was just practice, so *too* bad. Would you like to try for real?"

The trouble is that twenty-one and five is not twenty-five, but you never thought to quarrel with a man who says that you have won. You did not think to notice with all the brawl of the shills and the joy of the fairground and your girl pinching your arm and squeaking with pleasure and my felicitations and languishing look at the Indian blanket — the one I would have been out. You want to win, why argue? Why see?

But of course when it's for real we count more carefully. And somehow the combination is seldom right. You can't very well have a 1 or a 4 when there are five marbles and each hole has a value. Somehow the numbers of the marbles and the numbers which win never come together, or they meet so rarely that the Indian blanket factory can go out on strike forever without worrying me and all I have to do is air the one I have and keep moth flakes in its folds.

Some men with a pocketful of quarters and that encouraging girl on the arm just love to keep on trying. If they lose too much, what the hell, we make them happy. We count them into the Indian blanket before they quit. Scores up to three hundred dollars happen: it's the nuttiness of the mark and his fist in his palm, *Almost made it that time!* I've scored over two hundred myself once on a Saturday night.

Or the babydoll for a friendly souvenir.

Or a pincushion at least if all they've lost is twenty or thirty bucks.

A mother says to her kids while they watch Pa at work on the marbles: "Don't tell me you don't like Francis. I'll spank you on the rear. You *do* like Francis."

"Mommy?"

Pa is busy getting 16, just one away from the Winchester, or 164, just a few away from the bathroom scales.

"Mommy!"

"What?"

"I *don't* like Francis." The kids brought after dark always end up bawling. "I don't like Bonnie, either." Mommy whacks and baby yells. Pa is too busy to notice. He needs a bathroom scales. He needs a Winchester.

"Man alive," I growl, "you're sure getting close, sir." I shake my head and put out my hand with the marbles again. His hand comes forward before he knows it. "My luck is really running against me today," I complain to him. "Already give away two blankets and a shotgun, yes, it's terrible. Well, you got to treat the client right so's he'll tell other folks about you, so I'll just take it like a man."

The countstore is so simple and so sweet that it's easy to love. You just have to talk nice and talk fast and be good at reverse arithmetic. It has to be nice-sounding arithmetic on the trial runs. You need a shill for friend, of course, when the crowd is only watching, to count him into a winning score and load him up with camping equipment that he can carry through the marks in their mouth-open admiration.

And all the time the kid rubs dirt into his eyes and bawls, "I don't don't *don't* like Francis." When Pa gets him home, trying to figure out how it all happened, the click of the marbles still rattling in his ears, he will give the kid a licking to remember. And tomorrow I'll be forty-five miles up in the hills, squeezing the larcenous hearts five and twenty-one times to make twenty-five.

Now render unto Stan Stan's.

Bossman was winking at dough and yawning at finance and counting his money on a cardtable when I peeked between the slats of Venetian blinds at his trailer window. He wore a cigarillo between his teeth, a black onyx ring like a lump of coal slipping up and down his pinky finger, and a baby revolver to keep the little stack of fives from blowing away. There was no wind. His trailer shining outside, messed with chromium and paint, always fresh under Simonize, announced the *Wide World and Tuscaloosa Too Shows, Stanley Chick, Onr.*, and inside the onr.'s place was pretty, too, with its no-woman tidiness. Every pinup on the wall had a thumbtack in each corner, and each thumbtack was covered for insurance with a square half-inch of adhesive. Oh it was lovely. He had even been careful to clear a place about his money so that it would not wander in the breeze (which did not exist) among the socks, collars, copies of *Billboard*, and proofs of handbills. A couple of his favorite bills were posted on the wall: *Come one! Come all! Every cent to charity! Our Lady of St. Aloyisius! American Legion Post #104! Firemen of Montgomery, Ala.! Try some Vitamin F — it's FUN!*

Stan's way was to make his trailer blaze with the Christmas tree lights he strung over it, so that everyone would know when he counted his money. It was a celebrational thing to do; I respected him for his piety before the dollar. Casanopopolous and the Bossman both shared this vanity, this awe, this socialized buck. Casanopopolous ironed out the wrinkled bills in public, on a board, wearing an apron; Bossman just lit up, but it was the same thing. One of the nice carnie habits is to carry a big wad and pad it with tissue paper if you

130

have to. To tish your money is no stranger than for a girl to tish her boobies, is it? All right.

Stan had a safe riveted to the floor of his trailer. He was a skinny hard little man with an overgrown Adam's apple and a blond mustache that you only saw for sure when he licked it over his lips and sucked at the hairs, a flat-headed carnie boss with pale blue eyes flush with his cheeks, thin sandy hair combed and looped across his scalp, ears like handlebars — he looked like a quartermaster sergeant in the Free Ukrainian Army, if there is such a thing and if it has quartermasters. Full of admiration in the head, he got to be a boss because he saved his money. His tie was in a huge knot over the wiry Adam's apple. He blinked at me when I pushed my way in: "What say, Bud?"

"I'm back, Bossman."

He winked, and then his jaw cracked with his deep, sick, palate-snapping yawn. The confidential boredom was a part of his art, but it was also his life. He did not touch either the money or the revolver. "What you been doing?"

"I ain't been with it, Stan."

"What you been pushing?"

"Just now? Been talking with Pauline at her mittcamp. Been seeing Joy."

He hardly moved, but I saw Stan the baby now, held down by straps, struggling, red-faced, flailing, fisting, twisting, and unable to budge. But he only winked and yawned, reduced to these twitches of passion, saying: "What you planning on your mind?"

"You need me on a countstore, Bossman."

"I don't think so, Bud."

131

"Yes, you think so, Stan."

He stacked his bills and put the revolver back on top. He sighed and said, "What made you talk to Joy all afternoon?"

"She's a friend, a kid like me —"

"Sweet kid," he said. "You're older'n her, Bud. I'm not that much older'n her, being still a man. I don't think we really need you so much now, Bud. You ran out on us once. Your friend Grack left us in a bad way."

I sat down on a chromium kitchen stool without being asked. I played my thumb against a match end to give it something to do. "I told you I was going, Stan. I didn't run out. It ain't my fault what Grack took it in his head. I wasn't even around. A first-cream countstore would be good for the whole show, bring some fun to the show, not to mention your cut. They tell me it's dead."

"Unh." Grunting, his Adam's apple bobbing and the wide nostrils working: "Joy say there's no fun in it for her?"

"I'll be ready to set up in two days. You got the stuff for me."

He drew heavily in his snout and played the nostrils with two fingers. "I ain't denying you're a good talker, a good grifter for a kid." He smiled painfully and showed the tips of teeth. "That what Joy told you about Stan's Show, that no fun for her, that Joy?"

Even Steven, he wanted an answer. Well, I would see. "You got any ideas about why Grack did it?" I asked without bringing a word to his hard, wet, jealous sound, *Joy*.

He shook his head angrily. "No, no, we was almost friends," — and impatiently. His feelings were hurt. "No,

132

Grack stayed with me longer'n anybody. We almost got to be what-you-call-em pals."

Okay, Stan, I'm sorry for you, too. But I said: "Listen, you been carrying the setup, Stan. You been looking for a flat store man. I'll set up in two days if I have to use adhesive to stick it together. I'll even do some painting myself, you supply the paint. I got ambition since I left the show, Stan. It's good for a boy to learn the facts of life." He nodded. Now it was time to say something nice to Bossman. First the mean and hard, then the nice, that's the way for a Bossman: "I'm almost glad to see you, Stan. Your face looks almost good to me. You ought to take vitamin pills, your skin is yellow. I had the jaundice once myself."

Never mind that sympathy, never mind that nice, his hands in-and-out stacking work with the money told me. The busy nose and the yawning never stopped. He asked without looking at me: "Joy been complaining about the fun in this show?" I watched with my mouth open for the yawn and the tic of wink that followed. Complicity, boredom — these were the meaning of his life. Slyness, dead with it — poor Stan! His winking eyes were those of a fox; his foxy muzzle reached open for the snare. "Joy thinks she's a sweet kid, okay, I say she is, but she ain't got no right to complain."

I laughed and touched the stack of singles. "Listen, Stan, neither Grack nor Joy is our business now. I want a countstore, you need a countstore, we're playing new dates: let's get decided. Later we'll cut up a jackpot."

"It's true," he admitted, "we got a couple new fairs. A Legion next week, a dunkers' church Friday a week."

"And they're fresh dates, not any kadotas?" This means

133

that the farmers were unscarred by the countstore trap and the larceny in their hearts would be nice and fresh and palpitating.

"It's true." And he figured, leaning back on the red plastic seat of a chromium kitchen chair. All the furniture of his trailer was of this sort, chromium, plastic, the flash of display window at a 52-pay appliance store off the main avenue where the greedy poor pay and pay and *pay*. The two front paws of the chair screeched forward as he made his decision, a decision squeezed out by the wink of cupidity instead of the fearful boredom of his yawn over Grack and Joy. He needed me. He would keep me. I would help him clean the marks and wipe their bones. "True, all so true," he said.

"I'll set up right away."

"When can you be ready?"

"Two days, Stan, I already told you."

"Just don't fool around with that Joy, Bud. And don't go the way Grack went."

"What does Joy have to do with it? You get your percentage."

His head shook as if trying to rattle loose a bad idea. "Okay, okay, Bud." He worked himself up to a smile, putting forward his hand, the other paw sweeping his neat little piles of cash toward his bosom. "Shake on it."

"That's right, shake —" But I left his hand hanging in air. "Fifty-fifty then, that right?"

He kept the hand forward, saying, "Whaddyah mean? It's my setup, my show, my space. I handle the fuzz and everything. You're just a greenie in the business. It's a natural forty-sixty deal."

134

"Unh," I tried to say. I wanted to be an ox. "No, Boss-man." I wasn't for giving him sixty per cent of my take, no sir, when all he supplied was a little cardboard and a sign and a couple of light bulbs and a board and marbles and an extra grin for the sheriff and some slum that would rarely leave us. No, no.

"Which means what?"

"Which means no."

"Then that's the answer," he said.

"The nice answer is yes, Stan, and fifty-fifty. That's plenty and you know it."

"Bud, be smart —"

"If I were smart, Bossman —"

"— Be smart, think smart, kid." His voice rose to a treble whine. "Look, you can gaff it for the extra per cent. You're in charge. You can even cheat me for the extra per cent. I got no check on you."

This made me smile; it made him wink and yawn at me, his palate cracking. "I don't want to cheat you, Stan, I want to play you straight fifty-fifty, not gaff you for fifty-fifty."

"What diff it make to you, Bud? What'll the folks say if they hear you talked old Stan into a fifty-fifty deal on a count-store when you're just a kid and it's all my marbles?" He appealed to me to rob him for the sake of his reputation for rough dealing. "Remember, kid, I got to spend the winter with them in Orlando."

"I don't care what you flash to the people, Stan, I just want to play you straight and ungaffed at fifty for fifty. That's all."

"Joy will think I'm losing the touch, please —"

"What diff about Joy, Bossman? Listen" — and I leaned to

him with my confidential grin on my face — "you say she's just a sweet kid, don't you? Okay, what diff? If you tell her forty-sixty and I tell her I'm gaffing against you, then what diff? You ought to brush your teeth, Stan." He had yawned in my face.

Greed won in this bright chromium, bright red plastic trailer. He needed me; I knew that he needed me. He also knew that I would really give him his fifty-fifty, not say fifty-fifty and then go on gaffing against him until he booted me out. He finally said, "Yes, what toothpaste you recommend?" And then: "Okay, Bud, I give that you're a good man for a kid. Stay out of trouble now. Come in and let's cut up that jackpot someday."

Now I took the hand as it lifted once more across his money, the revolver, and the pink plastic skin stretched across a trailer-size kitchen table. Stan was not yawning, but winking and winking me out of his home. He half-stood for farewell. "You're a bargain, Bud."

I was on the show.

16. Pleasant is as pleasant pleases

THE next day was twenty-seven miles further on and already I was hot at calling. The marks who diddled their balls in my game were used-up marks, brother, as used up as only Georgia crackers get with their long bony red faces and wrists and their sly ways at holding their pants. My own pockets pulled at the seams with a hard little roll without even gaffing Stan a teeny bit, not that I had anything against it; my luck came so good that the idea hardly occurred to me. I spent freely on a wide-brimmed hat and felt fine when the popcorn man said, "Right chere, Tex!" With a strap. With a sharp narrow band. With a feather. When I say I had luck, I mean my talk, my way with the crowd and the larcenous slickers who shuffled forward to my cackle. I was the cock of this meager barnyard, and when I went kokoreeko the marks fluffed their rearends and stepped up to get stung and then to drop their eggs. That ain't just luck: I was good.

Of course 1 was thinking ahead. The man who figures ahead makes himself some good luck. Yes, and Grack was no longer mine to do my thinking for me. I was ready to get myself money and a place to breathe in — although the money is only money in a penny-one traveling show and the place to breathe in is only cheap scorched Georgia air where even the truckers bound for Jacksonville keep their noses high, the better to peep with, my dears, and their pants buttoned if they can.

Once or twice, maybe tired as sometimes you get, I talked too hard and high, "Lookee here, lookee here, lookee here!" and my index finger flew to my eye with Grack's old come-on, a shadow of habit which I didn't mean. My talk and way with the people were really all mine, whatever you might have seen on that one purple-shadowed late afternoon, or maybe twice. Tired was all. For the rest, Grack would have been proud of me, and pleased that I was proud of myself. He knew hurry-in skill when he met it. He would have grinned to see how I had learned from him but got to do more and more like my very own Bud.

I had trouble with the setup that Stan let me, of course. It wasn't a fifty-fifty worth. It was two bits of slum. It had bad need of paint and nails and glue and soap and water. Joy carried a bucket and wore jeans and helped me sop it down. She painted green paint on the board and got her flushed face streaked with it and handprints of green on her hips when she stood off to wipe them: "Well, well, this store is an opener, Bud. Smells the sweat-money already."

"How do you know I want to stick with a countstore?"

"Don't you?"

"I don't see it exactly, but no, not all my life long. But first I need me a stake."

"Wipe off your marbles, Bud, they're getting sticky from hands." She wiped each one in an oily rag. She even patched the holes in the canvas with canvas-colored chewing gum —

that's the womanly touch. I'd never have thought of it. Her elbows jabbed me. "Don't you laugh, Bud."

I stood back and hawed.

"I'll empty this bucket of Japalac on you if you laugh."

I hawed and grabbed her wrists when she made as if to heave the bucket at my head. "Oh! Ouch! Ooh!" — the game was to wrestle and sway and hold the wrists of this slender, short-black-curly-haired creature in green-marked jeans and a Sears white shirt. That morning, while the carnie was still sleeping it off, Stan passed with his eyes all crudded and gave us his yawn. We were squirming, puffing, knees bumping, with paint splashing in the sawdust. A tongue of it hit the dartgame next door.

"Watch out for the property," he said. "This business ain't no playtoy for kids."

"Stan's mad at you," I whispered to Joy.

She shook her hands loose, scowling, and watched him down to the latrine shack. "Old nanny goat."

The rocking in the pit of my stomach I recognized for jealousy, a sick turning without reason, unsteady and crowding me, but I said only, "That a way to talk about the boss carnie?"

"*Dirty* old goat," she said, and took up a tin can of silver glow-in-the-dark paint, a surprise gift from Pauline to me. Her tongue between her teeth, solemn, composing, she wrote on the band above our chewing-gummed canvas, below the old *Ballo Game, Tri-Yr-Luck*, these excellent words: *Bud Williams, Prop.*

It was a fine thought. It gave me an idea of what I wanted, to be the proprietor of myself and of something, and to like those things. Those things would like me, too. I stood behind Joy and watched the motion of one green hand on her hip as she twisted and reached. She had the longest, the slenderest neck and the collar of her shirt fell floppily about it. She studied me gravely when she had finished writing my name.

It wasn't many weeks before I picked up a prewar Dodge, borrowing the gas money from Pauline but paying for the rest out of my chatter and gleam and the balls' jiggle and roll and the mathematical tricks they made, first counting them to win on the tryout for free, then counting them straight to lose. One night I let a mark pick off an Indian blanket: "A happy moment for the management, sir! We just love to please the client. Now will you have the genuine Gruen watch, the baby dollie that weeps and pees, the —"

"Gimme the blanket, damn you. Cost me enough."

"Pleasure, friend."

Sentimentality is good for the hardness, although the carnie most honest with himself is the one who gives nothing but a clack of the tongue to the mark's misery. If I was honest, it was another way. I wanted to give pleasure, to take it, and to clear a place where Bud Williams could move around. I needed a car for pleasure, for joyriding with Joy, and I didn't want always to be a bum on Pauline's half-truck, even if I did double-clutch her out of the mud and change the tires and file down the generator points. A man needs his own. Well, that jalopy started to cost me right away, oil it drank, gas it leaked, grafting cops who squinted and grinned and gummed their tobacco because they thought ("*maybe*, young feller") the Dodge should receive a thorough inspection for

140

brakes and wiring. The body was shot with rust, well-chewed by use and weather, but the motor could always be fixed. I had to borrow again from Pauline when we rained out for a few dates running. I had also spent on a couple of dinners in town for Pauline and Joy. "Credit running short?" I asked her.

"Gosh almighty, no, boy."

"When's that?"

She poked me in the ribs with a damp bluish roll of hand, shapeless from many readings. "When I pawn my jewels, that's when. They're all paste, glue, and glass." Her own false jewelry amused Pauline, so I gave her my laughter, too. Heee, I said. I appreciated Pauline, and even more as I paid back the loans.

I also appreciated Joy. One day she asked me, "Going into town?"

"I was just getting ready to ask you, why?" It was a breath-less middle-of-the-morning on the fairgrounds where we were doing good for the VFW, the popcorn slush and the cotton candy gray in drifts on the battened-down earth and our gaunt ten-cent Ferris wheel very small in the sky. The carnies have a sense for enemy weather, working against it even in their sleep. When the sun came up high over a lot like this one, they managed to groan and sleep again hard on into the morning. Joy and I had awakened early, a full working day ahead of the kiddies' matinee, alert with each other, teasing and taunting. We drank hot coffee to break the sweat. The sky moved closer with the sun, enveloping the world in the catch-tongue heat of homes we had evaded; we had the jitters, I think; the day would be a scorcher.

"Maybe I need to buy some toothpaste in town. Maybe I want a Coke. Maybe just for the ride," she said.

"Toothpowder is supposed to be healthier for the teeth. Dentists use it."

I had trouble getting the jalopy started, but then it heaved and jerked as if it really wanted to go to town itself. Maybe the way Joy had become a lady pleased my Dodge, too. Joy sat up straight without spreading her legs across the seat, lips pursed and level eyes watching, a touch of vain hand at the cropped ends of hair. I asked her to bring her swimming clothes, and she returned a quick wry grin because we were not to swim in our skins today. It was only for the others that I said it, of course. To take a chance like that in Georgia was next thing to walking right up to the sheriff and asking for Indecent Exposure and Disturbing the Peace. We rolled through town and out the other end of a one-minute Georgia main street (J. C. Penny, Rexall, Smiley's Eats, Shine Here — you know), probably named for Robert E. Lee or the galluses of Gene Talmadge. "You aren't buying me anything?" she asked. "A Coke's only a dime. Here, I'll lend it to you."

The other side of town was greener, which meant water. Since our time of swimming, water meant Joy and Bud to us — the rich blackness of a dive which ended against her wriggling legs and then her laughter when I came spurting foam to the surface. But probably no swimming today. We passed another thin pine clump of the sort which freckle Georgia, but I kept on moving, putting miles between the carnival and us. The wracked and panting Dodge helped make a few miles seem like years. We stopped at a roadhouse and ordered rootbeer at the counter, heavy fake steins of

142

foaming brown sweetness, Old Pappy's very own brew. I watched Joy dip her red lips into this sugared stuff and asked her, "Don't you ever want to leave the carnie?"

"What about you? You came back, Bud."

"Yes, but I came from markville. I thought about it and changed my mind. Don't you ever wonder if it's the right place?"

"Yes."

"Then don't you ever think about leaving?"

"Pauline doesn't. We have a taste of markville every year in Florida. I have reasons for staying with it."

A swift bitterness came to my mouth, a rootbeer hiccup, but it was also because Pauline would grieve if we left. My father was sad. Grack was sad someplace. "What reasons?" I asked.

She smiled at me like the little girl I remembered when I had said, *Go away, you bother me.* She explained now: "Pauline needs me, you need someone to help you sometimes, chew the gum for patching for you, I need myself here."

"That's nice, Joy."

She wanted me to repeat it: "Nice of you, Joy." Little more than a child with electric hair and skinny tanned legs, she nevertheless knew what needed to be repeated: "It's good that people need you here and you need yourself here at the Tuscaloosa Too Show and —"

"Maybe I'll decide to clean out someday. When I do, maybe I'll let you know. *Listen now, Bud,* I'll say —" She laughed and got off the stool and carried her stein to a booth, making me follow her, but it was willing and knowing of what I wanted to tell her. A tip-hungry waiter stood wiping

143

his hands in a towel: "Sandwich, folks? Cookies? Nice hot-dog with relish?"

We sat opposite each other at a front booth, looking out at my creaking heap of Dodge, our fingers linked in the handles of the rootbeer mugs. I was waiting to say it. She spoke first. "Talking of clean," she said lazily, "we might try painting the limousine. Put your name on it, put the name of your store on it."

"Paint your name on it, too," I said.

"Oh. Why, Bud?"

It's funny how almost any woman is twenty years older than almost any man, and at the same time what a man seeks is the spit and quick of girlishness. Joy here, ignorant of the world except of the carnie, too smart, too wide-eyed and level, having seen too much, puzzled out and knew the desire to be with it which I asked the whole world, Tuscaloosa, and the show to gratify. There lies a riddle: What gave her solution sense was that she liked me and liked me and liked me. And let me know it.

"It's heading for rain. We ought to be getting back."

She made no move. "Yes," she said.

"Joy?"

"Yes."

"I want you, Joy."

She let me play with her hand and push away the rootbeer, but she answered, "What do you need me for?"

"I didn't say that. I said I want you."

"What does that say to me?"

"That I want you? I love you, Joy."

She grinned stubbornly. "What do you want me for?" She

stopped smiling and turned to the gathering weather out the window. "Remember when I was a girl?" she asked. "I used to bother you. You told me to go away and you meant it. It was only a few months ago. Grack used to pinch me when he caught me hanging around."

"Don't laugh at me, Joy."

"Seems like I didn't know you then, Bud. That you would say things to me now just because you went away and Grack went away and you came back. I don't get all these fast changes. Maybe it's too soon."

"You've changed, Joy. You're a woman. Look at yourself."

Proudly, high and strong, she commanded me. "*You* look, that's enough." I could almost sniff the pride of her flesh. Her level arch of eyebrows raised to receive my devotion.

"Don't laugh," I said.

"Do I look laughing? What do you want from the carnie, Bud? You're not born with it."

"To get with you."

"With me and for me?"

I took her hand and looked at her to say, *Yes, that's it, Joy.* Was this love — to give everything to her and for her? I could think it, yes, but not yet know it. We got up together and she stood at the door while I paid and left the change in the waiter's hand. My lady waited for me at the door. She linked her arm with mine and we went out together.

17. Love is with Joy only

Iᴛ seemed as if the rain were due again, but it made
no difference. We had purposes together. I drove off the road
while the sky sulked with clouds and a strange cool breeze
flickered up and died, but still it made no difference. There
were no repairs. We had decided, and Joy slipped over the
seat by my side as the lurching Dodge took us into a lip of
woods. I felt her knees near mine. *This* made a difference.

The first drops fell like petals on the roof of the car. "What
if someone sees us?"

"The rain will keep them inside."

"Are you sure?"

"Everyone but us, Joy."

She smiled at my way of turning trouble into good. Since
returning to the carnie and finding Joy, I had learned the
way of being good — seeing properly, looking properly, and
knowing how to regard even the troubles. The first drops
steamed off the hood. The rain just opened the black oven of
the Georgia noon. Flecked by petals, the Dodge creaked in
its dusty heat. "For sure they'll leave us alone," I said. The
new rain tamped the dust and softened the morning for us,
while far away a rooster, which lived by heat, cried as if for
dawn. The dustdrops spattered on the hood. Being with Joy

146

was a way of teaching me to be with myself, because while with her, I cared only for her. And I was with myself in my black corduroy pants with the ribs worn pale by hipwork.

For both of us now I busied myself with a carnie setup. I opened the doors at my side of the car. I spread my raincoat over them like a circus top. Joy smiled and knew what I was about and tucked the corners of the coat so that it would not fall down upon us at a strange time, as circus tops sometimes do when the trick riders are still galloping in their act. The flurry of rain had passed for the moment, leaving only a steaming freshness of washed leaves and calmed dust. On the grass between the open doors and beneath the circus top I spread two Army blankets which were my bunk since I had returned to the show. Joy flapped them smooth.

When I pulled her down to me, her eyes, those level studies of the world, made one frightened turn for what they could see. "Nobody here but us trees," I said hoarsely, shocking myself.

"I'm afraid. A little bit."

"Don't be afraid of me."

"I'm not, I'm not even afraid of the others," she said, "but I want us to be alone here."

"We are, Joy. We will be."

And as if to reassure her the rain came pelting down. No one would come out to peek in this rain; a man caught in it would slog along home. We kicked partway under the high chassis of the Dodge and lay holding each other, clinging against the thunder and the clap of lightning, watching the warm flash shower open up the sky. Then the sun-laden mud stirred and tiny rivulets of water streamed about our bodies, steaming and pale on the drawing wool. We were still dry; the thickness of blanket took it. Joy's tawniness, fading at the edges of clothes, whitened in the changing light against the great dusty body of the world; my flesh turned heavy and muscled in her sight — this came with male pleasure, I knew, but it came for her, too. The smell of grass and sweetness, like freshly washed or green things, rose with her arms' rise and fall and her willing struggle. She smiled again, saying, "I like the rain."

"I know, I fixed it."

"Thank you, Bud."

I busied myself with her clothes. She turned equally to me, and I was all hands at her while she was the eager tugging and pulling at my flesh and then all within as if my entrails were turning with a force to burst my body. The warm rain swam through the blankets and we sank in it. I love you! . . . Love you! The holding and grasping and twisting went on amidst swimming words until one moment when Joy suddenly cried out and went soft in my arms, all collapsed and spread under the chassis of a Dodge, destroyed. I felt her pain myself. A moment later I came to wakefulness and heard my own voice; it said, "She was a child — *you* were."

The warm rain puddled and diminished about us. Her hair was streaming and there were flecks of mud on her cheeks. She listened to the rain before she answered, "You're talking to me, I hope, Bud."

"You were!"

"Sh! Don't say anything."

We let the dark rain off a mud road in Georgia wash about us, and we lay without clothes and took pain and pleasure in each other. We rested and rested. We talked. I leaned on one elbow. She pulled me down, hard as apples, and said that she did not hurt, no. I swam in the tide, hotly bathed, breathing you and me, Joy! We laughed with our mouths open together because love is pleasant. No, no, she did not hurt. We were tender with each other, knowing that we would return to give life again and again, and that to get with it meant to be forever and ever with me, for Joy, and with her for me.

Later that evening, sitting through the off-and- on rain which had killed the carnival day but did not destroy ours (these no longer the same), we huddled about Pauline's kerosene hotplate, drinking tea, while Pauline herself went out to see Casanopopolous in his trailer and gossip about old times. Cas, never a talker, sometimes let himself be lubricated by rain and enticed away from the care and counting of his dollars. At those times Pauline went to court him.

Joy and I, lightened creatures, spry and calm on our stools, sipped from glasses and munched from a box of soda crackers. She put jam on them for me and stacked them by my glass. She herself reached into the box as if they were peanuts. We sat amid the mystic symbols of Pauline's mittcamp, the zigzag painting and carving and filigree with which Pauline tickled or teased the marks. "What's so funny?" Joy asked.

I was smiling at a pair of torn stockings hung over a chart which showed the lifeline in a copyrighted palm. She followed my eyes but did not smile. Pauline was home to her; the astrological tools and the mitt books were kitchen matters to Joy. "What does Pauline really think about things?" I asked. "She answers the big questions for everyone, she tells them the future and the past, she tickles their palms and makes them promise to be good. But what does she really think about this business? Here and now."

"It's her business, so?"

I looked at Joy to see, just when she had become a woman for me, how she was suddenly a little girl again. I tried to explain. "All business is business, Joy. It's a racket at first: you need money for a house, a car, go on vacations maybe. My pop wanted things like that — also send your kids to school. But it gets to be more than reasons for the future. You work for it while it works for you. You start to believe in it. You dream about yesterday and tomorrow. You have to, and you're right to. You believe in something that you give your life to, otherwise you're only Stan —"

"Is Grack like that?"

"Never mind Grack. Otherwise you're only Stan, I was saying."

She pouted. Grack seemed a rival to her because our time now was Grack's lost time, but maybe she would be able to understand soon that I had been a kid then, needing a papa, and now I was a man and needed her. Maybe if Grack had stayed around she might have understood, but she could not have seen all that had happened since the days of Grack at the carnie. She could not have seen what I had made happen to myself — Pittsburgh and Pa and Grack's letter, touch football and Phyllis and Andy, kicking so many bad habits and working up the habit of kicking. It was happening to her, too — once only Pauline's pretty brat.

"Listen, you think Pauline doesn't believe in her business?" I demanded. "You don't know your mama, Joy. She believes, even if she knows the cards and mitts don't give it. She likes advice. She wants to take care of things. She plans and plans, that's fortunetelling, Joy. She's very hopeful about people if they only take good advice."

"That's only *you*, Bud — she likes you." Joy smiled and put a crumb of graham cracker into her mouth. "It's your future she believes in. You got the wrong idea about her. She likes to give you advice because she believes in you."

"And what about me? How I'll be a bossman like Stan someday?"

Joy ducked her head, scowling. She herself, knowing only the carnie well, surely knew that Owner was not the top of the world of men. In her confusion she turned girlish and coy, but inexperienced in teasing a man, she told the truth about what came to her mind. It was not what I would become that she told. She bit her lip, she worried, she frowned. She finished a story: "Stan used to. It was before you even came to the carnie. It was before you left. Stan used to try to hold me on his knees and kiss me. I didn't like it —"

"What? Neither did I."

"You didn't even know anything then, Bud. Once Grack stopped him, but people didn't always see when he did it. He used to come around at funny times and peek. I was only a kid — but I knew Stan was important. I didn't know what —"

"Didn't you tell anyone?"

"What could I tell? Anyway, nothing happened, but I knew wrong because of the way he watched out for Pauline. . . ." She shook her head, *wrong, wrong*. "His ears had points from listening for Pauline."

I imagined Stan with little Joy on his knees, his head

151

cocked and eyes rapidly blinking, a yellow grin on his face, waiting for the groan and pad of Pauline's varicosed feet. His fingers were touching Joy; his shriveled little belly was pressing against her as she struggled to climb down. My face was stiff as I saw it — no, no, I thought; and I fought to keep from seizing her with hatred. "Listen, Joy," I said, "how long ago was that?"

"I was a baby, but Pauline was just as old as she is now. No, it kept on happening, but I was a baby until you came back, Bud. Remember? Once Pauline —"

"Why do you call her Pauline now? Why not Mama? Stop jumping around, answer me." I struggled with this mood of asking every question, rummaging in her past which now seemed mysterious and threatening to me, trying to smile at myself because this baby Joy, this child Joy, this woman I loved, Joy, had become a person to me and I had a full bag of questions to ask her. I could not smile the doubts back into the bag. She was strange to me still, but the desire to ask questions made me realize that she was the woman Phyllis could never have become, the one I loved and not just the carnie brat named Joy. "Pauline is your mama, isn't she?"

She frowned. "So listen, Bud. When Pauline caught him at it, he said he was just playing with the kid, hon. That's what he said. He dropped me so fast I bounced. Probably scared Pauline'd take a knife or the stars to him. Funny thing, Bud, I don't remember as he did anything wrong or very funny. Just thinking he must have done. A lot of ideas he must have done, smoke in the head. Pauline never said anything. Maybe she had him figured out."

Relieved, I closed my eyes against the image Joy prattled

152

about. These were girlish confidences, I guess, of the sort that most women finally work through with the men they trust. If they do it right, they don't need women in this way anymore, they don't need telephoning in the morning and shopping trips and shrill lunches with the girls. It gave me a sharp pride — if I was right about this. I said, "Does a lot of wrong thinking for one guy, that Stan."

She relaxed and folded her hands in her lap. Each day she seemed to learn new gestures and lose those of a tomboy. Even in my irritability I must have passed the test for her. Her smile said, Bud, Bud, and was not ashamed to say it. "Probably has no fun in life," she remarked after a while. "We have fun, Bud." And this girl's eyes fluttered in the steady valuing of me and of herself which meant that we had found some secret and general good together — secret because ours alone, general because it enabled us to join the common world of mark and carnie. It was a good which drained and then returned to her the color of her face and changed the size of her eyes as it had changed them in her pain and ecstasy with her legs partway under the chassis of our automobile.

Later I asked Pauline about Stan. "What does he do for fun, Pauline?"

She rocked in her seat, malicious and fun-loving herself, figuring what I meant without looking at my palms or at the bumps under my crewcut. "All right, Mr. Bud, you are desiring to pry, but every soul on the lot already knows. So what about this owner? Poor Bossman Stan, his only girl friend is his left hand."

Joy was rinsing some cups in a corner of the trailer. She stamped her foot and complained, "The tank is dry again."

"That's what I meant about Stan," Pauline teeheed at me.

"Bud!" Joy said. "I thought you were going to tend to the water."

Contritely: "I forgot."

"I can do my own forgetting," she said sternly. "Lately that's what you've been doing for me." But then she ran and flung her arms and legs about me, so that we made a many-legged critter as I staggered roaring about the narrow space of the outdoors between our trailer and that of Casanopopolous. "See how I can nag?" she asked. "I'm just as good as any of those Pittsburgh twist-and-twirls."

Pauline watched us, purple lips spread wide, and then, still smiling, she stood up when she saw Stan's face peering through the window in Casanopopolous's trailer. She stared him down. She told Joy to go away, don't bother her; then she asked me to come to talk with her inside. I followed meekly with the respect due the woman who knows all, tells all, and was all Joy's mother.

She groaned and settled among her cards, her charts, her powders, and her waters. She waited for silence, put her hands over her great middle, and said, "You don't have the Grack to take care of you no more."

"I don't need Grack. I'm making my own stand. I'm doing all right."

"Yes," she admitted, "but you're not used to Stan. Grack could get away with things, he could help you get away, but Bossman is mean."

"So?"

154

"He had his eye on Joy. She's no girl anymore, and he's been just waiting."

I shrugged. "That's up to Joy." I had been through my turn of jealousy. "I'm not scared."

"Stan is poison, boy. He's deadly nightshade and milky dogsbane, he's goat's rue and thorn-apple, that man is hog-meat and snake-nut. Trobble! He's all thorns. He's bad for you if he wants to be."

I fondled the new glass ball she had ordered out of the magician's catalogue. "I can cook his vegetables," I said. "I can take care of myself. I can take care of Joy. I can take care of you, too, Pauline, if you need it. So don't worry."

She put her hand over mine, and the two hands slipped down the greasy and glassy surface of the fortuneteller's ball. It was the world's caress on this globe, a caress from beneath covered by Pauline's hot flesh which wished me only the best. It's nice to have friends. Grack had not been enough.

"Okay," she said, "but hold on tight to what you got that's good."

The next night I had a dream. I dreamt I was with it. I was no longer a fish, a nut, or a goose in the world of men. I belonged. It was a good dream, comfortable, thigh-turning, a dream without tiredness. The rich darkness of the Georgia countryside was a spacious thing in my dream. I woke up slowly, gratefully, finding Joy's small head beside mine on the pillow, Joy breathing warmly on my shoulder and her body soft and growing familiar when I reached for her. The dream awakened me to become true.

The dream gave me this thought: Joy!

155

The dream gave me this thought: We can be mother and father!

I woke her, and as she stretched and yawned and touched my eyelids, I said, "Marry me, Joy."

"Okay, when?" she asked, and fell back asleep.

18. Southern days and nights, with popcorn and crackers

WE said nothing straight out to anyone, but the word about Joy and me got around as fast as a hey-rube call. I guess she lounged by my side. I guess I leaned and gawked into her level eyes like a mark who all of a sudden really does win at the weight-guesser's. Once I sat wearing nothing but a pair of shiny starched new khakis I had just picked up in an Army-Navy, no shoes or socks, no shirt, nothing but the pants, while Joy squeezed a blackhead on my chest. That really meant love and forever to me. She kept her fingernails from biting by wrapping a handkerchief about them; she pursed her lips and squinted and, by God, tears came to her eyes when I said: "Ouch!"

"Oh! Did I hurt you?" .

"You're killing me."

"Then I'll stop, Bud."

"No, you might as well get it out now. Grow up, kid, things got to hurt in this life."

She continued squeezing and paining me, saying, "Yes, Bud, it's part of things, but I hate to hurt you."

157

She hated to hurt me and did for my own good and we dearly were fond of each other. I never knew it could be like that. Of course, loving even Joy didn't make me think only pure thoughts of love. Her small parts, her noises from the middle, her demands and complaints kept me busy. A woman is not just soul and hickie-squeezing, nor just body, nor even a simple mixture of both — she's a hook, besides. Imagine Bud the worm happy on his hook, wriggling up against it, snuggling and warming the hard barb.

And see me, like any worm that has turned, doubting, quarreling, inflamed by novelty. Dare I risk so much of myself in the mystery and illusion of love? That intimacy begins by illusion, the mysteries of body making sense resonate like a lovely bell — and false, false, because no permanent earthly knowledge can stay forever in a clang of music.

Therefore we quarreled, too. I was unsure. We made it up. We quarreled over nothing but my doubts, and then loved again. "All right, all right, that's all," Joy would say, touching my hand and making me sure once more. What difference about the excuse for fighting? It was always the same reason — doubt and need, fear and need, testing and dreading.

"I'll never talk like that again," I said, "never. I promise you, Joy."

"Probably you will," she said. "But you should try not to."

"I'll try."

"I will, too. We shouldn't worry every little thing like that."

Pauline even let Joy stop selling the tickets at her mittcamp so that she could join me at my store. She put on lipstick and rouge (I made her take off the rouge) and spent hours painting her fingernails and toes. She invited the customers, she smiled and chattered, she merely stood and her health and her pleasure gave the marks confidence. Funny that true love could help a talent for cheating! But this was only business, of course, and she was not being dishonest; she was only, like me, sincere about business and wanting to make out. "O sir!" she would whisper to some long cracker with straw between his lips. "O sir! You almost won that time." He blushed and scratched his belly and wondered who was tickling him and put down his quarter again.

The carnie had some good days coming: hot and dry for soft drinks, dark and crowded for shoving into line after wheels and girls, busy and lots of change for all of us to count. The coffee from our jug eased our throats. I did well. We were playing some unspoiled dates, fresh and sweet, where they had never learned how fast the quarters slip away in a countstore. Joy raked them for me, barely touching the coins with her fingers. It was a pleasure for everyone. I was getting a nut of cash, and it felt good: Joy was a responsibility which made the joys of money more than an indulgence. She would need things. We would need things together.

Afterwards, during the tense sleepless hours of early in the morning, when we had just stowed away our gear and turned off the generators and the Christmas tree glitter of the carnival twittered into blackness and only the braked Ferris wheel gave a quaver or two in the breeze, we would sit outside Pauline's trailer in the chirruping night and talk things over. In the nights I told her about Grack and retold it because I could not stop owing him: how he ended the habit which had been mama to me, how he sent me away from the childhood in which I had been revolving without

159

moving, how he made me set myself straight toward being present in the world.

Then, mornings, still sitting, Joy with her knees pulled up against her breast, shivering but not wanting to go, leaning for warmth while I leaned to her for warmth, I would tell her about Pittsburgh and Pop and the old neighborhood and how I had decided that this too could not be mama to me and my future had to be ahead of me, not behind.

At first she just listened. Later, as the days and nights went by, and I kept the cash in a box upon which I wrote *Bud and Joy*, she began to tell me, too. She had practically fallen out of Pauline under the palmistry table, between an ace of diamonds and a trey of spades. Her father was some enterprising mark, a clever absentee from the world of men. "But Pauline always had lots of friends," Joy said, not to be complaining. "They were nice to me." Once in a while she went to school, and Pauline insisted on her book-learning. Life-learning she picked up in the carnival, that absolute future, that American place which, descended from Rome and the gypsies, was the footloose moving image of the get-rich-quick, get-love-quick, get-ahead-quick of America. It was a world where everyone was his own mama and papa, and cash money the only promised land, and *signifying* (bragging, wearing Texas hats, flashing the roll) the only way station before heaven. It was a land of friends bound like good brothers and bad brothers, good sisters and bad sisters, all in one loyal family which joined against the world of markdom when there came a hey-rube or a hailstorm or some ugly dealing with the sheriff.

Funny that only Stan, the Bossman, was not a brother to

160

this family. Even old Cas, crazy for folding money, counting and ironing it, had a smile and didn't wish bad for anyone. Stan wished the bad for all. He got to be boss, but not by loving. He had only his left hand for girlfriend, as Pauline said, and his right for dealing and false friendship. One night Joy left my stand for coffee, then didn't come back and didn't come back. The marks were piled as thick as Junebugs, but she didn't come back. Well, maybe her stomach is upset, I thought.

Later I pulled down the canvas and closed up and went to Pauline's to look for her.

"Joy? I thought she was with you," Pauline said.

Funny.

I peeked in at Casanopopolous. He was asleep. I strolled about, chatting with all the carnie folk, droop-eyed or falsely alert after the busy evening. I didn't like to hurry. There would be talk if I looked worried or jealous. But I had bit a hole in my lip. I was kicking through the sawdust down the empty midway in the dark when I heard a faint shuffle behind me. I whirled and cried out, "Joy!"

It was Honest Al, the Retarded Kid. That was a long title for Al; he only assisted at the Ferris wheel, helping the ladies in and buckling the rod. "Hiya Bud," he said, "looking for someone?"

"No one in particular."

"Okay, then why don't you go over to Stan?"

I snapped my fingers. *That's it!* I was running and remembering the terrible disease which Stan had once told me about. It came from sex and there was no cure, partly because there were no symptoms or effects and you did not ever know you had it. You could live with it for fifty years and never know. Miserable. I remembered the thrill of dirt, like a shadow over his eyes, when he made this joke. As I trotted down the midway, kicking up sawdust like snow, scared for Joy, I felt proud even then that there was not an instant of waiting and no one had to con me with a finger to an eye. Stan, that bastard, was all I thought. He couldn't hurt Joy. He couldn't hurt us.

There was a hard yellow light burning within Stan's trailer. Somehow this relieved me. Once I would have peeked through the slats to see what was what, but now I just grabbed the screen door and ripped it open, tearing the catch clean out of the plywood. "Bud!" Joy cried out. She was smiling. This surprised me. She greeted me but, still smiling, she looked at Stan.

He was drunker than any other man I had ever seen who could still stand up. His nose and mouth had been shoved to one side to make room for alcohol. His arms and legs looked soft enough to dissolve in the next drop. His voice was sick and slow and distant, saying, "Ah-ah, Buddy, too late to find us."

"What do you mean?"

His eyes turned to his pants, gaping open, and his sex sick as an overhandled rattler gaping through. I spun Joy around and yelled, "What's been going on here?"

"Nothing," she said.

"Why didn't you yell? I been going crazy looking for you."

"Listen, Bud, the poor dope is dead drunk. I was just listening to his talk."

I jerked my head toward the open pants while Stan rocked

162

stupidly against a table and grinned through his square yellow teeth. "That what you call talking?" I said.

"Buddy-Bud," she said like a tolerant mother. "The poor man is all upset. He has to show to ease his nerves. He was just telling me —"

"And you have to listen?" I was frantic with anger and relief, and bewildered that she took this from him. I didn't know this Joy. I couldn't see what she was after.

"Poor pervert, the exhibit-himself," she whispered. She held my elbows lightly and drew me aside when he went into the bushes. "Listen, Bud, if I'd have made him really mad he'd have kicked you off the lot. What good would that be to us? Now all I had to do was hear his life story —"

"I don't need that to stay in business!"

Wobbling back to us, Stan said, "Lishen to the boy."

"Sh, sh, Bud," Joy said, "everything is all right now. Don't spoil it for us. He won't remember unless you make it rough for him. Easy, easy."

And so I held on. I looked at this pretty, dark, high-colored little girl who was the creature I loved in the world and tried to speak calmly. "Listen, Joy, I don't like that monkey-business. I like you, but I don't like it. Grack got in trouble with monkey-business, too. Don't do me any favors if that's what you have to do to keep Stan from tossing me off the lot. He makes a good cut on my store already without cutting in on you."

She pouted. "He doesn't have me," she said, blushing at such strong language. She blushed while Stan's sex, thick, veiny, and limp, hung near the table at which he leaned, standing half-asleep. "He only showed me himself. I seen

163

before. I've seen men before. That has nothing to do with us."

I stared and blinked at her. Joy was far from me all at once, though I loved her as I had learned to do. But the carnie was not Pittsburgh, and although I was with it and for it, Joy was with it without knowing anything else. She smiled and touched my chest.

"Breathe easy now," she said. "You'll get dizzy, Bud. Why should I hurt the Bossman's feelings? It wouldn't be good business."

"Whore!" Bossman was swaying and knocking his ringed finger against the table. The thick words came from a cavern, tormented and miserable, dripping out like mucus. Stan swayed there and muttered, "Whore! Babywhore! She been laying for you," — and then there was a rush, an avalanche of loose flesh, and Bossman Stan fell like a heap of rags to the floor.

Joy seemed delighted. "Just in time! We were needing that," she said. "You looked like you were ready to hit him."

I pushed her violently toward the door. Then I bent down to shout into his ear, although he did not quiver with a sign of hearing me: "I won't kill you, Stan, because you're lushed. But I want you to know it isn't because of the store. I don't have to stay. But —" And I stood up and pushed my counting finger hard against Joy, who had returned to tug me away: "But you try anything like that again and I'll mash you down to soup."

"Good thing he's drunk," Joy said, taking my arm and leading me out as if I were the sick one. "Otherwise you'd sure hurt his feelings with talk like that. Somebody should

164

have buttoned him up before he left, he'll be embarrassed."
She pressed my hand. "*I* didn't want to do it, Bud."

Furious with exasperation, high in loving anger, I said,
"Goddammit, Joy, we're getting married Saturday a week."

"Sure, how about some tea? I'll make it for you now. Just
take a minute to boil up the water. You need to sweat some,
Bud. Sweat it out, you'll have a headache if you don't. Saturday a week doesn't give us much time." She cooed and murmured, trying to calm me, saying nice cool soothing things,
such as: "Too bad, I'm really sorry, kiss me, Bud. There's
really no way we can invite your friend Grack."

Maybe I'm getting it over that the carnie is a funny place
for love.

19. Trobble, absent trobble

When you try to get married on a carnie, Pauline warned me, her eyelashes peeling mascara like black sweat in the afternoon sunlight, you're asking for it: "Trobble! Trobble!" Legal business like marrying is that way when you're with a traveling show. "It's like this and like that," she said with a weary gesture of her fat open palms, "ziggety-zaggety. My, I ain't slept for thinking since you told me. That's how life is, Bud."

"Pauline," I demanded, "you're not trying to tell me Joy is too young?"

Her eyes crinkled up with a smile. "Boy, if I wanted to tell you that, I would say it this-away: Git! My dotter's too green for screwing! But I don't because you already know her shape anyway and she knows her mind. You're a good boy for her, Bud. I'm just sleepless, that's all, rememorating all my trobbles."

"You've had a hard life, Pauline."

"The details would destroy you, boy. Once I lived on nothing but peanuts and chitlings. Another time there was that famous subverted stomach. But trobble is woman's estate, and I got the mostest estate known in any truck show. . . ."

The odd way she had of pronouncing *trouble* somehow

made it something special, more sad, more lonely for Pauline. I could sympathize with a friend's plain trouble, but her trobbles made me smile and chew a straw fast. Looking at her the way I measured a mark, I was ashamed of my single and everlasting thought: Joy wants me! And a worrying thought in the smile despite myself: that she would back out at the last minute, laughing and teasing, saying, Well, Bud, it's like this — I figure it's sort of early for me and you're not really a settled fellow yet. . . . I tried to say no to the idea that there's a Phyllis in every girl.

Each morning Joy's soap-scoured face, gleaming darkly, turned to me that asking way I loved, saying, "Good morning, Bud. Are you weary of me yet?"

I took a glass of tea in Pauline's mittcamp while Joy was in town at Sears buying her trousseau: dress, shoes, two plates, two spoons, two forks, knives, and the rest of the gear. The thought of Joy in shoes with heels made me whistle. The thought of the ceremony made the whistle come out dry. We had trouble getting a preacher, as Pauline had predicted.

"You're sure you don't mind deep down inside any place at all?" I asked her. "No sugar, please. That's right." I sipped the boiling green liquid and felt with pleasure the stinging sweat break out along my collar. "You're ready for a son-in-law, Pauline?"

"Boy, don't worry about me, you got other things. Take two lumps for strength."

"Don't be a mother-in-law, Pauline."

Her chins and the loose bellyflesh shook. She giggled hoarsely. "Listen, if I had jewels to pawn so you two kids could have everything — percale to sleep on, a white bedside radio with a clock built in — I'd do it, Bud. As it is the jewels is mostly paste, it's the fault of the life I led. I went to bed for love always, and made my cash on the mittcamp. When the men asked me how I was, I never told them."

"I bet you spent plenty on men, Pauline."

"It wasn't my fault, I was always old and ugly. Joy is heir to all the looks I had in storage. Course, there were them as admired my knockers. . . ."

I heard the truck pulling up with Cas and Joy and ran out to see what she had bought. It was the sign of a queer stubbornness in Joy that she had insisted on going to Sears to get her things without Pauline or me. She was in a hurry to have private business after all the trailer life of the carnie. Seeing each other all day, not even closing the door tight when they take a leak, the carnies guard their secrets and are jealous of the smallest lonely thoughts which come to them sometimes in the midst of their buzzing, busy, overyearning days. She refused to let Pauline or me accompany her while she put a pencil and a knowing look to her lips for the city, and bought fake alligator shoes with heels high enough for hammering, can openers and vegetable shredders, black underthings because some cracker salesgirl said, "Gee, girlie, you got a terrific figger," the way the New York buyer said to say it. Bright and young as she was, Joy remained a carnie girl, hard and frightened under praise, guarding herself, generous when sure of love and never quite sure of it, living on a knife-edge of risk and divided by it. She had been picked at too often on midways, and no father to tell it to. Having returned now from town, she kissed and clung to my hello, but would not yet show me the dress.

168

As I said, the wedding was troublesome. They expected it; it had to be done. I swaggered about the lot, scowling, stretching myself big, getting across the idea that they shouldn't drink enough for a hey-rube. When they shushed at looking at me, I thought they understood. Since Stan's Tuscaloosa Too carried no circus tent, we had no circus tent for the ceremony. Logic. Joy and I both had a feeling about the sideshow tent and didn't want it. Also logic. That left the medicine store, where pickup talkers and sometimes Stan himself sold herb tea and lanolin for the hair and a preparation that re-stores the fun in life for men & wimmen alike. The last time we had carried the medicine store it had been for the hair, and the talker used an Indian sitting and combing his long black silk to show what happens when you do to your hair like the Injuns do. This broke up when the Indian got unclear ideas, thinking that the marks were flicking lice at him, and went back to the reservation.

Anyway, we could use the medicine setup.

"But no kidding about it," I grumbled to everyone in sight. I wanted this to be a solemn, quiet, hard-working wedding, not a time for an on-season drunk and a free show. I even wished that I could bring my father from that other star on which he lived.

There were the witnesses. Joy decided on Pauline and Cas. With half a mind I suggested Stan, but that would be making for bad fun. "No," Joy said firmly, "leave well enough alone. Listen, would you be marrying me so quick if it wasn't for Bossman?"

Finally there was the hard nut, the minister. Holy joes and petes are usually trouble; they don't like the carnies, especially when they know us, as in the South. I refused to look for some suave city preacher with a little pot under his black coat and a story to tell his favorite sheep, just doing it for the lesson and the emolument. I wanted someone to believe that we were people, or almost. Because everyone was busy with one thing or another, it turned out to be Deprived Al who found the preacher, dragged him from his gritty mission house somewhere or from behind the wall of a bible college or from within the barn of a revival sect. He came all in black, like an undertaker, with a three-inch celluloid collar and an umbrella and a shiny new black leather bible, just to look over the happy couple. I took one look and laid down the law: "No snakes at this wedding."

"Not even a little rattler?" he asked plaintively in a hollow voice. "A nice little defanged one, just for appearances? I'll stupefy it on sweet wine and no kola."

"Nix, Your Honor," Joy said. She touched me fondly at the belt, hooking her fingers at the loop and then putting her arm about my middle, patting me for calmness. "Bud likes 'em with poison if he likes 'em at all," she added proudly. She corrected her pronunciation for Georgia: "*Pie*-zun."

"Ha! ha! ha!" screamed Deprived Al with military precision.

I was strict with our man of God: "No boas either, you. Nothing — and *nothing* — along that line at all."

Our preacher, the Reverend Hurly, skinny and black-clothed, miserable with his lack of fidelity to reptiles and his desire to make ten dollars, risked antagonizing me by speaking to his invisible devil. "A materialistic unbelieving atheist," he grieved for the record. "Don't care for snake poison, he don't."

He glanced at his feet and pawed the dirt, scowling at his shoes. He had been tricked. Instead of the black leather which both he and I expected, he was wearing high tennis shoes, laced with string. Maybe it was his wife's fault, who thought that sneakers went with a carnie wedding, but it sorrowed him deeply. He shook his head and shuffled in a circle to hide his shoes within his pants cuffs. With ridged, hammered-in eyes, high-bridged jutting nose, hair slicked down by water, and only the throb of his immense veiny Adam's apple giving a steady sign of life, he resembled the principal silent actor at a wake. The beast in his throat leapt with his thoughts, and if you put your ear to it you might have heard such mumblings as those of which Pauline was fond: Misery and death, die and save, oh prepare for the day, brothers in sin. Free booklets at the rear. Offer as the spirit moves you, but remember, brother, Preacher has to eat, too.

"You know your business?" I asked him.

"Married many a couple," he pronounced over me. "Tom Hurly's the name, Doctor of Divinity and Divine Science. You didn't even ask me."

Joy looked at him with her nose wrinkled up to ask what we were doing with an inferiority complex for a preacher. I knew her thought. You get that way when you're in love; that is, you both know your girl's thoughts and you don't like people who feel inferior. But nothing could stop our feeling fine, even about this snake-baptist, water-episcopalian, flagellant methodist, fulltime undertaker and parttime anti-

171

evolutionist, whatever he was, Tom Hurly, D.D. and D.S.

And Joy looked fine, too. She wore a long white skirt to make her look older, tight around the hips, which made her look more different than older. She was getting a hippy and breasty look fast, and I take some of the credit: me and the pleasure she found in me. And she was wearing a long-sleeved nylon blouse with her tanned arms visible through the cloth and the cleft between her breasts sliding to the rhythm of the Rev Tom's words, "Be ye all gathered, brethren?"

Sweet and holy as could be, I coughed into my best pitchman's voice, half ready to flash Grack's finger to his eye, and said, "Methinks the brethren are gathered, Reverend. They're in a hurry for their beer, too."

"Then we may proceed, commence, begin," he announced. "Tad blame it, these shoes make me nervous."

"That's all right, Reverend," I said soothingly, "the feet aren't the important thing about a marriage."

"The important thing," Joy sang sweetly, "is that we love, honor, and obey. Righto, Reverend?"

Consoled, he patted her head. "Sweet child," he said, "how did you ever get mixed up with riffraff?"

Pauline, who had drawn close to hear the holy man's words, answered very quickly, "Her father held me down, that's how, Your Honor."

"I'm no judge."

"You said it." Pauline had the jitters; her chins shook. "Let's hitch them before the ice all melts." She opened the door of the refrigerator in her trailer and stood next to the wedding cake, fanning the chill air over herself while the

motor labored and heavily throbbed. In honor of this occasion Pauline had robed herself in black taffeta, the slippery
stuff flopping over her bosom and shoulders and in vast folds
over all the mountainous regions of her body, giving her the
look of someone's widowed aunt except for the charcoal
smear of mascara over her eyes and the thick paving of
rouge on her cheeks.

The Rev Tom strode ahead of us in his black suit and his
tennis shoes, stretching the pants at the shiny seat; Pauline
and Stan hurried after him; Joy followed on my arm, stag-
gering and laughing on her high heels. There was a burst of
applause from the carnies gathered on wooden benches as we
entered the tent. Rev Tom looked about disapprovingly, the
undertaker in him aroused by the presence of so many living bodies, then padded to the stand where so many bottles
of Indian Hair Tonic with Vitamin E had been sold, not to
speak of fortifiers for the virility, celery concentrate for good
health and good sense, and little conscience pills to drive
away the demon rum.

"How mucha you paying him?" Casanopopolous whispered
to me as I walked by. "Was not a proper shoesa inna his
contract?"

"Ha! ha! ha!" said Deprived Al, barking with his auto-
matic laughter.

Jean from the cookhouse (or Gene) stood at the door,
wiping his or her hands on his or her apron, scowling at so
much stew just to eat a supper and join the sexes that were
already joined in Jean-Gene. Jean-Gene rubbed his or her
hips and grunted disapprovingly, although Joy and I were
perhaps the only carnies on the lot who didn't kick out with a

joke as he or she waddled by. But I suppose morphodykes are likely to take it personally when people get married; I forgive it.

A quartet at the back of the tent began to chant, "Da *dah* dedum, da *dah* dedum," — Wagner's lovely wedding music, here comes the bride, all dressed in wide. Joy gripped my arm, touched because they went to this effort rather than merely calling upon a portable phono with its scratch of soprano and electric buzz. We were touched also because no one but the flies had snitched from the sandwiches and cookies stacked according to color on the table at the rear. Deprived Al kept looking at the green-bread cucumber sandwiches, it's true; but this was just a habit worked up from watching for small boys trying to creep under the flaps into the freak or girl show. Now Al protected our cucumbers.

"Ain't she lovely!" someone shrieked. I jerked angrily, twisting Joy's arm as I turned, ready in my awful weak-kneed nervousness to slam out at the smallest teasing, but then, between the rows of carnies scrubbed and solemn, watching us, Al, Cas, Sam the Popcorn Man, Red Rosalie, Roly and Poly Hayworth, Jean-Gene, and all the rest of them, my heart leapt in my throat and the here-comes-the-bride singing in my ears almost deafened me and my knees fairly buckled with love for everyone. "*Ain't* she lovely!" I still didn't know who had said it — a falsetto cry by one of these spoiled actors: "Ain't she *lovely!*"

They meant it. Joy, that little girl they had all known snub-nosed and a pest, a tomboy scavenger, a busybody with her school books, forever trying to catch up with the class she attended each winter in the Jacksonville or Orlando browsing

174

grounds, this Joy was ankling down a sawdust aisle in a long
white skirt. They suddenly saw a woman given to a man.
They loved her for it. They were proud that it could happen
even on the carnie, even married to the life, with it and for it.
The physical and moral freaks, the patient artisans of con
who were our buddies, sprawled stiffly in Sunday array on
their benches and watched. They were silent and their eyes
were veiled.

Rev Tom, squeaking on the platform in his sneakers,
raised gnarled hands for silence and had it even to the cutting of their breath.

"Brethren! Gathered here as who can doubt it and we
surely are —"

He had a few words to pronounce about the condition of
holy matrimony, it seemed. To everyone's surprise, he was a
pretty fair talker. By the calculating glare on Stan's flat face
I could see an offer of a place on the show, selling snake
oil at fifty per cent for the Rev, fifty per cent for Bossman.
"Bundles of happiness are to come drop-dropping from
heaven onto these two young folks, friends," — and many
of us looked to the roof of the tent, expecting to find the
stiff canvas shattered by a rain of babies pelting through.
"Is the state of wedlock the wages paid to horrible lust or is
it a gift from the Lord to man in order to de-mon-strate how
he was never descended from mere monkeys, apes, and chim-
panzees? Yes, it was. And are the —" We received a dose of
anti-evolutionary philosophy free for the price of the wedding; the Rev Tom had been a good choice after all. "And
are the poisons of earth, friends, really poisons after all?"
If only I hadn't to stand on my two feet, supporting Joy as

175

she turned dizzy and swayed on her heels, I would have taken greater pleasure in hearing how the devil came down to our land in the body of Clarence Darrow, all filth and New York cleverness, with a body rotted by hard likker, so that when he died the gases in his head exploded and blew what remained of his brains straight out the window. Surprised his wife, it did. Lovely sermon for a wedding in Georgia.

"And in conclusion, dear friends . . ." With this phrase I knew that he was good for another gasping and spitting half hour. Joy pinched me, trusting to me to hurry him along, but I had decided to wait things out. I had been in a hurry enough in my life. Grack, helping to break my habit, had taught me that you can't hurry to happiness; I remembered the lesson. And you had to take from people what they can give you, not just what you think you want. All right. "Remember so well, yes, friends," Rev Tom was saying, "the day I took my own dear first wife to the altar, may she rest in peace. She was all in beauty, a healthy specimen. She had eyes like stars, but she insisted on eating canned peaches with cane sugar added. Died soon after."

It was a fine gaudy sermon, full of fire and death and the vanity of fancy feeding. Finally, when Pauline inched a leg forward and came down hard on his toes in the tennis shoes, he returned to the first business of this meeting.

"Will Mr. Bud Williams and Miss Joy DeLand please step forward?"

We pleased to step forward.

He raised his hands over us again. I dodged, in case his knuckles fell off. The rest is rather smoky in my memory; I'm not sure as I recall exactly; he groaned and pronounced

176

too fast for me to follow: "Mumbledy-jumbledy-higgledy-peg."

Pauline was talking to herself behind us: "Fruits and vegetables, coffee and tea."

> "Sickness and death, trouble and clover!
> Rover, Red Rover, let Rover come over!
>
> Joining in wedlock for better come worst!
> Health is important and loving is first!
>
> Honor-obey, death-do-you-part!
> Linen and kettles and string beans to start!"

I rubbed my eyes. Pauline and the Rev were swaying and chanting. I stood silently with Joy, feeling her arms at rest next to mine, loving her, deep in our dream of the future to which we had pledged ourselves. Suddenly Pauline stopped her murmuring and the silence from our carnie buddies turned deafening, and Rev Tom's finger leapt toward us: "Do you, Bud Williams?"

"I do."

"Do you, Joy DeLand?"

"I do."

For the moment he did not quite recall what came next, so he asked me again, "Do you, Bud Williams?"

"I really do, sir."

And Joy did not wait for the repeated question, crying out with a high peal of laughter, "Yes, I do!" I slid my arm about the long skirt and lifted her high toward me to kiss her. Her thigh-warmth rewarded my arms; her lips promised me many things, such as *yes* and dizzily *yes* again. The hullaballoo of cheers from the benches broke into our sealing moment. The thought came through to both Joy and me, standing there still before Rev Tom: Yes, we are married. It was done. Our present duty to the world of our friends was to let them eat and drink.

Pauline minced forward to take the Reverend Tom's arm. "It was a bee-yootiful ceremony, never seen one like it," she said. "Really most deep and profound, such philosophy. Have you read Doc Connor's book on how to tell a criminal by his ears? Come with me and have a cracker with patty on it, Reverend, before all those louts finish off the eats."

20. Last space on the guest list

LIKE hungry cockroaches they galloped about us for the food and drink, lifting their feelers, scampering happily. Their muzzles jumped with heavy spices. "Ha!" cried Deprived Al, and washed down the butt of a pickle with beer. Even Stan tried to feel good, firmly gripping a corner of the board and wooden horses that served as table and pouring himself one shot after another of the good legal stuff which wet-eyed Pauline, my mother-in-law, had provided.

"Drink! No more trobbles! Drink up!"

It wasn't really that they were so hungry or so thirsty, but the carnie folk have a sense for celebrations and did honor to legal wedlock by taking communion with it in the form of Ritz crackers, jelly beans, and maybe a hundred dollars' worth of free liquor. Some of it was moonshine, of course, and delicate as carnies know how to be, our friends drank it with the same ceremonial gestures of pleasure with which they drank the bottled and bonded. To you, up yours, with it and for it, friends! You ever see such sweet kids before in your lives?

They let me stand alone with Joy at a rope-strung edge of the tent and played no tricks on us. Somehow this girl, Joy, remembered as a smudge-nosed child, had become a creature aloof and distant and chilling to their tricks, a bareback rider queen, someone as strange to them as Hungary or Bucks County, a princess because she knew her own mind. I tried to explain things to her as we stood amid the eating of our guests.

"I used to have a habit," I said, "because I expected too much of people." This was not reminiscence. It had to do with the job of life ahead of us.

"I remember, Bud."

"Grack helped me get rid of the habit."

She smiled and touched me. "Never happens that way. You did it yourself."

"I still expect a great deal. Grack helped me," I repeated, "and don't you forget it." In that steam and hurly-burly of celebration, I suddenly saw the cabin where Grack had led me out, holding my forehead when I was sick. "And don't let me forget it."

"You won't. But you had to kick it yourself."

I did not go all the way with her, but her assurance made me say, all the same: "Maybe so," — still not quite believing that I had done this deed before Joy and myself and that my demands on others were matched with their need for me. "Maybe so."

Sam the Popcorn Man came swaying toward us with a paper cup full of gin. "You buying, Bud?" he asked. "Give you couwage for the long pull. Heah! Heah!" He still smelled saltily of his trade. It was strange to see him without his machinery, his frier, the flying bits of snow, and the little pots of melted oleo. "Dwink up!" he cried, his r's deserting him in his face-splitting pleasure. "Dwink to mawidge!"

180

I took the cup to make him go.

"Then I went home," I told Joy. "You know about my mama. There was nothing there. I hung around the house, but I almost killed my pa. We'll have to go to see him. He'll cry all over you."

"That's all right, he's not a bad man," she said.

"I was good for nothing. There was no reason. I had to come back. I looked for Grack."

She smiled and pulled me to a corner and we sat whispering and huddling on a bench before the little pile of wedding gifts which we were too discreet to open now: Oh a set of percale! Oh a matching towels! Oh a gift certificate! Joy said: "You didn't find Grack, but you found something better, Bud. You went into business for yourself and you did well."

"I was John Peel. I was running, then walking, then strolling. I found you, Joy."

"I found you!"

"I got a long way strolling, and I'm not for a habit here or for monkey-business with my father anymore, and I did it now without Grack. Yes, I did."

"You found me, Bud. I'm so glad you did."

The party went on with songs and scuffling in the sawdust and old jokes relaxed at, and we talk-talk-talked on a back bench of the tent, sometimes interrupted but never troubling, content to stay amid the light and warmth of our friends under the high bare bulb which someone snapped on at dusk, realizing that we had come out well when even Stan came to wish us good luck. He yawned. He did not try to kiss the bride. We watched him return to the place near a bottle where his pawing feet had shredded the wood peelings to dust.

"You must have had all sorts of troubles, too," I said to Joy. "I know about some of them, but you don't tell me much."

"You knew me when I was a baby."

"I was just a child then, too."

"All right, Bud. . . . But trouble isn't over. This isn't the end of trouble. Never. Trouble is what we're bound to have, too, only maybe we'll know what to do about it." She leaned forward, touching my two cheeks with her two hands, suddenly older and grave, solid with flesh, the tomboy finished for good by Rev Tom's words, saying: "The bad thing about trouble is not being able to meet it. Now we'll do that thing."

"And you were practically playing with dolls a year ago —"

"A month ago, Bud. Maybe just yesterday."

And together until the earth fills our mouths.

I would like to say that Deprived Al came up to us through the party exactly then with his message, but it happened another way. We lounged and watched and had a little indigestion from eating and watching, our sweaty palms touching, without work to do, faces hurting from smiling, just waiting. Stan, supersaturated, returned to ask if thish wash the way for young loversh to live it up. Pauline, swaying, a queen in heavy seas, pinched his ear and dragged him off, winking like a topmast signal. Out of liquid and the dizzy laughter, Sam came to throw popcorn balls like confetti, Jean-Gene sniffled and said it was only hayfever, not emotion; many friends gave advice and told us how sorry a thing it is never to be happy. "But when you're with it —" Shrugs and shrugs. Seeing us together made them wonder why they had never tried that gaff, love and constancy. We talked about the little trip we were making to the seashore, where we would rent a cabin. We were leaving the show tomorrow for a week, planning to spend a good part of our nut, doing what a carnie never does unless he breaks his back: taking a vacation midseason. Almost as much as our marriage, this decision set us off from the others. They saw that business was not first with us. They saw that business was a way to something for us, not the end of human affairs on earth.

"You'll never be a boss carnie thataway," Bossman had told me.

"That's right."

"It's not the way to get with it and stay with it, boy."

"I know," I repeated, looking at him in the eyes until they rolled over like bugs playing dead. "I'm with it and for it, Stan, but that ain't all. I'm for Joy. I'm with myself, too."

With the generosity of carnies they accepted our taking the week off. They could not understand it, but they grinned, shrugged, shot their hands into their palms. Someone brought us two bottles of beer and, lounging amid a tangle of rope at the back of the tent, we watched and waited out this first married evening.

Deprived Al came in from out-of-doors, shivering as if freezing in this warm Georgia evening, headed for Stan, who was now too drunk to do more than sprawl and mumble in his childhood's Polish, shook him, gave it up, was shouted at by Casanopopolous, turned to Cas, shook his head again,

183

decided on me and ran in his foot-dragging shuffle. "What's up, Al?" I asked.

He stuttered.

"Seen a ghost?"

"Yes, that's the truth."

"Did you get sick outside?"

"I did, fact." He snapped his fingers. "Oh, fact."

"Can't hold yours, eh?"

He stopped stammering and looked at me dead sober and said, "I got something to show you, Bud. You better hurry. Fact."

Outside the tent, the carnie was drawn up to do battle with the Indians. Machinery and housing had been pulled down and stowed. The trailers were set in the traditional crescent, ready for motion when we sobered up. Tomorrow, groaning and complaining, heads and axles heavy, crankcases dripping and eyes gluey, Wide World and Tuscaloosa Too would move on to the next date. Now with the brave skeleton of the Ferris wheel down, the show huddled timidly on its bit of Georgia earth. Only from inside the medicine tent, where the party went on, there came the noises of stomping and eating, the banner of laughter and the shake of pleasure. The trailers were dark. The night was black. Crickets twittered by the millions, fiddling to keep warm against the black night damp seeping up from the swamps some miles away. It was one of those moonless nights when nothing is seen clearly; a faint bluish haze, starlit but not lighted, made the most familiar fender strange; guideropes came reaching for our legs no matter how we walked.

"Take it easy, Al," I said.

He hurried in his sideways shuffle to the lead trailer. It was Stan's. He pushed me toward the slatted blind; I felt his elbow; then he retreated fast into the darkness. By the time my eyes finished blinking I knew that, yes, there was a flashlight working behind Stan's closed blinds. I stretched on tiptoe to peek in.

Then, through the slit at the bottom of the Venetian blind over the window in Bossman's trailer door, I saw a dim light working back and forth, pulsing regularly. There was a body kneeling next to the refrigerator. Yes, Stan kept his safe there. The flashlight was moving and the body was swaying, counting, rocking as if in prayer. No, he wasn't praying. Yes, he was working the lock.

He stopped and began again. He was touching the lock, probing it, playing it. The swaying began once more. Back two, back four again, forward. No. Forward three, forward four, back. No. I watched over this black animal patience. He was touching and listening to the tumblers. He was trying and trying the lock. The shape grew clear to me as I watched on tiptoe outside, with the crickets shrill and an occasional night insect bouncing against my party pants leg and then away.

Yes, yes.

He listened to the tumblers and knew now that it was two forwards, then one back. Just the number forward to figure out.

It was a marvelous patience he had. Thus far, thinking of it as a skill game, I remained contemplative and muffled by wonder that he could do it. He swayed over the safe like a priest at the sacrament. It was all work, all effort, which made him sway. This was the musical concentration which I looked for in my own life. Aching on tiptoe, worried for the thief about the sounds of laughter and eating at the tent, I peeked and put a stilling hand on the door.

His skill and thoughtfulness and judging of the task were a marvelous thing to see.

The thought came to me: What if Joy comes out to find us? Only then did I face my recognition of this crouched body and fall back onto my heels for a moment to ask myself what to do about it. The door came easily sliding open under my hand and he turned with the flashlight full in my eyes so that I could not see anything but the blinding light of him and I put my arm across my face in a movement of protection, but it did not stop my having the first words this time.

"Hello, Grack. Did you know I got married tonight?"

PART THREE

You drink from the cup of wisdom? I fell into it.

But I learned to swim.

21. Let me tell now how I became a father to Gracchus

Yes, boy," he drawled softly, holding the flashlight steady at my eyes, "but you never did invite me. I don't care, I'm glad to see you. But I was just going good for getting this wall open —"

I walked toward him like a blind man reaching for doors, my arms outstretched to keep his flashlight from my face. I touched him and he jumped away and I said, "You're in bad trouble."

His laugh was answer.

"Don't mix with Bossman, Gracko. He'll kill you if he surprises you. He'll kill you if he thinks about it."

"Bossman got no other way, does he, Bud? Well, well." He sat on the floor with his knees poking high in the air and put the flashlight in his lap and the harsh laughter went on. "Who'd you take to wife, kid? That little Joy? She's nothing but a baby, she don't know yet."

"How did you find out? No, she's grown up fast, Grack. What do you need? How much? Listen, I'll give it to you if you need it, Grack — all I got." My eyes learning to see in the dim light, I squatted on the floor opposite him, the safe another face between us. He was thin; the wart, pricked up with hairs, had grown larger on the diminished skull. He cocked his head to study me.

"She's still wet from borning time," he said.

"You ever know a woman like that, Grack? I always find them plenty grown up," — and grinned for this nice conversation on my wedding day. Night it was already, and not a night for discussing.

He returned my smile in the wiry whining darkness where the carnival electric generator hummed. It was wedding time; they spent all those kilowatts on Joy and me while I listened to an angry Grack: "Dogsoup, son! Eat dogsoup if you like! Married!"

He had grown gaunt, stretched-out, bony and fleshless. He had the look of a fanatic. For a moment I thought of that undertaker of a minister who had married us, but the blue pads of flesh beneath his eyes made me understand: He has a habit now. His hand on mine was stiff with that control which needs to be renewed through the large vein at the crook of the elbow. The old coals were lit in his eyes, but it was fever that crackled there now. It used to be that he turned his eyes on like searchlights when he needed something. He was a sick animal, and yet he was Grack, monumental in the dark, his teeth glittering with that Frenchie grin, happy to see me. "*B'jour*, kid," he said, "you been growing up without old Grack."

"Grack, I said I'm glad to see you."

"I got the money, but why didn't you answer my letter?"

Pop did for me. I didn't. I deserted you more than you

know. "Grack, I can't explain now, I had troubles. But I'm glad to see you. I'm answering you now, Grack."

He patted my hand. "That's okay, kid. How's business?" More than anything else, what made me see the change in him was the way he lipped his lips, which seemed to be cracked and dry, as if he had come a long way from the north and licking unhappily on that journey down home. Even the wart was dried now with stiff hairs. "You got your nut back?" he asked.

"I took the store on sharecropping with Stan."

"He must have wrung hard."

"Sure, but that's the only way I could do it."

"I made you an offer from Utah, why didn't you answer? Not want to go in with old Grack?"

"Just didn't, that's all, Grack. You want me to explain?"

He shook his head. "Never," he said. This casual acceptance, without reproach, without prying to find out if I had done the best I could, came of a deep fatigue. He had always tried to look after me. He must have guessed that Stan had combed my hair good and left me only the lice I hid for dandruff. "Well, well," he said. "News."

"How did you get here?"

"Through the woods, boy."

"Where you going, Grack?"

"On my way. Maybe back to Canada. I don't think about it."

"What they pick you up for, Grack?"

He twisted a knuckle in his funny pink small-little ear, shell-neat and shell-shiny and close and not made for listening. "Mopery with intent to gog," he replied, chanting. "Spitting on hermits without a permit and stabbing a streetcar and stealing a transfer and gross graping of grapes while forgetting to peel it. The usual. Hotel dining. Wading on the High Seas. Loneliness across the State Line. You got business with me so's you have to hear?"

This, of course, is the carnie word for: *Mind your own!*

Even in the dark I must have showed white knuckles and hurt white eyes at being treated like a nosy first-of-Mayer with an itch for lifting pots and prying. You don't tell a friend to bag his head that way. He was sorry and said, "Bud, poor Bud, listen to me. Old Grack got himself some troubles, but it was old Grack himself got himself swindled up. I'm sorry. Don't make me chop it up tonight." He looked at me close and squinting and said very softly, making me listen hard, saying it once, I believe, with just his lips and then finally aloud:

"I'm tired, boy. Later maybe."

All right for that, Grack, I tried to tell him by nodding. But there was another question besides history. Was he on the sidewalk or did they have his picture at the postoffice and why did he lean away from light and honest con work and using words to tell just a little truth? And so I risked repeating myself.

"But what's the matter now, Grack?"

He sighed. He put his arm out to me, smiling his invitation. "You know. You tell me. I'm on." He gave me the flashlight. I squinted at his face, trying to see nothing but what I remembered, trying not to know, and then I leaned forward and lifted the sleeve. The blue skin at the crook of the elbow was crawling with black antspots and red, half-healed scars. He smiled and shook his head at me and I wanted to cry. There was no sense in his taking my place. There was no need for that. I wanted to rub my hand on his arm to erase this history of desolation, this fever and chills and the floating coolness which crashed to a bone-breaking horror, but it couldn't be done that way. He was tied to being without now; the addict has grown up without, and then gives to heroin or whatever all the love from which he has had no reply. Heroin is a silent lover, a bad one. I could not touch her away by stroking his arm.

Pretty soon Joy would come looking for me. Al would send her out. I had to stop him from clipping Stan even if I hit him myself. That kind of trouble would kill him — the image of Grack in some dripping Georgia jail, or picking peaches for some drunken sheriff, made my stomach churn.

"I got money," I said.

"Quit signifying."

I buttoned the sleeve for him. "Listen, Grack, we're going to use that cash. It isn't like the last time in Pittsburgh. I'm answering your letter now. Listen to me. We're going to kick your habit —"

Tickled, tired, he waved the flashlight in the air to mean glee. "Boy, listen, you never cure the addict type, for God and our mamas made us that way." His effort at laughter made me think about what he had done for me in that cabin in Colorado and whether he was now Indiangiving his gift. Could Grack have changed so much as to wish me this evil all over again? Could I have changed so much for him that now he wanted me to be with and for a habit only? I would tell him anyway. I would ask him, "What about me, Grack?" and I did.

"And what you used to say about me, Grack? How I was the kind but myself anyway and could kick it and get out? Don't you remember?"

"You're not the kind anymore, kid. You've done something to yourself." He squatted cross-legged now with the flashlight in his lap. Muffled through the humid Georgia air, sounds of singing rose and fell from the tent where they celebrated my wedding. Joy would be wondering if I were sick or only thinking. Grack said: "I don't forget, kid. I remember how you were. I was another way, too, but I see how it is for you. You changed yourself, you cured yourself that way, kid."

"You helped me, Grack."

"You did it yourself."

"I needed you."

"Well, well. . . ." And he stood up in that dreamy boneless way a habit gives you. He had lost the swell primping and posings of the carnie with a boodle in his pocket. He stooped to the safe. "Back to work now," — and he listened to the clicking tumblers as he tried them.

"Listen, Grack, don't do that. You know Stan'll kill you. We got to get out of here now. What are you after?"

The face turned to mine was drawn in stiff creases, the wart dead, the great black eyes washed of that immense command which had brought the marks buzzing to him. "Get the cash," he said. "Get home to Canada. Go to the country I came from, where all we ever made was quintuplets. Did

194

that from shivering in a block-of-snow woman, I'll bet he did. Run back like a licked dog to finish myself out. . . ."

I put my hand against his and had nothing to stop him but my will to be his friend. *No, no, Grack.* He shook me off with an angry shrug. No, a gesture not enough. Again he felt for the combination of the safe. I put my hand on his again, my fingers confused with his. *Ah!* came his shallow breathing, hot and dry and exhausted.

"Grack, don't, please," I said. "It'll make a trouble none of us can help you with."

"I already got that much trouble, Bud."

"No, no, I'll carry some of it for you now, Grack. Listen, I'm going to stick by you now. Forget about that letter you wrote me. There were reasons I couldn't say or answer. Listen now, Grack, I'm with you —"

"You got yourself a wife, Mr. Williams."

"Joy is with me all the way, too."

He stood up. He drooped from all the limbs of his body, like a wornout plant. He had stretched out taller and skinnier since I had seen him last, unhealthy loosening taxing him at the joints. His feet, his hands, his nose seemed swollen. He nodded assent, he nodded submissiveness. I told him that I would go to explain to Joy and that we would get him out of the South, out of his trouble, up to Canada if that was where he wanted. I didn't enter his habit in my argument, but I thought it hard at him. He was to hide outside in the woods until morning, behind Cas's half-truck, and we would come for him in our jalopy and no one would know. He wanted to see no one. Al would keep quiet about it. That was important to him.

195

He didn't fight me.

Jail and no job and the wanders and the habit are hard on a man like Grack. They're hard on anyone, but the one used to a crowd which flies straight to his beckoning eyes is put down hardest. All right, I thought, we'll stand you up again, Grack.

If he saw the look of pity, he helped me to cure myself of that, too. The broad, malicious, black-toothed grin took his face, and he lifted his head with its enormous eyes, and it was like the sun coming up. He nodded. He said nothing. He gave me the smile and the wart. He opened Stan's door and loped past the crescent of carnie trucks and disappeared in the darkness. I knew he would wait.

I went to get Joy. The party had picked up. Our friends all hooted when I invited her for a walk. "Don't catch the roo-ma-tiz," Pauline yelled after us, and the braying and titters followed us onto the debris of the midway. Joy took the news that we would have company on our wedding trip as she took everything, with that wait-and-see caution which comes of the risky life on a lot. You can't help surprises, it seems to say, but you can wonder about it. Her flushed face and her slightly swollen lips were those of happiness, how-ever, possessed and possessing — even if the bitten pout came of holy matrimony's kiss before all those oddball buddies and that black-coated undertaker in tennis shoes.

"Let's walk."

"What happened?"

"This your woman's intuition already, Joy?"

She looked at me straight on and said, "We only just been married, Bud, but I won't take you coming sly on me just

196

because you got some kind or other of trouble. I've seen trouble before. Tell me quick now."

I tried to say thank you to her without speaking, but she only laughed at my squirming and added:

"I accept the nice apology."

Then rapidly I explained, taking care to circle her away from Casanopopolous's half-truck and the patch of woods where Grack might be watching for us. She already knew all I could tell her about my debt to Grack. She saw that I was asking that she help to repay it. She took my arm tightly and reached her hand around to rest on my sleeve. She accepted. *Yes, yes, Bud, I'm with you all the way.*

And with you, Joy.

We would carry Grack with us, not knowing all the trouble he was in, and try to set him down in Canada if that was where he needed to go. He had never, in that other time, asked to know what trouble came with my habit. Nodding yes, nodding, Joy said to accept the gift of a nuptial boodle from Pauline which we had both first decided to refuse. We would repay it later: friendship under hardship is a constant making and repaying of debts. Pauline could do without fresh glass for this season while we carried Grack, afraid and backward-looking, crouched on the floor of our jalopy. We would do what we could for his habit. We would go easy. He must have had reasons. Willing to pay the debts which I had incurred, Joy understood that I was what those debts had made me. She had not wed a carnie; she had married a man with a history.

I kissed her behind a truck to seal our bargain.

She pulled away and let loose with what was on her mind.

"Don't close any deals with me, Bud Williams! I don't want you kissing me like that — kisses ain't contracts."

"What? Joy! I thought you're with me all the way —"

She armed me away. "Never you mind that, I'm with you. Yes. But listen to me, Bud, I'm not saying it's right. I'm not even saying we should. I know you have to. Yes. I don't think it's the beginning of being married, it's just before the real beginning. Yes, but I know we have to."

It was that *we* which I heard most surely: *we* have to. "Sure," I said, trying to see it the way a woman would, "sure enough, dragging Grack along in the back seat on our wedding —"

"That's not all I mean. I don't mean just Grack, I mean bringing your debts with us. You're not free yet to be married only to me."

"Yes, yes, Joy, I know what you want to say. But marriage is a new critter, that joining makes something new — still I go along with what went before. No husband comes to his wife absolutely free that way —"

"And the wife?"

"And the wife," I admitted.

Now she stretched on her toes to kiss me. "Well, we love each other. We'll cop out together. Maybe now on this trip we'll see Niagara Falls anyway, the way you're supposed to."

What she had said and what there was in our marriage for Joy was something to learn out of the days to come. Mysteries, puzzles, and nothing permanent except desiring! No, also the possibility of giving within time an adequate response to desire — that was marriage.

As if barely remembering him, Joy asked to see Grack before we went to our brief sleep alone together. I led her around the caravan into the dark where an arching spark stood for the cigar which Grack was having by his lonesome, crouched on the ground and waiting to hear from us. The pleasure of the partying carnies rose above us, distant as the stars in Georgia.

She stood before him until he came to his feet, ambling, grinning, making a politeness of the head. He nodded. "You been growing up so fast, Joy girl," he said.

"What did you do, kill somebody that you're running like this?"

"Nobody so much as myself, Joy girl."

"You ought to tell us. Why did you take the habit, Grack?"

"I hurt someplace, Joy girl."

She was impatient with his tricks and his gaming with us. She waited for him to tell us. Instead he repeated, but in a softer voice:

"I hurt someplace."

"A toothache?"

"Yes, that's right, a toothache right here. . . ." He put his hand on his breast, as if to make another bow, but kept it there.

She looked at him in her bridal white, her fierce animal's mug scowling, the sweetness of her person hidden under clothes and a harsh, demanding stance as she put it to Grack. "You were the king carnie of us all," she said. "You talked like no one. The marks could never say no to you, Grack."

"I had it," he said. "I was good. Yes, yes."

She came unknotted and moved to him; she peered up into the flesh-gone face of a man no longer needing food.

There was a forgiving labor in the work of her mouth. She made her effort. She said: "Grack, I'm sorry."

The hand turned to his chest and the bow was nice to her. He grinned and lightly touched a corner of his eye in the old gesture. "You been growing up real fast, Joy girl," he said.

Get to the woods now, we'll see you in the morning.

22. Muffler, tailpipe, mudguard, and journeying

AND this was our wedding trip. It would have been an odd one anyway, with stops to fix the carburetor or the fuel pump with chewing gum when they leaked and an occasional day in town to pawn Pauline's beads. My way was to spend what I had on a time with Joy, doing what the good carnie never does, leaving the show in season. He doesn't do it even for the death of his old pa. I would for him, too. I would to celebrate Joy.

And for Grack. And that was the way it happened. We opened the door for Grack at the roadside near the woods in the morning and he rode up north in the back seat with us, ducking with his head between his knees when he saw the cops' black Fords, smoking his cigarillos, leaving us in the towns and coming back dreamy and high. In the towns Joy and I were often alone. I bought her nail scissors, balloons, a bracelet from some Indians, funny things like that; I tried to make it a holiday. It wasn't. Nor for Grack either. He would return with the wart sleek and his eyes renewed for a time. Feeling good with the fresh kick in his veins, he talked. Old carnie legends, tales from his Kiskeedee village in Quebec, advice for lovers from a master at con — such things. When he felt bad, he usually kept shut, a private sufferer, except once when he needed to admit to us: "I got in some real bad trouble for real, Bud."

"I know, you were right not to say."

"There was this —"

"You were right before, Grack. Don't tell us about it."

"There was this doctor tried to hold me up. I knew he was peddling, he even said okay, then he tried to hike the price on me —"

From the front seat Joy whirled about to him in a fury. "Listen, Grack, didn't you hear him say about not to tell us? You ought to know for your own good. We *know* you got trouble, now be quiet about it."

"Oh girlie," he said, smiling and shrugging.

"Grack," I said, "she's just saying. You understand —"

"You want to be able to tell the fuzz the truth if we're picked up?" His voice rose to a ferocious falsetto: "Oh me oh my, so this man is a criminal? But officer, he was always such a perfect gentleman!" He shook his head and added softly, "Man oh man, Pauline's brat has really gone and growed up on us," — and the secretive smiling.

No matter, it was a fact that he was taking orders from Joy now. In the old days Grack was Grack's only chief, and there was that gorgeous hey-rube he started, and the gaudy way he had of jumping into a fight, feet first and roaring. Now he fell into silence down the eight miles of a dirtroad detour, smiling to himself, showing the yellow edges of his teeth, nodding in his misery of need, smiling without pleasure, and finally said, as we bumped out onto the blacktop road again: "Okay if you don't want to hear, but you're accessories after the fact anyway. Aiding and abetting the escape."

"You need to be funny?" Joy demanded, keeping her eyes on the long road ahead. "We know, we're not babies now. But we weren't with you when it happened, either — I got a story all set."

Joy's plans, pride, and craft were something new to me. I tended to my driving. He tapped me on the shoulder and I tilted my head to him, keeping the wheel steady. "You kids don't think I'd let you get in any trouble, do you? Do you?"

"No, Grack."

"No? For sure?"

I moved my shoulder to get his hand off it. "I know, Grack."

He grinned. He groaned. "Lord of mine, how long before we get to town?" He rubbed the long crease in his blue-black, unshaven cheeks. "I'm not sure I got the address straight in this town here. It's a pusher runs a shoeshine parlor in the big hotel."

And I was figuring (and Joy knew it): All right, all right, go easy. Don't make us be mean to you. Don't make us look mean to each other. Remember how you were once king of things, Grack. . . .

Joy knew also, because I had whispered it to her head next to mine on the pillow, that it was not time yet to tell him to kick the habit. We had to wait. Truth to tell, besides, I was not strong enough to help him do it. Not that I was tempted for myself — I had much better things, I had a chance in life — but you need muscles all the way down to hold a man while he kicks his habit. And Grack had to be readier for it than he seemed to be on that slow trip up north. Sometimes we gave him money, but he seemed to have a boodle. I wasn't even sure that he hadn't gotten to Stan's safe after all.

And then at other times Grack was cocky and tough and once he shook off his shoes and put his stockinged feet out the window to cool them as we ran up past a pleasant blue Virginia stretch of sea. He aired his toes like a drunken cracker on my wedding trip with Joy. I gritted my teeth. When he needed me it was easy; when he bragged like any carnie signifier, then I wondered where and why I was going. He cost a great deal in ease of spirit. It was expensive that way. My plan had been to come back with Joy, work up a nut, and then leave the carnie for the second time and for good. "Friendship is an interference," I told Joy one night.

"You're right to be interfered with," she said. "You were picked out for it, Bud, but that's fine. It's a good thing about you, even if it's trouble."

"Turn over, honey, I got a headache from driving."

"You call me honey and I won't turn over."

"Turn over."

She laughed and reached for me. "I won't anyway, honey. Where does the headache hurt?"

"Not where it did," — and it was my turn to reach for her.

And we struggled and pulled and wrenched in the hot darkness of our motel cabin. Once she ran to make sure of the lock at the door, and I ached with wonder at the simplest thing, her balance on two tiny feet and all of her on tiptoe when she liked. And now (potent loveliness of girls) she stretched beside me. A young climbing animal, fierce and un-

204

governable, she had a way of suddenly flowering softly alive to me, and all my staying and staying with her said: Beautiful, I love you. And I loved her.

"Do you, Bud?"

It was too bad that afterwards, instead of sleep, came talk of Grack. It was like having a kid, I think, Mama and Papa Williams rehearsing the day: What did he do all afternoon? What will he get into tomorrow? What will come of him? She interrupted: "Are you sure you love me, Bud?"

The days went by like this, and the days. We three could not hurry like hotrod kids: we had more voyaging to do on this journey than merely to trip Grack over the Canadian border. The inner voyage together was slower even than our Dodge with its choked carburetor and wickering fan belt. We climbed from the South slowly, almost with reluctance — red hills and pine barrens and sandlands and the swamps of the bony-wristed, leg-dragging crackers. They sprawled on their porches in the evening with their jugs of busthead and their hatred of the Negro, and then came the soft moon-burning beauty of the Southern night. Sometimes Grack said, "Step on it!" through the milltowns, and once we drove all night. Hurry, hurry, take coffee, go on. In the Southern morning a flood of yellow sunlight pierced the pale blue haze hanging in the valleys; the air smoked as the sun came up, smoked again as it settled back. Once a pretty girl, calico and eyes averted, awkward and shy, stood watching us stoop into the Dodge after stretching our legs and yawning in the Carolina air. She moved into the woods with a flutter of thigh and skirts.

Grack paused with his head cocked, watching her swing down the path. Not interested in the girl, watching only Grack, I thought of how finicky he remained despite everything, constantly washing his underwear in motel sinks and putting it at the window to dry.

Joy pulled at my shoulder. "Bud, make a pillow for me. Ouch, you have a pencil in your pocket."

We were dawdling up the coast, later heading inland with Grack's idea to cross the international bridge at Detroit into Canada. A man is tired when he wants that much to go home, and home to a place which is no longer home to him. I knew this tiredness for an old companion. Pittsburgh had been my Quebec. The funny thing, of course, is that the direct way would be straight to New York or maybe New Hampshire, but many thoughts ruled us. Grack had a route of pushers up through Detroit, neatly spaced where he needed them, and this was the route we took. They were picked by their good reputation for not overmixing the stuff with powdered sugar.

Sweet honey and travel, heroin and discovery, we motored north and west, eating, going to the pot, putting Murine in our eyes, Joy and I whispering each other asleep, chugging over the miles of our pet America. We had a sandwich in a juke joint of this big place, and it seemed small; we made love and made it big. When rain, there was mud for company; when sun, there was light, and the many lights of American skies. It rained and sunned and the weather changed. We unpacked wrinkled sweaters. We worried when Grack coughed; we smiled at each other when he finished his plate.

206

Fine honeymoon.

Once we were stuck and I had to back-squirm beneath the car to see what I could see. I learned machinery from that old Dodge; I learned to crawl on my elbows, face to its innards. The drain oil we burned was cheap, but it seemed to give the gripes to our motor. I crawled out finally, satisfied, having relieved the pain, my tongue furred with dust, to find the road sifting in the wind and Grack and Joy sitting with their feet in a dry ditch and not talking although they were three feet apart and both watching me.

When a breeze stirred the dust, it flew into a cloud, so thick and red that we could look straight at the sun through it, the sun swollen to a mass of glowing red fiber, and our stinging eyes were veiny and swollen. There were smudges at Joy's nostrils. She was breathing now with her mouth open, and I could imagine the dust dampened to mud in her lungs. I wanted to protect her from the heat. I wanted to command the dew to settle the soft and sifting world for her. She took a handkerchief and tied it about her throat. I put one around my forehead to keep the sweat from rolling into my eyes. Grack was breathing quickly and shallowly with the sick, hopeless gasps of desperation. It was easier to give up his breath than to take it. But somehow at this terrible break midvoyage, although it was the heat which stifled me, there was something more which made it hard for me to breathe: the curious, patient, and guarded looks which passed between Joy and Grack.

Stopping again that night for the last time on Route One near the ocean before dipping inland toward Pittsburgh, Cleveland, and Detroit, I came outside to stretch and wring out a handkerchief that Joy had washed for me. Grack was squatting on a stoop, doing nothing but busy. He was catching flies in a quick fisting gesture, holding the closed hand to his ear for the buzz and struggle, flinging the flies to the stone walk to break their backs. "You're worried, Grack," I said.

"You mean you didn't notice it before? I always look like that," — and he looked at Joy, who had stuck her head out the door, a bath towel wrapped tightly and clinging after the shower. We were in the usual row of motorcourt cabins — dry with asphalt and sun, thick with many sleepings, presided over by a man who thought he knew everything because he knew how people go to bed. Joy glanced at us and then retreated inside.

"Yes, it's how you are now," I said impatiently, "but more and more worried you look, Grack. Is this what you have to do?"

"I don't like it either, boy."

"If you're in so much trouble with the law, maybe you just better take the trouble. I don't mean snuggle up to it, but if it's no use . . . I mean they'll help you kick the habit, too, Grack. They got ways that's easy on the heart."

"No, no."

No, those tapering-off drugs and hot baths and wiggle-the-toes aren't easy either. "No what, Grack?"

"Not this trouble, boy. You don't just walk up and say you're ready to serve your time. They want me —"

"Don't tell me, Grack!" I found my arm raised as if to hit him down. "Don't tell me, I don't want to hear."

"I already told you."

"Let's make it" — and the shrillness of my own voice — "you never said."

The long mirthless smile and the eyes closed with grinning answered me: "Why, sonny, afraid to think about the reward?"

"Grack!"

He stopped smiling and looked with full and placid curiosity into my face. His hand moved, but he let alone the corner of his reddened eye. The tear duct was swollen and angry. He said: "I'm wanted for robbery and homicide on a man —"

"Attempted?"

He shook his head no, slowly, solemnly, *no* to that, and caught a fly in his fist and took it indoors with him.

That night I fell dead asleep in a hurry, as if to dream my way out of this trouble fast. As I already had occasion to know, this pleasant way is not the way to escape trouble. The trouble was not just what Grack had done outside and what trouble might come to us from outside. It was inside, what Grack felt about Joy and me and what I was coming to feel about that heroic Grack the Tuscan, Grack the Frenchie, of my first carnie days and nights. Disloyalty is a trouble to the disloyal man. What Joy thought of me in this was not the least of it, either.

You have to make something of the trouble you are given or else you will be made by it.

I had things to do besides dreaming of trouble.

All right, one way of slipping the trap was to bring Grack back to the way I remembered him. We would kick his habit as he had helped me kick mine. I felt that he was not yet ready, but we would try to do it. I dozed to the image of Grack the Talker, flagrantly playing the marks, finger to eye, wart wet and compelling, long and tense and hand drumming on his stand as he brought them in: "Step up! Oh you Tricksie! Step up! Come and say hi to old Grack. . . ."

And woke with a start of my legs and shoulders: Past the trick of the eye and the wheedle and tease and the hoarse croak, could he ever have been the way I remembered him? I had needed him to be that way.

Yes? No? Not fact about how he held me to that cabin until we untangled the habit wrapped in my brains and guts? How he told me stories of the free man I intended to be? How he put the bed over me to stop the threshing and crazed arching of my back? Then he held my forehead and made the lovely harsh words I needed. "You did it, chief, you've done it. . . ."

Fact, fact, had to be.

Despite Joy by my side, sleeping her calm sleep with two corners of smiling at her mouth, I dreamt one of the harried carnie dreams: Stow the stuff, load, unload under the morning sun. Fork and spoon the chow, push the table away, run to the crowd. Make it big! Flash your boodle! Signify! Talk, jingle change pockets, hear the calliope all day long, and calculate the dumb marks, the smart marks, all the many larcenous hearts. Go slow and score on Saturday! Get with it or be without it!

If the fret of my sleep meant that I wanted to leave Grack and run from him now, I would not do it. The day of flight was over for me, although I might move and move with Joy over the roads of America. I was a traveler. I was no longer pursued. I would wait and tinker under the hood with chewing gum and follow Grack through as he had followed me. The thing which he had tried for me was to kick the habit and kick me back among the living. It had been done.

"Do you really belong to me?" Joy asked almost every day. "I need to know, Bud."

The softness and wrongness of my life did not disappear by her side, of course. Irritations with predictable presence doing female work, dreams of an impossible freedom, smug certainties and dry doubts, and what astonished me most of all — once a heart-turning nostalgia for that first fainting excitement when Joy and I swam together in a Georgia pond. Already I could look at her and see this wonderful, hurtful time of first discovery lost.

She turned away and would not kiss me. She read my search for mystery in my wife's face. Vanity, vanity! Did I want to love and hate myself alone once more during such moments? She had a right to veil her love in scorn and lock me out.

These times passed, passed. We had much to do together about Grack now. Memory helped me, too — what it had really been like was something I could never dress up in fine colors. Or always beneath the fine colors of the grass-eating dog and John Peel's high pleasure, I could remember in my own body the faulty balance, the murder of fever, and the deprived flesh.

"Joy! Come here and sit with me on the stoop."

"In a minute," she said. "I have to hang up my stockings. And you got to finish what you're thinking up about me before I sit with you."

And these bad moments passed; they came on a Thursday morning and a Sunday afternoon. I promised myself that the next Thursdays and Sundays would be different. I went to pull Joy back into the light with me.

23. Some do, some don't

AND in still another pink neon and fake log motel, this time out of Harrisburg, Pa., when I realized how thin the cash was covering and how deep the habit was fixing itself, growing celebrationally and killing the tree, like mistletoe, I decided to put it to Grack again. The way you know about a habit is the going-away, the separation, the cutting of the circuits between people. Grack had that. It was not that he talked less and less; we are all like that sometimes. It was that his talk buzzed, clouded, and cooled in crystals about his head, meaning: no difference anymore. His mouth was pinched and white. The entire center of his face, badly burned over, was a bleak waste. He no longer touched his finger to his eye in that joyous gesture of domination which had brought us all to him.

Just a fellow living off his friends — that's still a hard way to put Grack in the box. He had a sly sideways looking at us, at Joy and me, because we liked to chatter and sit beside each other and touch and play. By Joy's covert glance at him, I knew that she sometimes intended to prove that she was alone with me. His long staring at her gave me the chance to ask one evening, while Joy was off ordering some sandwiches before bed: "You always used to like Joy, Grack. Why do you have that grin about her now?"

"She's a good kid. She still is."

"You don't act like —"

"She's turning into a wifey-dear, that's true. But your fault more than hers."

"It sure is, Grack, at least as much. I sure hope so."

And I received that smile, sly and spiteful, full of flat yellow teeth and detaching itself more and more from our old sense about each other. I knew, I *knew* that Grack used to like me for real, when his smile was a stuttering thing, quick as light, not this long patience.

I took a cigarillo from him. I remembered the way Grack had been and demanded an answer. "Why not?" I asked. "You once told me a habit is like a wife, but a nagging one that does no good and you can't score or get rid of it. No dee-vorce, you said, remember? You got to grab it by the neck and strangle."

We squatted on our haunches at the stoop of the cabin. The metal furniture had just been hosed down; I got wet pants from trying a chair. We did most of our talking at these times in the outskirt evenings, near towns at nightfall, with jukeboxes and automobile exhausts from the road nearby reminding us about voyaging. Joy was saying a sausage, please, balonny, a Swiss cheese on rye if you have it, a bacon and tomato, three bottles of beer since this county ain't dry. Iced. How much?

"A habit is nobody and nowhere. You told me yourself, Grack."

He put his finger to his eye to try to please me with this

dry and tired lifting; it said nothing. "What did you come back to the carnie for, Bud? Wait, I'll answer. To make your nut. You wanted to count the marks in, then clean them out and be a nice boy till the show comes down. And that's all you wanted. Is that being with anything? At least the carnie believes in the life."

"You don't, Grack —"

"Me? Me?"

"And you don't know what I was after, either."

"As to me, boy . . ." He stopped and showed his teeth. "Well, smart boy, you're right. I don't believe in the carnie no more, and that's why I got me a habit," — and he calmly waited and looked at the new muffler and tailpipe which we had put on the Dodge this afternoon to replace the rusted and busted ones.

The man in a roadside garage smelling of gasoline and bag lunches had said, "Yes, sir, in an hour or better, sir," and made humble washing movements with his hands. I had gone to the toilet to look at myself in the mirror and see why he had sirred me. Still long and bony, I had put on weight. The baby flesh had dropped from my cheeks; there were mouthlines and a fierce offside jut of broken nose. Kicking the habit and Pittsburgh, finding and taking Joy, these things had used my face. It was a shock to see that I could no longer be mistaken for a college kid. Each demand marked, desire and struggle were written into place on my head.

"No, Buddy boy, like I was saying, you're not with us anymore," Grack finished with a long breath, straightening up and stretching.

"I didn't belong in the carnie this time, you're right, Grack.

215

But I got more good out of the second time — I got Joy. It wouldn't happen if I was really with it. Grack, I'll tell you, the closest thing to a lover in the carnie is old Cas ironing his money. Or Pauline, talking six different ways, trying to accommodate everybody. All right, Pauline then. Or Cas. He's the only man who lives for somebody else, only the someone is the dollar bill."

"Go open a little store with your wife, Bud. Sell stationery and penny candy to the neighborhood kids. You'll have kids of your own soon, too."

Okay, Grack. I shook my head because he meant this to be bad and ugly, but the taunt had no bite despite my present engagement in helping a former talker now with a five-dollar habit run from the cops. It seemed that they wanted him in Fayetteville (was that the place? I always forgot) for violence done on a peddling doc. I could not forget that part of it. We watched a truck fight in first up the hill. I helped it by straining forward.

Grack held his knees, squatting on the stoop of this motel, while couples with big purses and no suitcases crept into their cabins and the doors shut softly. The tickling fumes of automobile exhaust arose in the evening breeze. Waiting for me to be and talk angry, Grack finally sighed, shook his head, and added: "I always lived for myself."

"Grack, you just said I was square for coming to the carnie for my nut and for Joy. You just said I wasn't with it."

"Kadota!"

"Then that makes us alike that way, no?"

"No." He grinned and tapped my hand. "But just suppos-

216

ing, would that be so good about you? Would it? No. And is it you against me? No again, friend. But yes, you're right, I'm heading for the Kiskeedees, I'm not with it either now."

It was a mystifying thing, topsy-turvy and wrong and true. Once the best carnie on the lot, the man who held our midway together and made all those palms flash out with green, he was not with it and for it. He used to slap his fist into his palm with tales of the collect telegrams he had received. He used to. He was chief. Angry and pained by memory, putting it behind me, I said: "You were a friend to everybody, Grack."

"I lived for myself."

"You were good anyway, Grack."

"Tried to be for myself."

"But you were!"

"Was, was . . ."

Joy, unpacking loudly, rustling and unwrapping, played the sandwich like a bugle to remind me that she wanted me to come to her. She disliked to be interfering and interrupting, and I wanted to sit and munch the eats with my wife, and I stayed, learning how hard it is to be a husband, saying to Grack: "And you only got yourself, that's all, when you do like that. But it isn't true, Grack, you were good to me." I looked at my arms as if reading it to him. The scars had vanished, but I still knew — and by heart — the invisible stiffness when I gazed into the crook of my elbow.

"Don't you remember how I told you? Sure, Bud, I wanted you to kick it then. I was nice because I liked you. That niceness was for friend Gracko, friend, just for me."

I gave him fake laughter for bad philosophy. Universal

selfishness, eh? Look at me, I'm only good because it makes me feel good to be good — oh it's nasty to be nice! . . . Nonsense. The medicine show grind is cleverer than that. "Don't kid yourself into ugliness, Grack, we don't need it. The way you talk it, everything's for you. You felt good to help me out, but is that wrong? You're sinning? Well, I'll tell you, that kind of sin doesn't scare me. What I want to see if I'm boss carnie of them all is how you do for us on earth, not how you explain it —"

"Pick pockets, lad. Play the tumblers when I can. Pass rubber checks. Talk to the larceny in their dogsoup hearts."

Sweetly he smiled and waited. The smile showed his broad flat yellow teeth.

"Never mind, that's only business, Grack. But what you did for me — you meant it to be good to me. Fact. That's what it meant to the world and to me, and Grack, listen" — I tried to close his smile on him — "Listen, it was, it *was* good to me. That was no kind of larceny there. Do you think you can take it away from me? No, no matter what. No. You did the good for me, Grack."

"Aah," — a sick wet exhalation. His thumb jerked over his shoulder to where Joy was standing, hands on her hips, openly listening. Dis-*missed*, the thumb said.

I went on stubbornly. Joy knew anyway. This was the affair of all of us now; Joy had joined me; I said: "You're thinking zig-zag, friend, you want to think yourself soggy. Don't change what was, you can't. I won't let you, Grack."

"That true you're a loverboy like they say, Bud? No kidding?"

"Ziggety-zaggety, Grack. Maybe I take that from my pa

218

and my ma was a lover to Dad before she died. Now she isn't anything. But —"

"Maybe I was a choir boy before I died. Now I'm a former gash-hound. Now I'm a monkey with a habit. I'm not much good, whatever you say, never was. Never was no good to myself, either, so why not a habit?"

"Best talker on the show, Grack, and you were fine to me."

He paused and made none of his slow scratchings for attention. This time I felt that he had listened. He said: "The show scores without me, Bud. You got yourself a Joy. I got no others and no score either."

I got no others, no score either, got no others, got no others: And the throb of traffic on the great highway answered, Truth, truth. The screech of tires about the graded curves came shrilly at us, *Truth, truth, he got no others.* The tires and the leaning springs shrieked because the curves were graded, but graded not steep enough for the speed of America. We were all careening around curves and shrieking against them and following the grading with a brakeslip of unwillingness. But there is a difference between the crazy straining joyriders and me with my Joy: I had an idea about going home to that home I did not have. I would make it, and I would make it with children, of which Papa Grack seemed to be first. He got no others (truth, truth) because he did not know that I could be a friend to him. But I was. I know it. I had someone.

A place in the world of men is hard to make. I would not be slotted in like a nickel whirling in the bank's machines; neither would I scurry forever like a rat in the bank's cellar.

Truth, truth. We need gas? Service station coming up.

219

Grack was saying, "Even when I helped you kick the habit I was doing it. I was making you liable to me."

No matter how he said *no* to himself, he could not destroy what he had been. I would be stubborn to guard it for him.

"You were getting another habit, Bud, the habit of liking Grack — that's what I was doing to you —"

"All right, Grack." We crouched like the hillbillies we used to see, dragging sticks in the gravel or whittling or just resting against their violence like that. "I don't mind, Grack. I want to have obligations."

"I was weakening you. I was making you grateful."

"Grateful didn't weaken me, Grack."

He stood up angrily, shaking off our oldman's rambling. "Idiot!" he said, and dusted his pants. But he did not go away and leave me with Joy. His chin was crammed to his breastbone.

Dizzy, swaying in my crouch, I looked up to smile and nod because I couldn't stare at the floor and say nothing. I preferred to look at him, although a few months ago I would have either counted the cracks on the floor or hit him (close to the same thing) for calling me an idiot. The floor could be a safe place to look and the eyes the unsafest of places. I looked at his eyes, thinking that Joy would be pouting and angry with me for leaving her alone so long and she would wait for me to ask her for something so that she could refuse and we could quarrel and then forgive each other. Dear ritual of family love! Although Joy was first for me, Grack came first into my life and I owed him greatly. Though he might cost me something with Joy, I had to fight him through as far as we could go.

While I watched and thought of Joy, he must have read my thoughts. Abruptly he turned and was ambling downhill on the road into town without saying what-for or when-back. I ran after him.

"Grack! What's on your mind? You want me to drive you someplace there?"

"I got a friend in town," he said, "friend I never seen before, but I got his address. I'm walking."

"What you going for? You don't like friends."

He grinned at my catching him that way. "This friend has something for me, I hope."

He was moving faster and I had to hop to keep in step with him. "Grack, I'll help you, I'll do everything, I'll make you kick the habit, Grack! Remember how you did for me in the cabin in Colorado?"

Half-turning in his stride, he winked. This meant: You have to kick it by your lonesome, boy, I already told you that.

"Grack, don't go into town now!"

Then, while the traffic roared by, heavy trucks and light cars, booming and hissing, straining up the hill and flitting down, he told me what we were in for. He explained all his hints so that we could no longer pretend not to know. Patiently he repeated that he was pretty sure he had killed a man in Fayetteville, North Carolina. He didn't know for certain sure, and he didn't altogether wish him dead, but he believed it had happened. It was a doctor who tried to dig him for more money, a doctor known as a distributor. "Not much of a doc," Grack said, "probably one of those Texas baby-doctor schools. But he could get his paws on what I needed. Was a wholesaler, he was."

221

Of course it would be like that. I watched the vans go by, milk, furniture, hunched interstate express. And the sedans with their salesmen and valises, the mothers with kids from school, the delivery boys, the great ever-moving tread back-and-forth on the highways. We walked amid the hot vapors off asphalt and the stench of weed-burning from a lot down the road near the motel. No, Grack could never kick the habit now, but I would have to help him still.

"It's so easy, boy, after you do it once. Before that it's hard. You sweat. You do in your pants. You crawl around like an animal switching its tail and making up its mind. You're stupid. You got no sense but what you got to do."

"You were mad at him, Grack?"

He squinted sideways at me with fantastic disbelief. "Don't you remember anymore, boy, what it was like when you want it? I didn't care about him. I just needed, and he was dumb enough to try to hold me up. Wait, talk, argue. A guy in his business should know enough not to discuss cash unless he got a gun in his hand. This doc, he was a little skinny Texan with a big hat and nothing but huzzanga in it —"

"He got scared? Knew what was coming?"

"Boy, not even Grack knew what was coming. I just needed, that's all."

"I thought you said you figured it out, Grack."

He was silent and walked. "True, true," he answered, frowning. "Slipped up. But I figured on how to get snowed, not the rest. Later I knew from the sweat and the pee what I was really thinking. I just wanted it bad, that's all."

"No sense at all, Grack."

His hoarse harsh all-for-self laugh, and: "Yes, member?

222

Remember? You had no sense once either. That there doc kept it locked up. Maybe that was why he didn't worry. Thought a lock could stop me," — and he stroked the narrow tips of his fingers in a wiping gesture. We walked a few steps further before he finished the story. "After I hit him and hit him and finished hitting him, I unlocked. I got smart fingers even when I'm nervous. That lock didn't need more than a few educated twists, lad."

So we had to run with him from that.

There was no sense following him into town. This was the same old outside-of-town America, neon and drive-in and billboard, fruitstands and DRINK MORE MILK BY THE GALLON and unfinished brick houses at the end of mud driveways — Baltimore now. We followed a crazy route, north from one pusher to the next, and then sometimes back south a half a day, because Grack had to go in for his purchase where he knew someone who knew someone.

Joy was alone back at the motel, and what if I were picked up with Grack? And Joy all alone back there? I left him with the word to come back quick. No, there was no helping him break his habit the way I broke mine. His habit had taken hold because of his deepest need, and there was not a way through to his need now. He dwelled in it.

24. Patience is for those who know

It should have taken him an hour or two, four at most, and the day went by. Motels down roads and a motel here, we waited at another motel. I worried just to park where the patrolling state police might grow curious, maybe only wanting to check the brakes and seeing something wrong on our faces — we stopped like vacationers at a motel.

Grack was not back yet.

I had taken to smoking those sweet cigarillos. I let Joy share the rest of the bad news about Grack and felt better. She sat with me on the bed and fed me matches when the cigars went out. "Poor dumb Texas doc," she said. She had a small full mouth and a way of rolling her eyes with a perverse, solemn smile when we had trouble together. We waited, we waited.

The afternoon, that new chill northern afternoon, was graying away at our window and Grack still gone.

Joy tried to make me feel her sharing. I ached from sitting. "I like the taste," she said, "when you kiss me, that is, Bud. When I don't have to do all the work myself. I like the taste when you're thinking about me."

"I'm sorry, Joy."

"Try again. Otherwise the taste gets stale and I might as well smoke it firsthand."

I put out the cigar, kissed her, and said, "What's keeping him so long?"

"Pass the smokes, friend," she answered.

"Joy, I'm sorry, I'm sorry, but what's to happen to him if the cops pick him up? What'll he do if they got him now?"

She looked at me full on, her face turned chin-forward to me, hard and more dark than I remembered it — no, I hadn't been watching her these last days! so soon! — and she replied to my question with her own: "Yes, what will we do then, Bud?"

Was this just an increasing selfishness of the body? The new wife's resentment at the claims which her husband brought with him? There was a curious thickening of all the small bones of her face. The childlike Joy had passed quickly on this flight north. Maybe the sudden northern chill, I thought, maybe a weariness of traveling and nothing more angry. "He's been gone about five hours, going on six," I said.

"He's been with us for a week and more. We could have done this trip in days if you and he didn't keep wanting to lay over here, lay over there, see a man in town the other place. Know how long we've been married? Long as he's been with us."

"Honey, don't get yourself a mad on. What can I do about it? You know how Grack did for me back then, you always knew it, so how could I —? Anyway, we were married before," I said, putting my arm about her on the slipping springs of an overused mattress. Her back stiffened as I touched her. "Remember how we were married all that time on the show?" I was a young husband trying. I was a young husband learning. "Remember," I said with the young husband's eager, false, and hopeful smile, "remember, Joy, how we rolled up a boodle together? How we —"

She pulled away against my arm, stiff but not pushing, reluctant it seemed, hoping that I could talk sweetly to her loneliness. "It's that boodle we're living off now" — and she leaned stiffly — "running like this, always running, carrying our baby with us."

"Don't talk like that, Joy! Grack is a friend, we got to be good to him. He's in such bad trouble, what can we do? He's not a baby just because there's trouble for him now, or we'd all be babies most of the time. This is hard on you, sure, it's hard on me, too. It's starting to rain. Whatever happened to him?"

She moved my arm away and went to stand by the window, looking out through the first dusty splash on the glass. She clacked the slats of the Venetian blinds together to make a noise between us. "It's true about the baby," she said.

"He's not! Don't talk about Grack that way."

There was a commotion of metal and rope at the window and the blind came down, hitting her across the breast as it fell. She winced but only moved to let it slam to the floor and she stood in the gray dusklight, before the thud of tires which followed us up the continent, telling me, "Think about your girl Joy for a minute, Bud. Hold on. Look at me. Grack isn't the only baby we've got between us. I better see a doctor and we better have a test and read a book about living with a kid in a ten-year-old Dodge. My breasts hurt all the time."

226

Sometimes, at such a moment, the eyes clear out everything in sight — ashtray and motel dresser of deal and butts and wornout socks in a wastebasket and the rushing world of travel in the window — before the eyes focus back, all in an instant, on Joy the wife, this Joy who was my whole sense on earth and now more than only my life. I ran to her, laughing at my own tears, and pulled her back from the window and away with me, darling darling darling.

She was dry-eyed, speculating. Such a different dry-eyed calculation from that of Phyllis! Forgive me, and she forgave. Her eyes were amazed: "You like it, Bud? You're not angry?"

"Forgive me!"

"But why?"

Dearest darling, I could say, darling dearest, and nothing more for that deep inner tolling of celebration. I was winning the prize, a child, my own blood, when I least expected it, and the thrill of reward is a pious thing, given without my deserving it: and then my sight came back to a single hard bright point: *Yes, we do deserve it!*

She was tricked in smiles at my pleasure and touched my face. She let me fumble to tell about happiness, quick, quick, at her blouse where the breasts which hurt stood up at me now (hurting? hurting? But she smiled welcome!) and the tired day passed over to brilliant night as we shook ourselves together again.

We both slept briefly. I was still sleeping when she moved away, saying, "Maybe we better find Grack."

"Wh-what?" — and catching myself in the sighs of my father's waking sighs. The window was black and the jeweled flash of headlights rising, headlights falling, informed me and carried my father away again with them. The sleepy wh-wh-wh chomping stopped and I remembered Joy and brushed her cheek with my lips. I remembered myself awake to her.

But not to why she had awakened me. I was dreaming of how she had fought alongside, then healed the broken nose, saying, Soda paste is good for burning. . . . Let me heal by myself! . . . Soda paste is good to cool you. . . . Leave me alone! . . . I'll help you, Bud. . . .

"We better go hunt him up now, Bud."

I blew and stretched, wanting only to talk. "Joy, you did it so fast, we did, I mean — a kid already! And you know, just a while back I was a kid myself, playing touch football in the streets, nothing more than that — it's a game where you duck the cars until you —"

Patient, severe, she insisted that I climb all the way from sleep. She swung my arm back and forth, very gentle, very reminding. "He might be in trouble. He shouldn't be this late."

Bad. I splashed cold water on my face and arms, dressed from the heap of clothes, hitched my Army surplus belt tight, all the time figuring where to look. I would buy a sandwich and ask the referral, a geek in a diner, as usual, and leave the sandwich for some Andy or some other hitchhiker. Dressing, Joy had her back to me, that fleshly womanly back bending, buttocks and lovely new creases. Then, in blouse and skirt, and narrow narrow waist, she didn't seem to have room in her belly for a sandwich even with the cheese sliced thin. "I'm going with you," she said.

"Stay here!" No, no, that wasn't the way: "I mean why

don't you stay here, Joy? What if he comes back while we're gone?"

"We'll leave a note. He'll just have himself a sleep and wait, that's all."

"Why you want to come into town?"

She blushed, darkening as she did, and turned away. "Be with you," she said, but this was for loneliness more than love. She was ashamed. She combed, lipsticked, and used her hand to fluff out her hair.

"You're not tired?" I asked. "Why don't you stay and rest, take a bath or something, take it easy. I'll get you a magazine."

And she stood by the fallen Venetian blinds still scattered like kindling over the floor. This time the tears drooped soft as rain; she let them come, she opened to them. The kid, the dark gypsy at Pauline's wicket, the perky girl, that happy creature was now a woman and miserable. My breath got caught and made me laugh it free: Joy jealous! While she carried our baby, I turned away to go hunting Grack in town someplace: jealous face tussling with tears!

"Why Joy honey," I said, holding and tugging at her — really married, all this marrying us, this the ceremony now: "Why Joy honey, listen, come on with me into town, will you?"

"No!"

"Please, honey. Aw, honey."

"No, n-no," — plus tears and pouting. "You want to be alone with Grack, that's how it is," — not a question, but a question anyway.

Yes, she was getting to be a wife, and with a memory like

the Lord's for slight and wrong. It had once been true that Grack had seemed a person to me and Joy only a girl, only a woman, a need and pleasure, but now there could be nothing better in life than to stroll down the streets of Baltimore with my honey, looking into windows, dawdling and vain about her beauty, taking the air together, with no plans but to sharpen our appetites and then use food and a smoke.

But we could not check our baggage, none of it, and Grack the heaviest. To get him to the border and safe until he did himself in was a responsibility we could not shake loose; Joy and I owed it to each other. "Come on, honey," I said, "let's go look for him."

"You want me along? You just saying that?"

"Why should I go in if you're not with me, Joy?"

"That's better. Don't call me honey because you're afraid I'll cry."

"You know I have to learn, Joy, but I want to be good to you. You know that. Our kid will have a real mother and father, no fooling—"

And she interrupted me to answer, "I love you. It takes a girl longer, but you've made me do it. You men, you con yourself into love all of a night, and we're supposed to follow. But it takes time. Sometimes we manage. Can I go dressed like this?"

"You're beautiful."

"Looks all right?"

I turned her around and smiled until she smiled and I kissed the end of her nose.

Poor Grack, he was as I used to be. Maybe I could be the

way he never was. Now I understood how this was a matter which could come between Joy and me. There are risks to every responsibility.

"Okay, then I'm ready," she said.

25. *How to be absent*

Of course, we had an idea of where to look, but we gawked anyway like hillbilly marks down a midway as we drove past those fine, red-bricked stands of the English squares of Baltimore. Were they really English? As much as we were really hillbillies. Almost looked it, friend, built to the sidewalks on which men as long as rolled umbrellas hurried through the drizzle under fogged streetlamps. When I climbed out of our jalop at a corner to look this way and that for the diner where Grack might have been, I heard the water sizzling off our overheated motor. There was a stench of rubber gone wrong from the fan belt. Fan belt trouble was all we needed more.

I climbed back in, wet and steaming, rain and sweat and purly wool, and went off slowly again in second. Joy's hair glistened from sticking her head out the window. She had to crane for streetsigns. Windshield wiper didn't work; her curls were plastered straight, sleek, and tight.

Funny, eh?

Funny if you're not sick looking for Grack, and sick of looking for him; tired of moving, tired of wet Baltimore; fan belt frayed and trouble to fix it. What would we be looking for when we found Grack?

I laughed and Joy puzzled over me with smiles. "You a funhouse talker?" she asked.

"Not that," I said, steering and squinting, "it's something else. Reminds me, you sure your belly doesn't hurt?"

"*That* what it reminds you?"

"No, something else funny. Was before I knew you, three-four years maybe . . ." I had been hitchhiking, not free as John Peel but starved as Andy, when I saw this Model T driving down the dusty Georgia highway. It was flying at twenty miles an hour, having a time for itself, in a buzzing, spinning cone of dust. I started to hang out my swollen thumb, then jerked it back fast. That Ford was bouncing toward me with no driver at all, and then it stopped, a few yards ahead, and opened its door. "Listen, Joy," I told her, "I'm a brave man at times, but I'd have run, only my old pop never told me to watch out for the old phantom Model T." Anyway, it was a kid inside driving, not more than nine years and four months old, if he remembered correctly. We figured it all out together. "How can you see?" I had asked him.

"Cain't," he said.

"Whyn't you sit on a pillow?"

"Ain't got no pillows yet," he said. "Paw gonna send away to Sears for Christmas. To set on."

"How do you know when you're on the road?"

"Easy, feel it in my pants," he said, and gave me one of those smartkid grins that even a cracker can drum up when his pellagra is cured. "See them telephone poles? Jist keep my eyes on the top of them poles and stay down the middle."

As respectfully as I could, I had inquired of him, "Like me to drive awhile, sir?"

233

Joy put her head near my shoulder and we both felt better, although I still didn't know where to put this little mother and just where to find Grack and what to do about him when I found him. But it was good to go shares with my wife.

Grack's contact man cooked in a diner on the seafood coast of Baltimore, near the market where the pumpernickel grows, all humid sawdust and plump butcher arms and German beer in there through the swinging door. The universe of grackhunt still drizzled, darkened, but the coffee smell inside was pleasant even though cookie wasn't. I smelled him right first-off after the coffee. Joy came sniffing in with me and brushed at her hair with her fingers before the cigarette vending machine mirror.

"Hiya," I said, "seen my friend Gracchus?"

"Who and why? Never heard of him."

"Grack, has a kind of mole, a funny way, you know —"

He shrugged and stared up and down at Joy. Many men look with desire at her, with cockeyed grins maybe, but he was busy tailoring her for a policewoman's wool next to the skin and looking for Enna Jettick shoes.

"Never mind, she's with me," I said. "Listen, this Grack came in today, long fellow, touches his eye —"

"What you care for?"

"He's a friend, that's all. Looking for him. Now you listen here to me, I'm not saying you're a pusher or anything at all, fellow." Patiently I explained. No use pricking him up more, jealous as he was already about the pretty Joy I carted along with me. After all, I was asking a risky favor — to trust me without getting a cut of anything, not even Joy, and to

234

admit that he had sent Grack where he could buy what he needed. "Come on, mister, you know my buddy Grack — tall like I say, skinny, big blue hickie on the face, one eye limps sometimes, came in here this afternoon for a coffee and a bit of conversation with you and didn't finish his doughnuts." I grinned for friendship. This was a job of talkeroo for a carnie, only our cookie was no mark — a fat-armed cookie with speckled baldness on his biceps, a raw meat face steamed apart, no facebones to speak of, silver-rimmed glasses and button eyes hiding deep in the diner-fed flesh. The fat on his finger had grown almost all the way around the wedding band.

"Lots a guys come in for chatter and java, friend," he remarked with a delighted smile. "I used to be a regular bartender before I got me this diner. I prefer food better — steadier thing in a nice neighborhood."

Yes, I could guess. A contact bird finds it less complicated not to have the liquor inspectors coming around with salt shakers for his tail. What could be more innocent than a diner, a feathered nest with Campbell's Soup and steamed stringbeans? He probably had kids, too, all plump and unclean like papa.

"So?" he said.

"So you know the man I mean. Needed it real bad. Listen, he's a friend of ours, he's with us —"

"In the life with you-all?"

"Yes."

He grinned at Joy. "I say no," he murmured. "Now you and your lady like a couple hotcakes? Fresh batter today."

The smile was overcurved and mean around the too-small teeth. It just didn't want to say. Maybe cookie thought we were federal investigators, only because we didn't look it; maybe he thought we were police stoolies — wet enough; maybe he just didn't like to open his mouth unless someone put a coin in it. And after all, there is business ethics and his duty to protect the doc who sold the stuff.

"Friend, listen, we're not hungry, let me explain it again," I said. "This Grack is moving with us. You remember. He needed it very bad. I'll explain once more how —"

At this point Joy, who had been keeping quiet, suddenly cleared her throat and put her hand on my arm to stop me. Her eyes narrowing, darkening under the thick fringe of lash, she said sweetly, "For your good too, Mister."

"Miss?"

I looked at her intently. It's how to get the audience. I turned and frowned. I shilled for my wife.

"Personal favor to you, sir," she repeated. "What if they pick up our pal in a bad way? Think he's not going to say who his last referral was? If he'd have found it, he would be back with us now. Don't you think you better help us get him off your hands and out of town?"

That was the line all right, smart talker of a wife. The cookie said, "Doc Purdy, seventy-six Key Street, fourth floor. Listen, I don't even know if he went there, that's why I didn't tell you. Don't blame me — you come in here like this, not a word from anybody. But listen, Doc don't answer his phone. All kinds of funny business with Doc . . ."

We shook off the steam of that place without even asking where Key Street was. A gas station could tell us. I was scared — Grack's bad way with funny docs. What if the doc tried to hold him up? Why didn't he answer the business phone?

Cookie was already talking with a new customer: "How are you?"

"Swell."

"The wife?"

"Swell."

"Got some of that blueberry pie today. . . ."

In the street I pulled Joy's wet face to me for kissing **and** the angry eyes opened away. Smart good girl she was.

Now *hurry*.

Purdy's office on Key Street was in one of those trading neighborhoods which, evenings and Sundays, are as dead as mined-out mining towns. Heaped slag of storefront and echoing canyon of retreated affairs. At first we drove down Key Street without finding him. Then, the second time through, we caught his sign on a glass door between a surgical support store and a place that rented typewriters (*Rental Price Applies to Purchase*). The door let into an unlit stairway:

DOCTOR PURDY

By Appointment Only

My Pittsburgh sense of propriety made me remark to Joy that he should have a first name, or call himself M.D. — it makes dignity for a dope pusher. She looked at me and said to ring the bell. I peeked up the long hallway and thought there was no light, no one home. She reached around me and poked the bell.

No answer.

We stood on that empty street in the drizzle, our faces shiny with smoke and mist and hurry, needing a wash, needing a rest, and what would we find when we did find Grack? I listened to the wet movement of a corrugated box under the wheels of the Dodge.

"Ring again — you want me to?" she demanded angrily.

"I'm sorry." But she did it. I was thinking of her; maybe that's why I didn't want to ring. Why not just leave and forget about it? Why not just take off since Grack seemed to have skipped?

Now I leaned on the button and listened to the thin buzzing upstairs. This time a sick blue light answered through the hallway, seeping under a door and perhaps through a keyhole, but no sound of movement. "There, there's somebody," Joy said. She rapped sharply on the plate glass. A cutting rasp from the ring I had given her.

"Open up or we'll break it down!" I yelled into the glass. *Break-i-down,* came the faint echo from the brick front of the warehouse across Key Street. The rustle under our car was of an eating rat in the decaying box.

A buzz unslipped the door. We hurried up the frayed wooden stairway. Upstairs a long corridor was lined with offices for societies and probably a hall for meetings — Sons of Rumania, Lourdes Scholars, Antifluoridation and Cancer by Nicotine groups, the American Nationalist Party, things like that. Those stairs were splintered by dwarfs and pituitaries and by all the parade of the invisibly crippled who

238

were Doc Purdy's clients. What despair of profit he must have grown up with! He waited behind his door for a password. Cookie had not given it.

"We're looking for a friend," I said to the blank door under which the blue light sifted. "Gracchus. You know him. Needed it bad, fierce."

Again, as if pitching us by tumultuous silence, as if raising our price, Doc Purdy listened without a sound.

"Let us in or we'll tear you down."

The voice behind the door, a sweet and reedy voice, took place without needing to clear its throat. "How many are you?"

"Man and wife," Joy said.

A chair creaked and heavy footsteps started, shoes too heavy for the voice, heavy black shoes with shiny eyelets and a nice female voice, "It's so late." He unlatched but held the door on the chain and looked at us with a pocket flashlight. He admitted us into his cracked-leather, paper-piled, clinic-smelling roost — the blue light from a nightlamp crowding the room with dimness, filling the spaces between the auction warehouse furniture and the smears of wallpaper (did he sleep in an adjoining cubicle?) and the doc himself now sitting behind his desk with his cheeks in his hands.

"You come back for it?" he asked wearily. "No way to change my price. I didn't plan to go to bed this night, so no matter how late you come I'm ready. A stubborn man. Got to have stubbornness for staying so sick and living when you don't have to anymore."

I held my breath to figure him, telling us his life's story already, desire and illness and how he couldn't taste the good of peaches and pears nowadays, dreaming us to go on like that. Joy's start of comprehension at my side gave me all the sense we needed for him: Sure, a hophead himself, he made a moony wiseness. He and Grack had argued about price or about the powdered sugar in it or about something to do with getting, giving, or using. Now he thought the Grack had sent us back for bargaining.

"Not when you do like this to an old man," he said. "I'll sell, business is business, but I don't give no fear nor favors." And he showed the bruised cheek and the brownish swollen eye. Was Grack going hot-crazy, beating up the pushers? The doc's other eye, just normally swollen, closed to let us see. Holding it, he showed us that marvelous sad calm of the man with a heavy, heavy, satisfied habit. And the calm of a man with a weapon in his open desk drawer.

"No, no," I said, "all I want is where is he?"

"Who?"

"Our friend."

Doc wheezed, trying laughter. "You think I asked where he was going? He tried to hold me up, son. He hurt me." He touched the eye and winked. "Lucky I had my protection." It gave him a pleasure to be beaten up but to win anyway.

I remembered Grack's desperation. "You ought to know better'n to lift the tariff on a guy who needs it bad, Doc."

"Your friend ought to know better'n to try to fight down the price with his hands when he has the shakes already, son. Son," he added with satisfaction.

"Where'd he go?" Joy demanded.

The doc spread his hands, *who knows?* "Look at my poor

240

eye," he said, "contusions. I don't even want to show myself. Wouldn't even be fun at all."

He smiled happily and squeaked around in the chair to the full-length mirror behind him. He kept one hand in the drawer.

"No use," Joy said. "He isn't going to tell us anything we need to hear. Let's go."

"Oh I could tell you young folks lots of things," Doc Purdy cried out. "The life I've had! Ruined! Only thing, of course, I can't tell you where your friend is now."

"Come on."

"Was the brightest boy in my class, high school, second or third smartest, little college I went to, then medical school and I fell in love —" I stood listening for a moment, dreaming of my own habit while the man talked, knowing it for the reason I looked for Grack and the reason for waiting without looking while this goof goofed on us and my wife's ankles swelled and could get varicose veins from the burdens I had given her. The doc said, in deep amazement, shading his hurt eyes: "It never did stop 'em before when I held up for price, not if they really wanted it, unless he knows another pusher." A shrug of what might once have been scientific curiosity: "Now what do you suppose kind of habit he got, he could turn reluctant over a few bucks? And then not get it at all." Holding his sore cheek, he shook the gray unshaven medical head over such a phenomenon. His silence was philosophical about how it requires brains to push heroin and they ought to require only the highest types for it, men of standing who don't mind a fractured nest of capillaries in the cheek now and then.

"Come on, no use here," Joy said.

"You tired, honey? Let's give it up for now."

"Yes, I'm tired, Bud. Yes, indeed."

Without getting up from his chair, Doc Purdy called out behind us, "You don't want to buy in case he didn't find it anyplace else? You don't want to make sure? You don't even want to say goodbye?"

26. Round and round, the trick of want

Let's go back," Joy said. "Maybe he's back there already." I could not argue for looking when we didn't know where to look. Joy's face was cold and small with fatigue, her mouth drawn larger, like the muzzle of an indoor animal left outdoors. I had done it to her. If Grack had not found his way back, I could leave and again go looking for him. The steady drizzle over Baltimore, steaming off heated roofs down all the streets of the quiet town, made it impossible to hide her weariness. She had the right to rest now. Even the weather conspired. And where was there to look?

Here in Baltimore I only then thought of how close we were to Pittsburgh and how Dad and Joy would blush and stammer to meet. Well, Dad had waited; he could wait longer, until I saw this carnie business through. And if Grack had carried his doc-fighting habits somewhere else? Trouble, real trouble, trouble enough to forget my pa. But now enough for Joy to let me forget her, knowing that I wanted only to remember. She did know it, I believe, despite the hardness of knowing under Grack's sight.

"Right now," she said. "I need to go home, Bud — home to the motel."

I know directions. We found our place without a false turning, passing through a lovely square on the way, the red brick wet and all the patterned walls joined. I slowed down the Dodge and said to Joy, "Nice town — someday you like to live here?"

"We passed it coming already, didn't you see?"

"You're really beat, Joy."

No, she wasn't thinking houses yet. That's a mother's job, and she wasn't quite a mother, although tired. It's also a father's job and I thought of it the second time we passed the square.

There was no light in our cabins side by side when we finally drove up, sticky to the skin and worrying, nothing except the nolight glare of the spotlights which mark the parking places of a BEAUTYREST MOTEL. You come blinking out of the car, eyes shrunk by blaze of white, and it was so we came. Grack's cabin was dark. Not there. Ours was dark. We ran with heads bent to the rain. No, a cigarette burned straight up at our pillows.

I knocked open the door with a kick and yelled, "For Christ's sake, Grack!"

"Been out on the town?"

"Been out looking for you, goddammit!"

He should have swung around when Joy and I came in, keeping his feet high so as not to let them dirty our bed, and he should have sat up and offered us a cigarette. He lay there in the long trough made by his body in the used-up mattress, smoking and peaceable, waiting. I put Joy in a chair, then

244

furiously turned back to him: "What the hell were we supposed to think?"

"Calm down, friend, I'm satisfied. I got what I needed."

"That isn't what I said. I didn't ask how are you! How was I supposed to know how nice you feel? You tell us you're running, you tell me you need us to keep you hid, you tell us you're scared —"

"Maybe I shouldn't of said that."

"You tell us you're scared and then you scare us sillier'n the kids in the House of Murder by disappearing for a day like this. How do I know you're not picked up? How do I know the fuzz aren't waiting back here to tie on a rap for Aiding and Abetting?"

He breathed slowly, working his contentment around in his mouth. "Who you scared for, kid? Me or who? You didn't do nothing. I'm just a friend taking a little honeymoon trip with you, is all I am. Pauline knows you just got married — everybody does. So what's that aiding and abetting?"

One of the habits of a man on habit is not to worry about what used to worry him. The past is far past and behind, the future is far ahead and away. He was my friend; he had helped me; I had rights at anger — and yet there was no way to get to him. He floated on the springs with an unreachable smile. Human, yet less than human under a habit, he could not be found with reproach. Blind and protected, he lay puffing his cigarette with his blind and protected eyes amused over us. And Joy was watching me.

Having learned, I was ashamed for all those like Grack who fed without eating, loved without loving, died in ad-

245

vance. Yes, ashamed for myself too, but all for him as he lay without the will to kick himself free and giving no twitch of desire. (Yes, he wanted things better; yes, he wished, he was alive.) You might think I would diddle my toes in my shoes for shame and look at them. I looked at Grack's feet crammed into his black pointed shoes — too tight they were — and I thought as the carnie thinks: Feet hurt, head hurt. Poor man with not enough sense to buy shoes that fit him, just for wanting pointy feet. Still thinking feet, I said, "You can't do this kind of thing to us, Grack — running off to fret us like that. You can't. You're asking for trouble. Why get it from us?"

Yes, *us*. Joy and me.

I said: "You must be hurt bad, Grack."

He answered, "Wrong and right, Bud. I love the smell of my bandages, that's how bad I'm hurt and how long."

"You're not my friend anymore?"

"You've got yourself a wife."

"It ain't such a kind of being friends, Grack, that it couldn't be with Joy, too."

"You mean because she let me come along for the wedding?"

"No, no, no."

Joy's moving and breathing in the darkness behind me let me know that she was replying. There was a small hurry of thought in her fine balance and grace. She did not need to say it when she heard me speaking for her.

"Sure, things are different, Grack, always are. But we can still be friends like —"

"*No!* You can't play that one with me, Buddy! When you

246

come to the carnie you don't want things ever to be different. There's only one life when you're in it. We never change! The carnie is with it, enough!" Thrashing, agitated as a fevered man, he barely moved in his trough. His voice was cold and thin, a telephone voice from the never-changing past that I could no longer believe in. He turned his cheek on the pillow. "I'm no different," he murmured. "What you mean, pal-o, is you don't want the life no more. You're not with me."

Joy breathed her assent. I did not speak. To be not with it was once so sad!

I watched him on the bed, tough as a crisp-shelled beetle — but step on the beetle only if you are fond of gore. "Grack," I said finally, "we're with you to get you home. Isn't that where you're wanting?"

How can I say that he died in that instant of the word *wanting?* He wheezed, he choked, the cigarette flamed, Joy stood by my side; his eyes rolled and stared and the hatred and despair swelled to bursting within him — and the moment passed. Maybe it was only the moment of the passing of his high, but with its passing, the paroxysm of the beast, I could never again think of him as anything but a dying creature. We are all moving toward death, true; but we can carry life curled in our bellies, nicely squatting there, or swimming and ready to spurt forth for pleasure and the future. We have things left to do. Not Grack.

"You feel all right, Grack?"

"How about you?"

"You sleepy, Grack?" Joy asked.

"Why, you want to be alone with your loverboy? Use the

other cabin, I'm tired," — and true that he was thin and dim and very tired.

And I thought: He has no right to age Joy like this! And said: "How the devil'd you get back here? How'd you get the stuff? Where?"

He did not answer.

"I don't feel so well," Joy said. "I got the cramps. My back hurts. I'll wait for you." She searched my face solicitously before she left. Grack's death in my sight had not escaped her. She did not fear, but worried about our burden in her belly.

"Grack," I began again, "we've got to get along, you see? Otherwise you better take a train. We got to get you there and that's all, otherwise . . . Listen, Grack! We're going to have a baby."

He grinned. "You and the girl?"

"Try to understand what I'm saying now, Grack. It isn't like that time when I couldn't answer your letter. Didn't. I'm telling you straight on now. It's not just for me. You remember when you told me that? How you helped me kick the habit not just for me? How you sent me back to home not just for me? There are others, Grack."

"There's the marks, sure."

"There's Joy! There's our kid!"

His sallow face turned with the grin. "There's my ma, too, but she ain't with it. Old lady wanted me to go for priest. In French. Learned me to talk, anyway."

Trying hard to be calm and fast, I could feel Joy's belly-ache near me; she would not lie down until I came to lie

248

beside her. "You hear what I'm telling you, Grack? We got to cross that bridge soon."

"Detroit to Windsor," he answered to the everlasting highway headlights flicking across the motel walls. "What's there to giving birth? Once when I was a kid I put acorns in the pocket of my lumberjacket — fat ones for carving. Went into the woods for them. Ma laid my jacket up for me, and next spring when I went for that jacket the pockets were crawling with little white worms and the acorns were slick and died to dust when I pinched them. . . ."

Joy returned as I stood by his bed. "He's sleeping," she whispered. "Let's go."

"Sure I'm sleeping, girlie. Let me pinch you in my dreams. So Mama will say, *Bon jour, Grack, tu viens enfin?* That's Canuck for you ain't been a son to your ma. Can't you see by my skin and bones — I'm sick, I got a habit — I ain't my mama's anymore? She almost dead already — head gone. I'm just wanting back, that's all. Her milk is black. Hear me? You always in a hurry?"

In his addict's faint sleep he was crossing over to nowhere and to get away. Black milk was all. Joy and I went out on tiptoe. He slept.

27. She had a right

Joy slept out her cramps of the two-inch fish which measured our marriage within her, measured it by climbing and changing and sounding for union in our blood with a note deeper than the carnie haw and the chime of my loyalty to Grack. I watched over her and brooded and murmured comfort as incomplete as that of the radio on Sunday afternoon.

"I'm going to give you something nice to sleep in," I said. "Don't be sick. Just lie still. I'm going to buy it first time I get in town, lace on it, real pretty."

"That's so lovely of you. Please kiss me now, Bud."

"I'm going to put the money for it in a special pocket. I won't forget."

"That was nice, Bud. You already gave me nice things. Oh my legs are cramping."

I tried to make my own legs cramp, couldn't. "Do you want to sleep and then we'll get started again?" She lay white and still under the folded top sheet. I had not believed so much whiteness possible in this small and tanned, ankling, earth-scattering carnie creature who was Pauline's dark daughter; but now ice-whiteness, sheet-whiteness, bleeding-whiteness in her still and scared face. "No, Joy, you're not doing so good today." She gave me gratitude in a smile because I had seen it without being told. "I'm finding a doctor, Joy."

"Don't you move. I just need rest and it'll stop by itself. Too much running and wet, riding the car, that's all," she said. "It's okay, Bud, Pauline told me all about everything. Same thing happened to her when she was carrying me. Had to lay overnight and give up the reading of palms for Friday to Monday, but don't worry, it was all right and it turned out to be me who was born that way, with just a little birthmark to show for it. That okay, Bud? I'm cold."

I lay down by her side. She said:

"I like the way you take care of Grack. Will you take care of me that way, too?"

"Let me go find a good doctor."

She threw her arm across my chest. "And leave me alone? No, no. We had enough with doctors already. Anyway, listen, I know, Pauline told me. It's just my day of the month and even when you're carrying you sometimes feel it bad. A little blood means a boy, that's all."

Marveling, I said to her ear — and the pleasure I took in touching it with my talking lips! — "How do you know? A virgie like you were."

"No woman was ever a virgin for that, for kids," she said, and closed her eyes. "I'm not sleeping," she said, and slept.

I lay there quietly while her breathing came up and down, cool and warm, holding my breath for her sleep and proud of her need for me despite the pride about her womanliness. I touched her legs under the blanket. The muscles were

251

smooth and hanging slack in the firm flesh. She was at rest, then, and it was permitted to think of Grack in his dreamy high next door and of myself in my journey here by Joy's side where she ached with sudden alterations and became what she had never been. What we had never been! The carnie is brave, yes: he is always in a strange place and puts up with it, finds the marks in it, gets his kicks from it, is with it and for it. But Grack next door also dwelled behind the other face of his bold venturing: he carried a small, dim, and locked world with him. Not only the secrecy of heroin and privacy of morphine, no! The privacy of expecting so little — cash, kicks, calliope music — and a guarantee down in advance that only success is possible. Bravery for oddity, cowardice for patterns, a meagerness of demand — was there ever a surprise in the funhouse for the electrician who set it up? The wheeze of air which blows the giggle-girls' skirts above their bloomers is installed beside the same door at every fair: she always giggles, shows just the few cubic inches of pink thigh and/or panties, and then puts her hand to her bosom for pride in her quirk of nipples.

Dad had another way: cowardice for strangeness, bravery for his acceptance of the terrible repetitions of days. His life suddenly seemed heroic to me in its stubborn going-on, a gloomy heroism of day-after-day, a heroism of heavy breathing. Oh my poor dad who never saw how strange to repeat a life over and over! Ma must have taken a great deal from him by dying, and I must have punished him wickedly by borning, growing, claiming flesh and being. The thought that he never fled his day (up at the alarm) and never gave me up (fought patiently, fought) made me cherish him again even as I lay beside Joy, his daughter now, the mother of his grandchildren now, and she said in sleep, "Stay here, Bud, I'm listening."

Someday soon — I gritted my teeth — I would dress Joy in clever Maternity Shoppe clothes and take her, jut-belly and all, her fine legs spindly under their burden, to meet Dad. (Yes, yes, if Grack left us in peace.) My shame at thoughts of murder would not stop me now. That was previous. That was accidents ago, efforts ago. The time was past when I stood on the stairs watching my pa — sullen, eyes swollen, sleepy — for him to admit just one mistake and to try something new in our lives. The carnie was all new! Pa all old! And now the carnie was as familiar as death and Pa unknown.

"Bud?"

"What, honey?"

"Sleeping?"

"Yes."

"So'm I."

Dad, don't cry, don't you cry, I would say. He would bawl, of course, and Joy would just whisper to me, He got that habit? and then would put her arms around him and rock him like an infant. Not yet rid of the baby fat herself, she wasn't!

I thought of the rooster in the sign above the chicken shop where Dad bought the Sunday dinners which he cooked for himself on important holidays.

And then after dinner he read the paper with a flyswatter in his hand, looking up from Walter Lippmann to squash a beastie, until finally he fell asleep amid the bodies strewn terribly on the floor about his easy chair. Poor Dad! He only wanted his rest. The buzzing drove him wild — unsanitary, makes disease, he said. My father's love of the tricks of earth had not survived my birth. Ma's death had him wise to failure too early — no ripening through the long disaster of a life. He spit often into pieces of newspaper; I guess that said, *I'm sorry, I meant to be different.* Or maybe sinus trouble is only sinus trouble.

She was sleeping, my little girl Joy, the mother of my kid to come, and the fretlines eased slowly between her eyes. I slipped out of bed, heart ticking loudly for silence and not disturbing her. In our suitcase the two-dollar alarm clock ticked also, still packed from the last stop and running down between my socks and her sweater. I pulled the sheet up to Joy's chin. She lay still.

The door was open next door and Grack had not moved. "Bud, thanks for coming," he said. "I was thinking you here."

"What's up?" I smiled in the darkness and turned my head, although he couldn't see anyway — had he put his finger to his eye to call me?

"I need you, Bud."

"What for?"

"You're planning on dropping me off."

"What do you mean?"

"You're planning on taking me someplace, Windsor I guess, and just dropping me there. That's all."

"That isn't what you want? To go home? Back to your mother, you said."

"Yes, back to the Kiskeedees," — and again, more briefly this time, that jerk and fit of death stiffened his face.

254

Then he explained once more, "They call us Frenchies Kiskeedees because it's *qu'est-ce qu'il dit, qu'est-ce qu'il dit* all the time. Don't understand us. My mother spoke three words of English, learned to talk with my eyes from her. Listen, Bud, Ma was a mark . . . But you're just going to drop me past Detroit?"

I figured ways to say it nicely. I thought of Joy, ill, bled, and still waiting. I said only, "Yes."

He sat up abruptly. "No, you can't do it! You have no right! You got to come with me, Bud. We'll get with a traveling show together in Ontario, we'll pull 'em in together, kid, and I'll support my own habit myself."

"No, Grack."

"What do you mean no? *No?* You don't have any right to talk to me like that. Wasn't for me, you'd have a twenty-dollar habit by now or you'd be squirming in Lexington. Listen, kid, where'd —"

Listen, Grack, I was thinking, *don't be pa at me*. It hardened me to have my gratitude used against me; I knew enough about it already, and guilt for failures, and owings and borrowings and obligations. You don't even win slum like that, Grack.

"You're not listening, god damn you!"

"True, Grack, I'm not. Talk sense at me and I'll listen."

"I'm sense! I took care of you!"

"True, Grack," — and I spread my hands. What more taking care of him could I do? And yet the twitch in my legs as I looked was for following him, and the dry of my throat for hawing with him at a countstore in Ontario, and the ache of my arms for a burden taken up while all the other

255

burdens were not put down. Forever. Could never be. O a man without schools and clubs and neighbors and hours, having to make his life himself, has too much to do! Once the carnie had been my hour, then I took Grack for friend, finally I wived myself — and that led me straight on to neighbors, schools, and a box with my name on it. Maybe I had the right to break mindlessly, like a cresting wave, against my father: but what monster can rebel against the child his own will has made? — I did not forget those stirrings and that new pleasure even as I met Grack's harsh black gaze.

Grack watched.

Joy groaned and turned on our bed next door.

It seemed to me that I fled that evening from one scheming sleeper to the next, while each tried to master me in sleep. Grack lay with his finger to his eye, sallow, long on patience, furiously watching me as he watched the swarm of marks. He counted what was in my pockets. He figured how to get what was for the getting. It was no longer a question of being friends, although I could never forget those days in the mountains when he had waited and watched like a father to help me throw my habit, and held my forehead and thrown a bed over me when he had to. Now he only schemed.

"Once in the Rockies — remember, Bud? — you said you wanted to be with it." He must have hurt badly to use this as part of the scheme. It could be used up. "You said you were wanting it, Bud."

"Yes, I remember."

"You don't mean it anymore?"

"Yes, I do."

"So?"

I shook my head. "You told me you were sending me back. You said you were doing it, Grack, you said I was one going back for you. I just believed you was all. With it is someplace else now —"

"Ah!" And the tendoned lines of his face were making clefts of hardness again, pleasing me. It's terrible when a skinny man sags there in loose flesh at the chin and spongy under the eyes and dugs at the breast and a loose flat belly. He understood me all the way where he could never follow or lead. "You want to be a good little lad in a good job in a nice city. I know you now, Bud. She really tipped the bally on you. You want to be Joy's good little husband."

"Yes, Grack."

"I see you now."

That was all I said: "Yes."

"You do? You do? You wag your head?" His craw was jumping and he took pleasure in speechifying: "Well then you're nothing but another dumb-ass mark in the crowd, Buddy. Well I'll be blasted."

But you can say *yes* to the truth and like it and then not be pleased at all by the way your friend says it. His mouth twisted in little cleaning gestures over his teeth. He wiped and licked his lips. He was searching for the words to talk me down (not necessary, Grack) and his hand flew furiously, flew happily to his eye. I said:

"Sleep it off now, Grack. I remember what it was to be like you. Cover up, don't catch a cold."

And again I crossed the little space of concrete to the cabin where Joy slept. I bounced between these two solid

257

walls, played by the sleeping combatants, and grew a will and a skill of topspin as I bounced. Crossing through the night's wet chill, I thought of that other battling sleeper, my father, and of the one quiet sleeper which Joy bore. But first of my father, perhaps because I had hurt and meant to hurt Grack, as I had hurt and meant to hurt that father who loved me.

"Who? Who?" Joy turned in her sleep, troubled, as I entered.

"Sh-h, just Bud."

She had uncovered herself and lay in the rinsed window light like a child in uneasy dreams. The ache and kinking of her legs had pushed up her pajamas; there were soiled little-girl knees, an active child's knees even now with our two-inch baby tucked above them. I pulled the blanket back under her chin, dropped my clothes, and crawled in beside her. Thick with sleep, her voice said, "You keep me warm, Bud. Someday we'll have a kitchen, too —"

"To write letters in. I'll take you out to swell restaurants for eating, kid."

But Grack was right that I did want that kitchen for eating.

28. *America is voyages.*
We were American

NEXT morning the weather changed to burnt apple time, the Maryland fields crackling under the lip of frost on each leaf, good for blood and appetite. Joy's eyes played sharply over me, past the crisis, tomboy again, with no paleness but a dusky deep color at her fine cheeks. Grack too, he awakened refreshed by our conversation followed by sleep, and the bugskin of his habit let him free of scratching for a while.

He was trimming his nails when I went to wake him. "Let's put some miles between us," he said cheerfully. "I mean on the road. Let's go. Want to drive awhile before breakfast?"

I asked Joy. "Sure, good thing," she said.

It was our habit to undo a few miles before the first eating, clop-clopping our lips awake, rolling the eyes clean, stretching and deep-breathing until the right diner with the right coffee presented itself. These sharp first-of-the-morning minutes were the best between the three of us.

We did a few quiet days across Pennsylvania and then up through Ohio toward Cleveland, stilled by this medium country, fat farms and slow-moving people slowed down not by malaria or pellagra or mortgages but by their deliberations, pious and plump, sure of their soil. In Pennsylvania there were brick churches and steeples. In Ohio we saw colleges in every small town. The kids I might have been pleased me, and so did the bleating sheep that Joy had escaped being. We would stop for our dinner in a Campusburger Shoppe — jukebox playing "the popular classics," hands a-holding while the eyes tried not to notice, all the suburban children out for their few years without husband, without wife, and the parents not watching.

And how well we came to know that this outing doesn't end easily! There were imperfect moments between Joy and me, of course, as there always are. There were also still worse times, stricken by poverty, poor especially with my own failures in the past. In such hours, Joy struck out at me and blamed me for fixing her this way: "My bosoms hurt bad again tonight."

"Say breasts, please," — exasperated with the word and with her complaining.

"They hurt anyway. How would you know anything about it except what to say?"

"All right, I suppose you were just waiting for us to be alone so you could say you hurt, so you could say bosoms, so you could say this and that —"

"Yes, yes, that's right, I was just waiting to whine at you, you know it your way, that's all I wanted from you. . . ." And tears.

While my heart turned, I perversely tried to think of what they say about Woman's Tears — making them merely female, not my Joy's. I held her, saying, "Joy, Joy, I know it's hard for you. I *know*, honey."

And then, before she could be eased, my meanness had its reward. That rattatat would quiver in my legs as I held her, a wanting to escape these schemes about a wife, and I would recognize once more my old companion: the shameful dream of evasion. And words would come to speak for my impatience: "Why *don't* you try to sleep then if you're tired." Or: "Let's go for a walk," — when I knew that what she needed of me was to sit and hold her on my knees awhile.

"I'm in my slip, I don't want to get dressed. You can go for a walk if you want to, it's all right."

"Okay, okay. . . ."

"Aren't you going?"

"No."

"Go ahead."

"No, no!"

And I sat in silence, holding her but my silence of the no-saying kind, until she thought of something else she needed to do and we moved apart.

But it was not like this often. Yes, we had this *no* to learn out of our marriage, but most of our being together, even from the ignorant beginning, was as I said of it: "Joy, Joy, we love each other so much."

At first all I wanted was to be human like a few other people. It sometimes seemed that to be married was already to be more than human.

As we drew in toward Cleveland, where Grack had a friend, his skinny haleness seemed to flow back. Eating, he showed huge jaw muscles, talking muscles, biting in his sleep muscles. He ate with immense muscular chewing and grins and winks while we watched the college kids squirt from straws and play in chocolate. Grack liked to tap Joy's wrists and put his finger to his eye for me to listen. We were near Hiram College, I think it was — a main street, a campus, the kids in white woolen socks and very white teeth for making friends:

"Bob, this is Doris — this nice-looking doll."

"Pleased to meet you, doll."

"Doris likes to go for joyrides, Bob."

"Want to drive around the stadium, doll?"

From our booth Grack, Joy, and I watched them. It bothered me that Doris, the simple townie, did not answer Bob. They must have understood each other. Grack grinned and felt good and had another sandwich. He slipped his finger to the wart and asked me, "This what you like, Bud?"

"College? Little late now."

"Answer my question — this what you like?"

"It's okay for them, but it isn't either the carnie or this. That's not the choice. I got a wife already, my Joy, for instance," — and I pulled her to me across the bench. She slid easily. I made her sit that way with me, the two of us facing Grack.

"Boy," Grack said, "you don't answer me straight no more *no* way." He wagged his head and sucked at a tooth. He reached across the table and patted Joy's hand. She did not remove it, and this bothered me; but it was for my sake that she held so still. We had to get Grack through to get through with him. He wagged his head and grinned at both of us,

262

holding and patting Joy's hand in his own two, saying, "Bud, tell you what. I been thinking. You ought to go into politics."

Polly-ticks was how he said it.

I laughed at the notion, from countstore to county clerk! "Why not?"

He stroked Joy's palm and she rested quiet. "Settle down, make a name someplace, you got a pretty little wife to help you — run for an office."

"Why not?" Politics is to make out as best you can with what you have — all my life's practice was politics. He was putting the nasty carnie ribbing to me now, sheriffs and cops and the dumbest, meanest, most larcenous marks they are, but I thought only, Why not? He was telling me that he could stroke Joy's hand and be nasty to me without our turning on him because we wanted no trouble, because we had plans, because we were waiting to be rid of him. That was his idea of politics. He stroked her palm now while I watched and Doll went out for that ride.

"Politics!" Grack said, glittering with the joke of it on our way to Cleveland and Detroit and dropping him forever in Canada.

"Sure enough, Grack. Let's pay up and get moving."

When we all slipped back again into the Dodge, I noticed that Joy's breasts were slightly irregular, like a lift of birdwings, one slanting higher than the other. Grack jammed himself in too damn tight next to her.

Patience! his jerk of body said. You just wait me out, patient Bud my friend, even when I rub up against your Joy.

Thus up through Ohio to Cleveland, that great sprawled-out city with the Cuyahoga River its worm at the center. Grack had a friend with a motel just off the skidrow of town, where the carnies stayed when they sometimes passed through. The prop. on this busy corner was with it and for it, an ex-carnie who had sunk his gain in the G. Washington Motel for the girls and boys. "Old Itch Scardini," Grack called him, "needs to drink some vegetable water for the stomach." He made a quiet living joining out the odds, the odd lads with the odd lassies to come out even. He would know where Grack could get a little recreation for his habit, where we could rest and jolly up a bit before that last stretch into Detroit to Windsor and goodbye, Grack.

Grack touched the tapioca cluster of swelling on his friend's neck. "What's the matter, mumps?"

"No, swollen glands from a pimple on my collar," Scardini said. "Always get 'em like that. They cut off the glands for that sometimes."

"You got to be real careful."

"Yep, second worst place to have a infection in the glands. But how you been all this time, Grack?" — nodules of flesh on his neck and shivering false jowls when he craned and greeted. Goiter coming. "What say, Grack?"

"Mr. Scardini," Grack said, having greeted his old friend Itch, "let me present my dear buddies Bud and Joy."

Scardini took Joy's hand and murmured, "Why, hello there, Joy," and then looked his congratulations at Grack from a yellow-fleshed, oiled-down, slicked-up head. A saliva line of unhappy digestion creased Scardini's lips, leather-stained by blood from somewhere. I believe he was not a well man.

"These kids are true friends of mine," Grack announced, liking the sense of taking over after so long — better even than a habit for making the pride feel good. "Treat 'em like my friends. They used to be with it."

"Nice!" said Scardini's worn mouth. "Kids like them?"

"With it and for it," Grack answered him, "used to be."

Scardini risked the fissures of his mouth in a smile and lifted both arms to show us his G. Washington place. I could smell the camphor ice he had rubbed on his lips. "Then stay as long as you have pleasure here! How you want the rooms, Grack?"

Joy answered coolly, without waiting for jokes. "One for my husband and me, Mr. Scardini," she said, "and one for Grack — they don't have to connect. And thanks."

Oh, said Scardini's mouth, figuring this one out as best it could. The mouth cracked and opened for Joy, meaning, *a cute trick she is,* the eyes rolling to Grack for further explanation.

29. *Poor Scardini, he was only Fred Trapp*

I NEVER knew that Grack had such a friend as Scardini, a gutty, chicken-necked, flabby-breasted manager, gastric and troubled by piles, with a glove compartment full of special creams: "Me First Everywhere," — his motto. First everywhere, but he was Grack's friend, too, just like me.

A man with a habit rarely takes well to friends — does he need them? The answer: *why* does he need them? Grack seemed to need me, all the same, and this is one of the strange things that might happen even deep within a habit, despite its withering against the odd and familiar edges which define life. In a habit you need no more adventure, no more novelty; you need no more friends or family, no more job or pleasures — you need only to get your mainline when you need it. Grack wanted me not only as a help to getting to Windsor, but also as a reminder of his days in a life outside the habit, and maybe even because he liked me. I was fond of thinking of myself as an exception to habits. That Joy troubled him was the bother of friendship, exclusive and jealous, I thought. He wanted me to remember how he used to lead me although I now did the leading.

Well, now I wasn't sure just what about Grack and Joy.

He looked at her more softly through his red-rimmed, yellow-dusted eyes.

Scardini seemed to be a friend, too. Grack sat with him to talk the whole day through, in low voices in the next room, and twice I heard them clap and roar with laughter. When I came back from changing the oil and greasing our Dodge, Joy said, "Grack's been laughing next door. Almost forgot what that sounded like."

It made three times in one day, odd for a habit, which doesn't need the fast switch of laughter. Scardini must have been a close history to him. Joy and I shrugged for annoyance that Grack could laugh for his pal Scardini and not for us. Let him be as happy as he could.

"How do you feel, Joy?"

"Fine. Quieted down inside."

"You look like a kid."

"Wait a few months and I'll wheel my belly ahead of me. I'll be good for shoplifting, Bud."

"Never mind, never you mind. I'm going to get a job of work and we'll *pay* for what we swipe. That's the plan I've got."

She grinned. "Mighty sweet of you to do that for me, Bud boy. Want to kiss?"

I did. I moved my mouth over her loving frown, that warm tussle of pleasure and devotion in the face. What if I had nobody, nothing? What if I had killed a man? What if my friends were not my friends and not even my enemies cared about me? What if my habit gave me no pleasure? What if I were a Kiskeedee with a mother so old she walked sideways and nothing more in my life at all?

I would look for Joy to kiss and feel better. If I had no Joy, well, then maybe I'd look to cross over the International Bridge.

We were kissing again later when Scardini came to our door, lightly tapping and rocking on his too-high leather heels. Where does a man pick up shoes like that and does five feet four really like so much to be five feet five? His sick mouth contemplated himself with a little scowl. He was stretching to be taller, making his face long, while Joy fixed her skirt. Agitated and filming at the eyes, a grease of self-seeking starting from his nose and thick pores on his forehead, he was a cruiser in Cleveland and now cruised over my face, thinking, So you're Grack's Bud Williams, are you? He started into brisk words for us: "Hello, kids, hiya. He's bad."

"What?"

"Grack."

"What's up?"

"He's bad, so bad."

"What do you mean, Mr. Scardini? You deciding now who is bad and good? I suppose you get lots of experience in the hotel business."

Scardini smiled the thin-lipped scowling smile of the man used to being disliked. It was okay. He didn't need friends; he had ways; and besides, he had a pet friend or two. "Poor Grack," he said, "he felt good, but now our Grack has got the shakes. We better get out and get him his sugar he needs. I know a place."

He cocked his head at me. Joy looked something at me which I could not quite read: Don't go, go, something like that. There was one of those tense pauses which a carnie talker so much dreads: who's buying what? She waited me out.

"I'm carrying the boodle, I'll go with you," I said finally.

Scardini nodded and his plucked eyebrows shot up. "The whole family going?" he asked in a particular nasal voice.

Joy spared me his ridicule. "No," she said, "the rest of the family will make itself comfortable in Scardini's G. Washington Motel, thank you."

"Then come on, Bud," said Scardini, "we're going out."

The way he took to my name, *Bud*, made it clear that Grack and Scardini had had a long talk. He must have said a couple or three times, Bud, Bud, Bud, for this eaten-mouthed runt to say smoothly Bud at me.

"You sure you have some things to do?" I asked Joy. "You don't want to come with? You all right?"

Joy showed her teeth to say that what she had was not sickness but health, and we exchanged smiles. I kissed her goodbye the way a husband might on his way to the office. Her arms around me were finely downed arms, sleeves pulled up tight over the bare round flesh — that nice pressure of sleeve on nice arm! She strolled with me to Scardini's Cadillac and said goodbye again while he absently caressed a chrome strip. The stroke of his hand on the wheel told his satisfaction and still another story: Not yet paid for, Bud, but mine. When I took Joy's arm in farewell or hello, I did it the same way. It was the stroke of pleasure which my father had always lacked in Pittsburgh — for car or for girl — and no son could give it to him.

Of course, I gave him less than most sons.

He would have been heavy-faced and creased by disapproval and not daring to say it if he had seen me by this slick Scardini riding, touring in Cleveland. Without knowing where or why — that would do him in, it was so much like his own straining to nowhere.

"The name is Trapp," Scardini said after a minute, looking away from me. He wanted to be agreeable. He gestured with his hand off the steering wheel.

"What's that, Mr. Scardini?"

"No, *Trapp*," he said. "I took Scardini's name when he died — a tribute to the boss, you see. I'm really named Trapp from Lima, Ohio. Scardini is a better name for me in my business, besides being like a little heartfelt tribute to the genuine old Scardini article."

"Pleased to meet you," I said.

"No, I mean it," he insisted, *"Trapp."*

"Hi, Mr. Trapp."

"Fred Trapp!" He gestured in an angry way, waving the glowing cigarette lighter from the dashboard. The name must have reminded him of himself. When he slapped his hand back, the hot coil melted and stank against the plastic of the steering wheel. "I'm telling you the whole truth," he announced, beginning to regret it, "and that's Fred Trapp. It's because I like you."

"Okay, Freddie," I said.

"You like to work for me maybe as my night manager in the G. Washington? It's my legal name."

"No thanks, Freddie, but deeply appreciate. Joy and I are cutting out after — after —"

He grinned. It was something he wanted to know: *After*

we drop Grack. He didn't even bother to say, Well, never mind, think it over. He had spent his born name on me, he had won knowledge with this investment; now he could Scardini around the corners in his Cadillac again. But he was right that I had to figure about our unborn child after the couple of days left with Grack. Grack and a time of flight are not a wedding trip or reason enough for three lives. I knew Joy was thinking hard, maybe about seeing my pop and his trucking business and an apartment in the same building to start. She had a right to plan.

Was Pop thinking about me?

Would he reel and stumble when he laid eyes on my lovely Joy, the tears rushing because mothers used to die?

"This is the house," Scardini said, no longer Trapp, tires grating the curb. "Get out first, if you please. Don't like to get out streetside in this here neighborhood. Rough class of people. Wait a sec — let me tell you."

We were at a low office block on Prospect Avenue, shoe repair and while-you-wait and Hadacol for Health and a row of apartments upstairs. Could have been Jacksonville or Baltimore, was Cleveland. One apartment had Venetian blinds pulled shut. That must be Nancy. "Nancy's my contact for this and others," Scardini said. "Nice fella, Nancy, we're in so many little businesses together. We like it together. You just need friends in a world." His cruising eyes again returned. "Well, son" — and the eyes were fleeing again — "please let me tell you how I made mine one week, later lost it. . . ."

"With Nancy?"

"No, that was with another good friend, the filthy double-crosser." He too spat because he no longer wept, spit the tears of the tough, I believe. "But I don't let Nancy get anything on me ever. That's one good reason for you, Bud — you're my witness. I like a nice boy like you for preparing himself for me —"

"Wait a sec!"

"No, no, not that Nancy would sing or make me pay, no, I got things on him, too. But I like to show him your sweet face. You shave already, Bud? How you get your nose done in like that?"

He was a talker at curbs, Scardini was, locking his hands about his steering wheel, confiding deep within the motor warmth of his Caddy while the useless power creaked and slipped. "You sure you wouldn't love to go into a little business with me? Trust you to make collections, boy."

Then he meant it! "No," I said.

He jerked the door open. "So what we waiting for? Please understand me: I asked only because I need somebody to trust and you have a peculiar face. Honest. Come to Nancy now, boy, Grack's in a hurry."

I would have liked myself to claim hurry, hurry to finish the grackwork, but Scardini had feelings. Jeez, not hard for me to say, that word *feelings*, since his soft and rabbit-mouthed touchiness would make no diff to me one day after I left him. My pop, Grack, even Scardini and Doc Purdy, all these talkative ones were helplessness seeking a listener. Joy could sit quiet. Well, anyway, it would hurt him to think I didn't just love to rock on Caddy springs and wiggle down and chat like this with the radio humming for company while he said: "Grack tells me you were a good talker, a carnie who got on, but just a mark in your guts."

"Yes."

"What do you mean yes?"

"I admit it, yes, I am." And the radio said, Whiskey and gin, the trouble I'm in, please love me again, I'm yourrrs. "Yes," I repeated, wanting to slip through the door onto the street.

"You mean you got mark guts instead of stringy carnie ones?"

All right, if he was the great conversationalist, I would try to climb fast to the truth he needed. I explained. "That's what it takes, Mr. Scardini, to get to be the big boss, the man with the boots. You got to know marko. You got to know it by being it, but now I want out."

"How's that? Now you don't like getting yours, Bud? Grack *told* me you're far out, boy. You like that girlfriend of yours too much for good health and money? It thins the blood and makes the hair fall out. That how much you like her? That little Joy of yours we left back home at my G. Washington place with Grack? Yes?"

I did not answer.

"Yes? Me, sonny, I like hotel business, don't you? I like to touch legs, you don't? Rub up against the shaving, then where they forgot to shave. Don't you though? Oh I'll bet. I like a girl's legs more'n the girl, how about you, boy?"

Nothing to say, but the impatient foot turning on its ankle.

"Of course, that little girl of yours is pretty neat. Grack just told me how —" He stopped. I said nothing. Patience was always my trick in times of difficult talking and hard waiting.

"Nice day," I said, and put my hand out the window.

He groaned and we emerged onto Prospect Avenue in Cleveland for our business with Nancy. Scardini bumped me to jog my thoughts in case they were wandering. Poor Scardini was a reminder. We went for Nancy.

30. Down is the long way up

W HEN ripe with anger and righteousness during that
swell hey-rube that busted my nose for Grack, I had learned
something important although it took a long time — the
habit, Grack's helping me to break it, my father, Joy, and
now this far flight — to teach me what it was. I had fought
for Grack and my brother carnies because I had a mad on.
When my nose got busted, little-girl Joy helped to repair it.
All this was a fine wound, and fine to receive it for a friend.

There are two sorts of anger in the world. One is that
one — for the need of Pauline and other friends. The other
doesn't move at all, it is a stiff and self-seeking anger, the
Scardini thing. He had it as we trod the staircase up to
Nancy's. It was for nothing and for no one, and yet it was
as miserable and as angry as the mad I spouted for true love
of our false carnie freedom. We crowded and bumped each
other up the decaying stairway, coffee grounds and fuzzing
pine, off Prospect Avenue in Cleveland, Ohio. "For a buck
in Tennessee when I had my other name," Scardini said,
"talked my other way, said it *Tinn*issee, for a buck you could
get what you wanted, how you wanted it, sunnyside up or
poached, any age including virgins. Oh, wait, it's hot in this
hundred-dollar overcoat. Why did I need to wear it?"

He labored up the stairway, his back bent from behind, stooped and neck-sweating, with deep belly unease. Nuck and willy of love, that's what it was for him — jigger and yawp and withers. I stopped to escape the bad air behind. He turned to breathe and scowl.

"Hurry up. Nancy has all we want now, sonny."

He needed me to stick by his side, this heavy-lidded, thick-eyed, wheezing man, inflamed at the seams, always on the verge of tears, with a nose and ears that were three of the same shape — this man who liked to be called Scardini but could bring no Sicilian litheness to his straining on earth.

"Come on, you afraid to get what you want from Nancy?" His eyes bulged and teared with the attempt at laughter. Please smile back at me on this staircase, no one can see you do it, his mouth implored, breathing in wisps. Please. I have tried to please you. No? Then I will go on trying.

He took a step back and pulled my arm. "Come on, Nancy expects us, sonny." His face swollen by overheat of house, car, and fear for self, heat of ambition and heat of dread, he had veins, lymph, water under the skin, troubled kidneys, too. This was the bad stopped-up anger which above all Joy had helped me escape. (Yes! Kicking the habit had been before Joy, my own work, and I found her myself!) Tenderly Scardini bent to hurry me. It would be a fearful thing to hit a face like Scardini's — a blister ready to burst, boneless — and let all that full-to-breaking poison spill over in tears on the stained cheeks. Absolutely stopped up! What a stink if you lanced it! My rage of pity was righteous and pleased, because could his mother have died any earlier than mine, who died at my birth?

"You coming or you staying?"

"I promised Grack, didn't I?"

"Come on then, sonny. Once I knew another guy did all his thinking on stairways. Break-and-enter man, he was. Used to place his irons, shavers, electrical appliances with me."

"Don't tell me."

"I trust you, sonny. Come into business with me, the hotel part, strictly legitimate. What you want to grift for?"

"I'm coming, I'm coming. Which door is Nancy's?"

The door opened as if Nancy had been listening for us. "Come in, come in, oh come in!" This joviality on a Prospect corridor made me want to run. I even preferred Doc Purdy. What was he selling, this lovely Nancy in his beige corduroy shirt, all bending and smiles to Scardini and me? If Scardini's face had been gradually worked up from his stomach and kidneys, Nancy's came trippingly distilled from his cologne, male cologne for sweet sportsmen, musk and invitation. "Come in, friends, and sit down. I so seldom receive visitors before the cocktail hour, it's an unaccustomed pleasure. Do enter!"

Scardini laughed alone. He had told me that Nancy ran a notch-house for travelers who loved to see things. Exhibitions. He had artistic ambitions, Scardini had hinted, to make stag movies and live off the royalties. Nancy's wife, a woman wan and thoughtful as a convalescent, a bony hillbilly with hooded eyes, stood waiting behind him. "Be a pretty girl, hon," Nancy called to her, "and boil up some coffee for my friends."

She went.

"But don't try to use the perc, you're too stupid," he said, smiling to us and putting us in chairs. "Comfortable?"

Still wrapped in his overcoat, Scardini sank heavily with a sigh into the softest cushions. "Just swell," he said.

And so we settled amid the dust rising from fancy auction-house furniture, genuine louie for sure. Another conference, another friendship. Was all business like this? I asked myself as Scardini spread his thighs and Nancy riptickled onward with little pleasing sounds and I breathed the factory soot from the flats, drifting against the windows, wriggling through the blinds and the drapes. It was hot with head-drawing furnace heat: granulations of bad coal inside, brown oily slush in the street outside, a game but exhausted sun. It had to pierce too many elements to reach us — smoke, clouds, exhaust fumes, smudged panes of glass, the drainage and secretion of a city and Nancy's household. Even in the daylight I could see how Nancy, come nightfall, transformed this parlor for the performance. A false fireplace with plastic bricks, a turning electrical trick, red and sparkling, with a tinsel crackling made by gears — this was almost genuine fire and almost real sparks for almost virile men. A good living from that type john, Scardini had commented. If not greedy, he didn't have to sell mainline sugar in addition.

I knew what this sick dark room recalled to me — my father's flat. And yet I had to pass through both of them before I would be free for Joy.

"My son's picture, died," Nancy said, passing us the framed snapshot of a pink, rosy, curly child. "Maybe was the prettiest little baby boy in the world, I wouldn't say yes and I wouldn't say no. What do you think?"

"A rotten shame," Scardini said. "Taken off by the polio

278

like that. A dirty rotten shame. And just when they got an injection for it now. They could have stopped it, couldn't they, Nancy? But they were saving it for the rich kids, the doctors' friends, those brats."

"You got that coffee yet?" Nancy trilled to the kitchen. "You let it boil over again and I'll mop it up with your hair."

"Mind your company, I'm watching it," his wife answered sleepily. I knew with a pang of regret the slow hill drawl and the drowsy hill face. She might have been a pretty girl three years ago, pretty in the hill way, calico and blushing at the fair, the kind that Grack used to love to pinch. Nancy's dwelling brought back the fair, partly the smells of coffee and grease, partly the destroyed prettifications of it. Ever see an abandoned fairground, that one in Orlando, Fla., for instance? The dead gilt, the moldering wood sweating its paint, the rickets of pleasure sprawled out in rain and sun, washed clean, silted over, washed again. Nancy's place of entertainment was like that, with more overboiled coffee than a carnie, less pop, but the smell of hotdogs, yes — and I could even imagine the banging of skillets to attract the trade. And the grease and fatty pork. And Scardini with the gristly, bloated face of the spice-blooded cooks.

Repetitions! Even to the sad young woman, so recently pretty, watching the coffee in the kitchen. But I missed Pauline.

"Haven't had a good cup a coffee since the kid died," Nancy explained. "Nothing I ever say helps, always, *always* boils over. Bought her a perc, no good. Nothing. She uses the pot anyway."

"Shame," Scardini said. "And they still try to collect money from me for that polio racket. I threw one of them out of the hotel, bad for business to do it, too. I was thinking of my pal Nancy."

"But the wife was a sweet kid," Nancy went on, "I can't complain, always nice to me, do whatever I say. The least I can do is be nice to her right back."

Scardini agreed with shaggy throbbings of his cheeks.

"Don't you think we better get back to Grack?" I asked.

Scardini closed his eyes. "Terrible, terrible, the polio. . . . Well, sure is nice to drop in on a friend like this, Nancy. Otherwise it's hurry, hurry, hurry." He folded his hands across his belt and put one inside his pants.

"Come into the kitchen, she got another picture of the kid there. You too, Mr. Williams. Or maybe it's in the bedroom. She takes it to bed with her."

We sat again, this time in the kitchen, because this had to be a social call which included Mrs. Nancy, all coffee and grits, dishes in the sink, windows more dim than her eyes. . . . And surely Mrs. Nancy had been pretty. The thin faded face and lanky limbs troubled me. She sprawled in a kitchen chair, watching the coffee, scratching herself and dozing and must once have been almost as sweet as Joy. She had fine pale hair, country sunlight burnt into it, and golden eyebrows over the perishing eyes.

Scardini described his delicate organs which took neither whiskey nor coffee. He drank a great deal of soda. It spoke frequently. The two, Scardini and Nancy, managed to get me between them, at the long end of a chipped and enameled kitchen table, facing Nancy's wife, who scratched and stretched and sighed. I had learned my patience from was there in it for them? Pleasure? But they knew this about Belle. I jumped up, still sticky with the love's slime with which they had intended to glue me down, and said, "Yes! yes!" to her plaint:

"Ain't you even going to kiss me goodbye, not even once?"

"Yes, I will."

"You won't even do anything else for me after all Nan and Scardini and their little Belle wanted to do for you?"

No, I wouldn't. I never even said her name, *Belle*.

"You ready to go?" Scardini called down the hall. "We been cutting up old times, friend Nancy here and me. You feeling better now, boy?"

Stiff with fury, I waited at the door.

"Coming, coming in just a sec," Scardini said.

Nancy accompanied him. "She says you cracked the picture. Pretty kid, wasn't he? Now she likes it too much, I can't make her happy a-tall noways, Bud. I need friends for helping me out."

Scardini smiled and pulled his sleeves.

"I gave friend here the sugar for your other friend," Nancy said. "Byebye, and come around any time."

Why didn't I figure it all out in advance? Who knows when he is being put in purgatory or a wife made to suffer for him? How do you see these things when the moment is hot and sad and a creature once pretty, with golden hair, says, *Look at me, I need?*

It is a duty not to oblige all the suffering in the world. That way lies madness, sainthood, and no wedding or fathering.

"Wait a sec, wait up," Scardini said, puffing. "I'm driving

waiting out the marks. I waited. I counted the brown chitlings in the sink and the soap and the white bread from the A & P and the old slippers and the dust in the corners and the way the G and the D in blue on a Grand stove were loopingly joined by the artist. Mrs. Nancy took her coffee in an enormous white dimestore cup and gave me a smile with her new bridge. Scardini and Nancy gossiped without looking at me.

"You like kids?" Mrs. Nancy said.

"Sure do, Mrs. Nancy."

Nancy interrupted me. "Belle, that's her name."

"Sure do," I repeated.

"You just come on then," she said, "let me show you a picture." Scardini and Nancy looked up together, grinning, and said with limp waves of hands, Go ahead, what diff, she's nuts anyway. Maybe it helped her to show pictures. While studying and refilling our cups, she had prettied herself for the trip down the hall to her bedroom. Only natural. I knew that Nancy ran an advanced hookshop, so maybe his wife had learned from the advanced hookers.

She showed me the picture and I sank deeper and deeper into a sprung armchair. Poor rosy kid, poor mama. She sat on the bed and cried and I tried not to look at her. She had a soft and pretty drawl despite the fading and wanness, the caught breath and the tears. I stared and stared at the tinted photograph of a fat little two-year-old, *Remembrance Home Portraits, Call On Us,* stamped on his blouse at the navel. The tinting, performed too rapidly, had run the pink of cheeks over into the chinablue of eyes.

"Oh you can't know, you're only a boy yourself," she said. "He was so cute and warm and mine. He was an accident. I didn't have the right to him. All I had was Nancy, now all I have is Nancy. He suffered so! He died and they wouldn't let me see him until after he was dead. Nancy cried too, but right away he started to fight with me because I wanted a little silver coffin for him. Oh I know coffins don't help none, but I didn't want the worms to get to him —"

The worms come from inside, ma'm, I wanted to tell her, polite as can be. The only way to keep the worms down is to live them out.

"Oh I don't know anything now. I don't remember anything, I don't want anything. I don't care. I only want him back. But you know, I got it figured out. I tried to talk with him in outer space, but I couldn't get to him. I know why. His soul isn't there. It's here, here, in this room here. He's waiting to come back. He will be born again. I feel it. I know it. Look at him, don't he look back at you? Don't you feel his eyes on yourn? He needs a young father, a strong young boy, not all that nastiness Nancy made me do before I could have a baby. Before he would give me. Look at him. . . ."

She was moaning and rocking and the springs of the bed were creaking. I was stifling in that room. An echo of her rocking was taking me. I could hear the furnace laboring below. I tried not to look at Belle, I tried straining my neck every which way, away from her, to the picture, everywhere, but her chanting and moaning took me to it.

And I dropped the picture. The glass cracked, splitting across the infant's face.

"Now you've got to!" she cried.

And I had to look, dizzy and the black coffee stinging in my mouth and Belle smiling, smiling for me to fumble with

myself. She was on her knees and arms in the b[e] at her clothes, her bottom straining at panties, al[l] pink and creamy at the edges, and rocking and say[ing] baby baby." I wanted to help her as best I could. [I] that I obliged: she was skinny and long and hang[ing] small long breasts and hard red sore nipples that w[ould] when I touched them. Asking me to hurt them, hu[rt] please.

One minute it would be?

Less of my valuable time?

Joy was obligations beyond dreams of obliging this [The fury of temptation, of course, had nothing to d[o] Joy. Maybe it had something to do with that Phyllis known, but maybe not much. I watched Belle's shut face slowly compose with fatigue in the early evening [She had not closed the door. She opened her eyes and sm[iled] "You're not vexed with me?"

"No."

The dreamy trusting smile did not change. "You do[n't] mind how I wanted — ?"

"I don't mind," I said, "why should I?"

In the distant whirl of my ideas, it made no differenc[e] what she asked or answered. "I told Nancy I had to, but h[e] couldn't look. He said yes, he promised me. I told him Mr. Scardini couldn't look either." She reached to touch me in the chair where I slumped. "I see you," she said. "I thought if you saw how I could love you, maybe you would believe . . . Nan doesn't . . ."

It was this I see you which awakened me to all the plans about me, and the cunning of Scardini and Nancy, and what

you, so wait. Don't hurry. Donkeydust, eh? Ain't that what all women are? All wives? You're no holy joe yourself, but that Nancy's wife is really a pip, ain't it? Every woman alike. They don't sell out, they buy in. You like it with her? You enjoy? She used to work for Nancy as a pro exhibit-it. All women the same. Who can ever tell what they like to do? Now take our Grack, all nervous, so nervous for his sugar, and that little Joy of yours, also nervous — who are we to judge?"

Without time for the pleasure of hitting him, I jumped into a cab and said, "G. Washington Motel on Prospect, fast!"

Thinking: No. No. No. Please Joy, please Grack, please God, no.

31. A child is forever

I COULDN'T see out my eyes. I could not see through them; I saw something in them. Cleveland was scarlet and dripping in haze.

I rubbed my face and crouched behind the cabbie for the few minutes it took. "Paint it any color you like, so long as it's red," — Grack's carnie motto. The storefronts of Cleveland were red. The December evening sky was red. My innards tasted red in my mouth. Monotonously all the long history of Grack echoed in my head, singsong, memorized, that metallic voice of the mind-made-up, the changeless spirit, determined on death before life: "I got me a daughter up there with the Kiskeedees, want to see her picture?" O Come all ye faithful, it was Christmastime for late shopping. Trees, tinsel, tinkle, snow in the oily gutters, muddied cars waiting, the city procession home after work. Prospect Avenue was longer going back! Grack had gotten humpbacked and meanlipped with knowing himself. He was ready for anything. He was ready for anything. He had arranged with Scardini, Scardini had arranged with Nancy, Nancy had arranged. And only Nancy's wife meant anything, poor Belle, she meant it.

I should have said Belle to her!

What about Grack's habit? I was Grack's habit.

And yet once he had been the man who saved my life, strong he had been in that world where the dodgem has funny accidents, jolting and wheezing and spitting electricity, where almost every night someone's kidneys let go — that's how funny it was. The tent got to smelling bad. "We're in business for fun," Grack had said.

"That why we're with it?"

"With it and for it."

But you can't do everything, no baby. Enticements are for the refusing: just look and admire. Exercising the rejection muscle makes the body strong. Pinch me and see if I yell. Wink of lights and shouts and climb of laughter — but you can't have everything. The boys and girls, heavy-legged, tussling, refusing, consenting, ran off to their lonesomeness after banging dodgem car against car. They shared their fun, they were lonely together, they came back to play skillo. And in this world it was all true about Grack's giant shadow over the lip of stage — Grack the talker, that fine old prince of con. It was a world which really signified, too, although it soon stopped meaning.

"The rolly-coaster, Mama."

"You just came out of the Funhouse, Laff Yourself to Death."

"But I want it!"

"I'll tell your paw to give you a hit, where'd he sneak off to?"

"The rolly, rolly, rolly coaster!"

"Here's a dime, you brat, just leave me in peace."

"It costs twenny cents, Mama!"

Step up for this, for that, for love and forget. And Grack was the king of it, not Stan, not Pauline, not anyone else. In the hey-rube it was Grack who was king. Afterwards Joy repaired me and I snorted blood and was brave for her. Pauline, a heart-reader, a palmster, should have known it for love: so much exasperation! so much sullen bravery!

"Women all slime!" Grack said. How frayed that song. "Now take that little trick of yours, let me give you a for-instance —"

And Grack hated each town we passed through, hated the people who fed the pigeons in Southern squares, hated the cute tricks, hated the houses and steeples and their careful ways. Once we had driven through together in the cab of a circus truck. He refused to look at this pleasant Utah place (it was that time). "Notice," he drawled, flashing the single finger, single eye, pulling down the lid. Without looking upon the town, he gave it his evil eye. "Notice, friend, these are homes where the marks breed — chow, dodo, wiggle between the legs, that's how you make a mark. Do you see one looking out at you?"

I stuck my nose out the window into a fresh spring morning, peachy, too early for a town of grandfather farmers. "No," I admitted. It was truth. "No, they're minding their own business. But I would like to peek in and see their breakfast. . . ." And I dreamed of missus plucking the toast from the Toastmaster, buttering it, blowing kisses and handing toast across the table to mister. He would have a masterful profile, even eating buttered toast, and gracious and flowered with a print dress and cheeks still pink from bed she would be. Their identical children, differing only in that the girl was blond and the boy dark, stamped from a set of cookie cutters which they received by saving boxtops, busily did the housework as a surprise for mommy. Then . . . But no, the point exactly was my knowing that no cookie cutter made them, although I could not yet guess at the sense of these living souls in a sleepy town in Utah or wherever else we passed through. I tried and tried. Grack knew how I yearned toward them.

"Not me!" he said. "Not on your life! Just let me get away without looking, just let me give them my eye and make their fists come loose. Sheep with pig heads! They don't have the right to spy on me that way, they all got larceny in the heart —"

"But they don't, Grack. You think they care about us? You hardly ever see anyone at all in those windows."

"Worst of all! They hide behind the curtains. They feel themselves and see me. No, it's the houses, the lots, the porches, the rent and the bills looking and looking at me and asking, Why not you? No, no, no, they never get me. Nowheres! No-one! Not for me to stand still and be looked at! Well, they say screwing is better when you move, too."

I laughed and broke it up. "Have to try it that way someday, friend."

And another time he knocked over a girl, just walking, a kid, bowled her over and left her crying. Oh yes, he picked her up again, he dusted her off, he kissed the top of her head. But it doesn't stop the truth that he knocked her over and laughed because she was in his way.

He was John Peel? I wasn't. I had Joy. What would he have done for that mark Andy? Rolled him for his marbles, that's all.

Cleveland was stuck in traffic now. I was pounding the cabbie's window and he was saying how he didn't care about the tip, I had better just quit goosing him or he'd throw me out right where we was, here next to a chicken shop with a familiar sign:

BUY ME IN PIECES.
I AM FRESH TODAY.

Okay, okay. I fell back and waited.

Joy once said she was a granddaughter of Pocahontas. Yes, I had said, from the Neapolitan branch of the family. You sold John Smith ice cream bars.

Drowning in fear, I recalled Grack's brag of what he had seen. The carnie. Baptism in streams, the preacher up to his hips, dipping those ladies in his very own arms. The carnie. Hillbillies stood on the toilets, only way they knew how to use them. Quebec where they buried it for making the corn grow. Jail where the sheriff bothered the punks for sex: Nevada, that was. The carnie and the carnie.

What was my brag before Joy? How I gave my father whatfor? Phyllis? One year of college? Belly slamming in the snow for prizes and the sidewalk play in touch? No, I knew it, how I kicked the habit and the carnie, how I took help from Grack, how I *earned* Joy. That was my brag before Joy.

"Goddammit please god hurry!"

The cabbie believed I meant it, but you can't jump a ramp

290

over the traffic. That too I had learned. This is a world of others always in the way. In the stream of cars, there's nothing but figuring out better what to do when you get there. You have to reckon with the others. It's best if you enjoy traveling with them, but no matter what, you have to reckon. There's no way around except onto the sidewalk, where you smash the people and the stores. Just wait, just figure, just see the nice kids looking at Santa in the Christmas window.

Oh a good thing I never hurt my father with the knife I had ready for him!

I counted hotel doors from one identical room to the next. When I slammed into my room, Joy was spread out under a sheet. Grack was slumped into a sagging overstuffed chair with a flowered cotton cover. As I had sat before Belle.

"Did you hurt her?"

He shook his head no. He had a bruise the size of a prune under one eye. "Did you get for me?" he asked.

"Scardini's on the way."

At the bed I wondered why Joy lay so still under the sheet. Her face was pale, but just as Grack had a prunespot under one eye (his mark-taking eye), so Joy wore two small blotches of red, one on each cheek. "You missed it," she said flatly. "I missed."

"*What?*" The time spun around for Joy and me, whirling Grack with us. I thought, Given Brown's cow! Given Brown's cow! In the carnie we gave Brown's cow when we cut the performance for a rapid turnover. The room had a stale greasy smell, like the counter of a frankfurt joint where the frying has gone on without cleaning. Joy's face, like Mrs. Nancy's, had the used look of the bereaved woman. It was inner-turned, but turned to me with her question. Where had I been?

She looked ill, Joy did, it had hurt. "We're not anymore, Bud," she said. "Where were you?"

This was our child made outdoors in Georgia on pine needles, this was our first fret-fingered, mum-mumbling babe who would never kick the day except for our kicking together then and Joy's anguished straining here with Grack trying to serve her.

"*Where?*"

"What did you say, Joy?"

"We're not going to have our baby now. What you been doing?"

I never believed in a connection between Nancy's wife and Joy's miscarriage, but I asked anyway, as if it mattered: "When?"

"Been happening almost since you left. Why were you so long?"

"Did Grack make trouble for you?"

"Right after you left, a little. I hit him. He stopped."

Grack lay in the chair, watching me with one flaming, unblinking, terrified eye, waiting for Scardini with his arms struck against the restraining chair, needing Scardini as the diver needs the weight of sea when he is brought up too fast and his blood is like to explode. There was no way to hurt him now, no matter how I needed to hurt him. He watched but did not see me.

"Don't worry, Bud, it wasn't his fault. *Wasn't,* Bud. It wasn't carrying right, cramping like that. I was afraid about it all the time. I felt it coming even before."

"Joy, Joy, Joy."

"It's okay now, Bud. Grack's been helping — towels and tea and things. And he needed his stuff bad, but he's been taking care . . . But where you been all this time?"

And where had I been for Grack? And what had I done for him except let Nancy and Scardini manage to make me watch poor Belle? Did he really believe he could make me see Joy any differently? He was at my back; I did not look at him — the collapsed watching in the chair, the bruise on his cheek, his serving Joy with towels and tea because I was not there. She moved and obliged me to admit what I did not want to see — the bloodied sheets, the packed towels between her legs, the mess of linen tossed in a corner of the room. Grack had tried to help her.

"Why didn't you get a doctor?"

"Money, time, no time, and anyway it's okay, it stopped now. Pauline told me all about it. She had it all the time. I was the one that didn't happen on a towel."

"Why didn't you call me at —"

"Nancy's? But you said you'd just be picking up the stuff for Grack, just be coming back. . . ."

She shut her eyes. She would let me replace the towel. Grack knew how to put it to her, she said, but she didn't need a fresh one yet. She didn't want to move. It was stopping.

I sank down onto the floor by the bed and put my hand on her head. It was warm with a low steady fever. Grack lay waiting in his chair. She seemed to fall asleep. Too tired to worry about Grack and think about the struggle between Grack and Joy, I decided only that it needed to be that way. Grack had to be Grack; it had nothing to do with what he could choose. I could choose, I can make my life; but Grack could only watch slyly for me to leave and then, shivering with his habit, dry as a bone, paw toward my Joy. Ugly for sure. He had been a sly pincher when a hero in my world. And a hero and ugly when he saved me and my habit broke in two and the pieces stuck to him and grew there. (But he told me I had broken it myself! But all the same, it was Grack who told me.) Without sense, without fun, without the deep agreement of flesh, he had tried to take her and they had knocked the furniture about in a furious whispering and she would have missed anyway. It wasn't Grack's fault to be Grack. I moved my hand in Joy's hair.

Now I was tired and we rested, touching and near, until Scardini came looking in. He nodded to Grack. Grack was up in an instant, gasping for his mainline. I opened one eye to look at them. It was a private matter, like love, to peel up the shirt and open the swollen blue vein, first heating the needle over a wick, swabbing the arm with alcohol, nursing the stuff in through its hypodermic stinger and waiting the breathless instant for the big kick of death-in-life. I opened one eye, but I would not know if Grack squeezed out a single thick tear like the one that was my habit when the sugar hits blood with its wow. These two, Grack and Scardini, left us for this business. One eye cocked, I winked at my brother Grack's new brotherhood with Scardini — the dry spitline of sick digestion dividing the inner membrane from the outer lip.

They left us alone.

"Are you for loving me, Joy?" I asked her.

She did not answer. She slept.

294

Nancy's wife meant no more than Phyllis, though Phyllis was for the failure in my life and now Belle for the new richness of spending. "I'm for loving you," I said to Joy's wide sleeping forehead.

And sitting on the floor amid the mess of bleeding, within the sight of a drop of blood near my leaning knuckles, I closed my eyes and dozed. Scardini and Grack must have had their heads together. They returned in the space of a short dream.

"How you feel now, Joy?" Grack asked her. He was lean and springy as the old carnie now with his newly spiced blood. He bounced and sang into the room.

She opened her eyes without speaking.

Grack pulled open his own eye with his finger and looked it at her, at me, at the room and the mess of towels. He could see that Joy was going to be okay now, that she should eat liver and red meat and then be okay. He started to laugh, a high carnie cock-a-doodle-oo of roosterish glee. The wart shimmered. I got up. He danced and tweaked my ear. I waited. He said:

"That Bud of ours, Joy, what a fella! He laid Nancy's crazy wife, that hot hillbilly bitch, and Scardini here says they didn't even take time to close the bedroom door. A carnie takes his piece where he can get it, quick with it and for it, that right, Bud?"

Head thrust forward, Scardini was breathing softly through his wisp of a mouth.

"Nancy works hard for his peace of mind, supplying that wife of his with fresh meat, I mean," Grack gasped, having trouble with his breath, "but you could have shut the door!"

He was shrilling his laughter even while I swung on him. He fell and I fell with him, clawing and slapping at his face. He laughed like a cock in a barrel. Scardini, behind him, did not move. Scardini grinned and passed gas at the doorway. He said: "Please, please, I can't call the bulls after all this. A respectable house I keep. Please, dear friends," — but pleased, delighted, sparkling and digesting with rapid satisfaction. I heard everything. I heard the television down in the office, the car tires on Prospect, even the movements of Christmas weather in Cleveland. The rush of blood to my ears was nature.

Grack tried to heave me off his chest. I knelt by his side, however, and slapped his face, back and forth, forth and back, careful not to touch the nose but hurting as much as I could. One ear, then the other, slivered against the floor. He chortled his glee. "Hit me! Hit me! You been mousing Nancy's wife!" Without fully knowing what I did, I closed my fist. His face, dead white, a brackish white at the beard, turned blue and richer colors where I hit him. My hands hurt. There was spit on them. The knuckles felt huge and heavy and wanted me to stop. His laughter was immense and that of a broken chicken. I thought of breaking the hard Adam's apple, that talk thing, that crazy bony deadbox of racket.

A low voice occurred, occurred. It was Joy. "Bud," she repeated, "I can't get out of bed or it'll start again, but stop. Stop now. Stop."

I looked at my hands. I stood up with my hands heavy

and the fluids puffing up the skin over my knuckles. Lymph.
Grack was spitting blood and whispering shrilly, "Didn't hurt
me at all, Joy, not at all, didn't a bit." And a whispering
flutter of laughter. He lay with his lips ballooning. He did
not move, although the long chest jerked.

I stood above him with his head between my shoes.

I stooped and held him under the armpits and began dragging him across the floor. I kicked open the door.

"Don't make a fuss. Don't spoil my business," Scardini
said.

I lifted him gentle over the sill and dropped him outside
the door. He did not laugh loudly enough to spoil Scardini's
business. Scardini started to help me, then to remember, then
to back away. I just stood and waited until he backed out
the door. I closed the door and turned, very tired, to look
at Joy. She sat up in bed with the bloody sheets and towels
gathered between her legs. Her face was working silently, lips
moving, eyes fixed, in that bereaved fatigue which I had now
found twice today, the first time on Belle's tormented head.
Women bereaved! I moved to say something, moved to move,
and fell in a faint.

The best thing for a faint is just to stay there and rest.
Joy knew enough and had patience. She let me rest and
watched only to see that I had not crumpled something under — an arm, a leg, a chance for the future where we need
all the limbs we have or can acquire.

She waited for my good time to sit up.

When I did and felt all right, I ran cold water over my
head, bending over the sink to rub it into my hair and over

the back of my neck. Then, still working a towel and my teeth beginning to chatter, I returned to the bed and asked: "Do you believe him, Joy?"

No answer.

"Tell me. He's worse than a mark! A county fixer!"

She watched me dry my face and ears carefully, tenderly, with my bruised hands at the towel. Frowning, she remarked, "Grack's no different because he said that. Always wanted —"

"Do you believe him?"

"It's all right, Bud."

"*Do you believe him?*"

"Never mind, Bud."

"Tell me!"

"What do you want me to say now, Bud? No? You might notice how I couldn't help hearing —"

"But it's not true, Joy! He's not telling the truth! Scardini didn't see it and it didn't happen — it didn't happen like that — it wasn't —"

"Never mind, never mind."

I stood up and raised my fists to make her believe me. "I swear it, Joy! I know I shouldn't have — I couldn't — I don't know — oh I wish I'd stayed here with you! Maybe I'm not — *believe me, damn you!*"

"Please don't threaten me," she said. "Hush up now. Sit down."

"Tell me you believe me!"

"You're for me, Bud, you are, exactly. It's just you had a funny look, almost a soft look, when he said that woman's name. It doesn't matter."

"You believe me?" I asked, sitting close to her.

"No matter."

"Do you love me the same?"

"Do you love me, Bud?"

"Yes," — my yes.

"Yes," — hers.

"Then why do you say it doesn't matter?" — and now I was jealous of her unconcern. It should matter.

"It was a bad thing if you did it, but it's done. The baby is done, too. Maybe that's what I'm thinking about. Do you guess maybe it was a boy? It's no matter now. It was a bad thing to do, Bud. But I'll tell you more later. . . . What are you going to do about Grack?"

"Get rid of him fast."

"Do just like you wanted to do before. Makes no difference, Bud, I knew it was getting to something like this. But now you know."

I stroked her hair, damp at the forehead.

"All this was there before," she went on, "only not love yet. Just there in a different way now, Bud."

I stroked her hair and asked, "How do you feel about me now?"

"Later. I'll tell you more later, Bud, hold me now. What I have isn't catching."

She stretched with the smile of her trouble and pale thoughts on her lips, suddenly drawn, thinned, her mouth calmed by steady pain. But her movement was of yearning. She had to lie still with her legs bent to put the bleeding to sleep. Her face and hands were open to receive my face and arms. And that's the way she made it for us, the way it should be even in time of trouble, forever and ever, although the risks of marriage can never all be known or predicted:

More later, love now!

32. We ask to be admitted

In the morning Joy said that she would not go, would not move, would wait. She would rest a day or two at the G. Washington Motel in Cleveland while I carried Grack the hundred and eighty miles to Detroit and the International Bridge leading toward Windsor in Canada. Bruised and mashed, Grack wished us a good morning. He came in with coffee and toast for us. His long talker's mouth smiled as if it knew a secret between us. The head huge and swollen, lolling on the skinny sprung stalk of a neck, under-fed in his habit, he wore his beating with no comment except, pointing to the adhesive tape on his neck: "Cut myself shaving."

And the yellow-toothed smile. And the wart's fat squiggling on his nose.

"I'm sorry, Grack," — while Joy and I reached greedily for the pot of coffee, the bowl of cream, the heap of toast and four kinds of tropical jams in little paper cups and butter spilling over itself. It's fine to eat after an illness. When I looked at my sore hands, Joy took the toast and buttered it for me.

Grack stood there while we ate, munching and reaching,

clinking tools and spreading jam, covering and uncovering ourselves with the sheet as we used knives and spoons, busy. We leaned for butter, creamed, lifted cups. He said: "I'm going."

"Where?"

"Canada."

"And don't I know? We'll start out soon's I stow some vittles in me."

"No, I mean right now." He studied my swollen hands and said, "I can make it alone, boy. Eat hearty. I don't need you."

"No!" Joy, already recovering, sang this *no* as if to welcome her returning health. "Why no, Grack, Bud will see you through to the bridge, that far exactly." She popped a bit of toast into her mouth. "And then he's mine. Try this kumquat, I think it is, hon."

Grack shifted and turned away, his addict's eyes squinting, granulated, red-rimmed. "Okay, just get me to Detroit so I can cross over."

"To the bridge," Joy said.

"But he don't need to."

"To the bridge *exactly*."

"Okay, I heard you, carnie girl. Come on then, let's get this truckshow moving," — and he lifted his thin shoulders in a high humorous shrug over our domestic breakfast with crumbs on the bed, and his forehead wrinkled, and he smiled and turned his palms out. I had not seen resignation in Grack before. "Okay," he said, "let's roll."

But of course the old knockdown Grack could no more jump into his clothes at the snap of an hour. The mainliner

302

jerks, but turns so slowly — *so-oo*, just like that — like a Ferris wheel on its last strange run against the sky, bare of lovers, turning to be dismantled for scrap. He squeezed his eyes, trying to force the cooling fluid from the ducts, but they remained parched and cracked.

And we made this drive alone down Ohio Route Two along Lake Erie, past the tall flimflam captains' houses with the wooden roosts at the top where they stood watch with their pipes over the frozen lake, through this stiff gray Ohio farmland in December, with the chicken-and-steak shacks shut in the suburbs of Cleveland and the kids out of school but attentive before their blue-glowing teevees in one cold town after the next, Bay Village, Avon-on-the-Lake, Sandusky. . . . The country is strange to me. No matter how long I worked the carnie, no matter how badly I once needed to eat grass after Pittsburgh, pastureland remained the queerest of towns. I didn't see farms on the land; I saw motels and burg joints. A show is a metropolis with portable skyscrapers and willing women who dawdle by the funhouse, a many-faced ashy mob of strangers, sweating and tricky with whim, a rush of urbanity even in blue jeans. City things happen in private city ways within the crowd. Ashes to ashes, sawdust to sawdust. He leads her under the ropes and behind the tent.

Now in December, here in Ohio, alone with Grack and Joy's unspoken presence between us, there was open winter farmland, brown and quiet beneath its snow. Well, I didn't have enough lives for those board houses and barns with the rented space that said, "Richman's Clothes" or "Meet Your Savior." We stopped once for hot soup.

"Got an upset stomach," Grack said, "thanks." We ate in silence at the counter, looking at each other in a mirror below the Campbell cans. Grack's harried face, long and sick, the huge eyes swollen small, fried dust on his eyelashes, was consumed by secret and unexpressed understanding of me, of himself, of everyone — this comprehension deeply corrupting because unexpressed, because unmoving. He could know nothing by his own will now. He could only know how to devour himself, and tread lightly back to the car, skirting the blotches of snow with his thin pointy black shoes leaving no footprints, only a shadow.

We paid and drove on. Although this was the last time we would sit and take food together, we had nothing in a hurry to be said. I could not repeat what I had so often thought: Grack saved my life, and now he's worth nothing but the remembrance of a mighty nose, a wart, a trick of hand to eye. This thought, with the stale soda crackers that came with the soup, stuck in my mouth from Sandusky all the way into Toledo. Who can tell what was on Grack's mind? Maybe his level gaze at the road ahead looked straight north to the Frenchies of Canada. At last he spoke of that.

"Back to my Kiskeedees, that's what they call us, that and Canucks. *Qu'est-ce qu'il dit?*"

"But you learned English, Grack, and how to be a talker."

"I did. I did that. Don't you think it's funny how a Kiskeedee got to talk those marks from all over America into the corner of his eye? I see good out of that eye, but okay. Man, just let me brag a sec. Just try to think how it was for me, not believing this language, frenchifying it to myself, but pouring it on the town-monkeys with that sweet old lying sincerity. Man!"

"You lived in it, Grack."

"No, not that far. Wasn't my dwelling place, Bud. Never believed my own words. . . . I finished my brag now. You can put on the speed," — and my foot on the accelerator assented. "I'm going home and they'll tell me I'm an American up there. Don't fit noplace but the funhouse, the flat joint, racked up front of the marks. . . . You not so mad about Joy? I didn't mean a thing."

Not about her, I would have said if I could. About Nancy's wife, poor Belle. About fixing it up with Scardini, that's to be mad. But as to Joy, that was our business together.

"Not much," I said.

In the bleakness of the lake road, Toledo suddenly announced itself with a City Limits, Kum Inn for Liquor, Save Our Children, a clamor of drive-ins, a last-chance-for-gas, a stop at our home cooking. There was a county fairgrounds to pass now, emptied by winter. We had never played this date, but Grack knew all about it — Frankie's Truck Show, modified grift, quarter for the Legion, half for the sheriff. The kiddo whip, the crystal maze, the flat joints, and the War Horrors See It Now were all put away in Orlando, and the glass-ringed talkers, hairy-knuckled and faces oiled with coconut, were all scattered, sprawled in hotel lobbies, shuffling decks and awaiting the thaw when they could rub their mouths limber with their palms and again sing that lovely song, all for charity and the sweet sheriff: These Original Jap Tortures from the Muntz Collection! The secret they dare not tell you! No minors under sixteen without a mother or father — and girls, get yourself a boyfriend *now!* Too horrible to describe in words! Show starts in *pree*-cisely one minute!

In the shade of the old Standard Oil refinery, yessir, fellas. Grab her quick, and if she hollers, tickle her tickler!

I slowed passing the grounds. We both looked, sniffing for cotton candy and feet, putting the wet sawdust under slush, dragging out the cardtables, the splintered benches, and the franks steaming and skinny as worms on hot pavement. But now we had winter and no use to stop. A permanent Ferris wheel preened its bones to the Toledo sky, done up in grease but waiting like death. Passing and away, my tires gave me Ferris wheel music, klip klap, klip klap, pumparump, klip klap, pumparump, the revolving whir of the great cradle. Whatever happens, whatever love-making or death-making comes of it, the klipklap music falls from the motors and the shifting cages. We screwed down the windows and stared as if coming by chance on the house where we had grown up.

What if we had stopped?

Grack would say to the watchman, "I'm with it."

"Who, you?"

"With it and for it."

"First place, she's closed. Second place, you pay like everybody. Third place, sonnyboys, run off now before I run you off."

We wound through Toledo without stopping, licking our lips to talk, not talking. The Cherry Street Bridge — I remember its grillwork *wong* against the tires, finishing off our Ferris wheel music. Then, once again on the road, this time the busy trucker's Number Twenty-four that leads from Toledo to Detroit, Grack said, "I got a daughter-a-mine, too, up there with the Kiskeedees. Want to see her picture?"

"Why not?" I slowed down, but he did not reach for his wallet.

"Just about your Joy's age, too."

"That's nice."

"I'm telling you the truth, you don't have to say it's nice. Thing I did as a kid." And he stopped as if he had said nothing more than the weather or the time. He was drooping and distant down the seat from me, leaving space for our invisible Joy who had been patient so long up from the South. The carnie had given her that at least, patience, and not yet taken from her desire and will. At the same time, I could think of Grack without feeling the pressure of his body at the other end of the seat. The unhappy man is never present, never absent to himself. Like the carnie, never out of his own pocket. Like the carnie, never out of the mark's pocket. Grack was whistling a little tune, not hearing it. A bent stick of winter corn, discolored, the fine nosewart now only one more bad kernel among teeth, eyes, bruises, blotches, liverspots, his cheeks cracked by winter, he shivered. He kept his hands between his legs. He watched me force the jalopy toward the end of our friendship, and whistled.

Love makes a man both present and absent, as I was then, thinking of Joy, thinking of Grack, full of pleasure in the trials we passed, thinking of myself and knowing I was really there, taking Grack someplace, leaving Joy someplace, dropping him soon and returning to her. Near me on the seat a parched mouth tried to whistle.

307

And so Detroit came to us, flat and brown and planed by car-bearing trucks, a huge prairie built over with cement and girders and spilling its burden of steel, rubber, and people at every change of light.

"Marks every little one," said Grack. "Look at the town-monkeys."

"No, only for fun. Other times they do things together, cars, kids, they make politics here —"

"Politics now! You getting interested in that already, Buddy boy? You going to nominate or run or vote for some-body? That's past the very end already, boy. I don't believe in politics. I don't care. I'm going to need another dose over there in Windsor, that's all, but don't you come with me, there's likely to be trouble getting through."

"I'm not coming. I'm going back to Joy tonight."

He nodded. "I know, I'm not asking. I *said* no." He took his hands from between his legs and cracked the knuckles. "I'm a little stiff from sitting. Skyooz. I *said* I don't believe in those things anymore. I used to think you were my friend. Now I think I'll go back to have a look at my daughter. I bet she's a pretty one by this time. Run a bally together. She'll take care of me if I can get by the border."

If.

"If they ain't got a good picture who did that doctor down in Fayetteville. Don't I look different now, boy? I changed?"

I looked to make sure that there was enough gas. The best thing would be to set him down without stopping. Knowing how much he had changed made it hard to tell him. Once a wart had been his honor, a waggle of immense flaw! He had shrunk like corn in the winter weather.

308

"If they're not watching for me at the border — for that doc in Fagleburg . . . Wouldn't you of helped me out, kid, in the old days? Now you stop ahead of the bridge, Buddy boy. Got to think of the little woman."

I thought hard: Joy is waiting. It was not enough to think it. "I'm going to get back to Joy tonight, Grack. She'll be resting. She won't be sleeping. I told her."

"Who asked what you say to her all the time, Buddy boy?"

We were threading through the city and near. In Paradise Valley, that swarming sharecropper land, chicken shacks, orange crate street fires with black kids dancing for warmth, frosting exhaust of used cars, we passed a walled city cemetery. The old ofays had not moved their dead, anyway. Grack saw that there was no more stopping. We had had our last ham sandwich together, had stopped in our last beautyrest motel, were finishing up forever and closing down the show. Grack peeked over the wall, raising his long tendoned stalk of a neck. "You ever think of the graveyard for peace of mind, Bud?"

"I'm not with that there permanent attraction yet, Grack."

"Just a place for resting is all. Member I was a kid, I used to eat sandwiches there — summer, you know, used to get a kind of polar heat even in Kiskeedee land. Air never once moved, that dark summertime, friend."

"Not yet I don't want to get with eating sandwiches in that place, Grack."

He peered about him as, honking, I switched lanes again. "Jeez, boy, you're in a hurry. How you know the way in this traffic?"

"Just follow the map first, Grack, then the signs. They show how to zag to it. Can't you see the signs?"

It was a mean thing to say, somehow, and put him in silence. With his hand he eased the places at his cheeks where I had hurt him. I should have been hot for sentiment during these last minutes. It was practically Christmas, too, with all the Santy Clauses peddling in the streets, the loud-speakers doing Bing Crosby's "O Come All Ye Faithful," the sidewalks thick with women, the streets blue with cops — tires, tinsel, tinkle, gray snow, brown snow, muddied cars waiting for lights and the walkers to cross, the great city procession aiming toward the winter holiday. Of course, both Grack and I were oddballs outside Christmas.

"Lookit them marks, boy!" He jittered on the seat, racing awake now. "Great love for each other, *chacun l'enfant naturel du bon Dieu*, great cost. God's bastards, I said, kid! Rich! Thighs under their coats, women, why not? But not for me, I wasn't brought up to pleasure. Lookit that girlie got her buttons spattered! Stay off the streets next time. Lookit —" It was the scratchy, jumpy place in a high, a Christmas itch of heroin, and it was still Grack meaning what he said: "Lookit those windows — all pretty! Don't hurry, Bud, it's goodbye. I had a serious-minded mother, don't care much for girls. My own kid and your Joy excepted always, you know."

"Take it easy, Grack."

"I never talked the truth, let me do it now. It's goodbye." And indeed the windows were rich and lovely for Christmas, the plastic mannikins in stiff gestures under their clothes, the shoppers shuffling in a hurry, wearing rubbers or pliofilm galoshes on their shoes. Grack admired Christmas and went on more quietly: "Maybe that's why I could lie so good. Truth is only my own way of talking, but you can say anything in English, it was a talk I learned. It didn't matter. I didn't belong with you."

"Yes," I said, "it's goodbye pretty soon, Grack."

"You, Bud, you felt bad about the marks — you're a holy joe at bottom — it makes you look crooked at the eyes and they don't trust you. That shiftiness people talk about — it's conscience. The real con makes a fellow happy, sleeps nights, functions regular. Yes, I know it's goodbye down the next block, Bud. I saw the signs. Goodbye."

"Not all that hurry."

"Yes, all that hurry. Listen" — and the finger conned his eye — "Listen, you better write it down, Bud, you like talking. Or maybe you want to forget it?"

And now the line of cars was formed for the International Bridge. Grack knew that I would let him walk over, passing the inspection himself, taking him to the edge and that was all, because there was noplace left for him with me on earth and noplace for me to follow him. There was no longer a fair for us, and no cabin in Winter Park.

The police on the bridge were careless, but cops all the same. There were the Canadians and our own, with the same bored policeman faces and breathing the same international exhaust fumes. I tried to take Grack's hand. "I won't forget you, Grack. I'm with you. I won't forget the good things you did for me, all the way back there —"

He pulled away angrily. His harsh laughter sealed off my wish to make a healing, softening farewell after his talk of

311

last night and my hitting him. The dark wart on his nose was swollen and doubled, a pale second wart of infection joined below it; with the shudder of false life in a sick woods animal, it moved when he moved. He cupped his hands to light a skinny cigar. "Forget it, you've forgotten already. You don't even talk carnie anymore, but write it down. You're with her and with yourself now, nothing else. You weren't born to be with it, Bud. Don't even get out of the car with me. I'll turn the tip myself."

"I'll be watching you, Grack," I said.

He climbed out with a cigar in his grin and reached into the back seat for his cardboard suitcase. Before he started walking, he paused and, thinking of the letter from jail to which my father had replied, I said, "Need a few extra bucks, Grack?" He was terribly shrunken and yellow. His face was shriveled to the bone, sharp Indian elevations in his cheeks, a mass of wasted cartilage supporting the blooming wart.

He leaned back to my window. "Need nothing at all. Need to get hiking. You turned the bed over on me, Bud. Now need to get with it."

And he was moving down the sidewalk toward the control booth at the bridge. I watched. In the sight of his walk, that tall swaying amble of the tricky carnie, nimble and free, for an instant my thigh twitched and my spirit assented to him in the old way, Yes yes yes. And then he kicked through a pool of muddied slush, not knowing where he was going: No. It was only my one leg that had wanted to join him, and it only from memory.

Near the control booth, he started to run, wobbling crazily

from side to side. He was a wanted man. It was a marko giveaway to run. Two policemen in square hats with big cop rumps came out shouting. Whistles. Traffic stopped. They drew their pistols and shouted. He went on running with his blind addict's waddle. They yelled again. One banged into the air and the bullet made an awful warlike screech. It was not necessary to shoot him. He dodged phantoms and careened off a railing. For an instant it seemed that he would clamber up and jump. No, no, he bounced and ran.

There, five steps more.

A boy, a third kid cop, brought him down with a flying block at his legs, and he did not even try to get up while they stood over him and decided what to do with this live beat body waiting to be done to. It wiggled on the ground. It had been hurt, but it started to talk in an old habit. The talker-tongue worked. I could not hear from where I watched, pushing close now, but I saw the clop-clopping of pleading and, while the body writhed with a brutal between-the-legs kick, the arms flew about and one finger came to an eye to pull down the lid and show the hoarse angry cops, stamping out of cold and nerves, a gaze of red fury, malediction, and dreamy persuasion.

The persuasion for me. *Clean out now!* the eye commanded, streaming tears, and the mouth went on entertaining the cops. One had removed his hat, the better to scratch his head. They had never before heard this high gobble of cajoling song from a man floored, kicked, and head-first into trouble.

He turned the tip for me. He talked and talked and pulled

313

his eyelid at me. The ring of policemen closed about him. Grack was right. Now there was nothing left that I could do for him but to go back to Joy.

All the same, he had been a friend. Joy and my own father came to be good friends to me, too, and stayed that way because they could be friends to themselves. We found a job in the trucking business in Pittsburgh, and a place to live, and Joy and I got with a child again. Grack's troubles went on, but he would not answer my letters. Dad asked me please to never mind, just bring up my son to be with it.

Joy and I had other ideas. We will not — and cannot — pull our son out of the way of our own hard times. They go on. There's a good and with it way to be not with it, too.